"This isn't the end of it, Rowan,"

Max assured her as he returned to his car. "We've barely begun."

This had to be the end of it, Rowan vowed. To get involved with Maximillian Donovan, knowing what kind of man he was, would be more than stupid. It would be suicidal.

She watched in silence as his car pulled away; then she fumbled with her house keys. The sitter was sound asleep on the couch in the study, while zombies terrorized Honolulu on TV. As Rowan watched the badly made-up monsters tear the hearts out of helpless citizens, she couldn't help but chuckle mirthlessly.

It was a fitting end to what was perhaps the most bizarre day she'd ever had. Starting tomorrow, she was going to have to be a great deal more careful about whom she ran into.

Dear Reader,

Welcome to the Silhouette **Special Edition** experience! With your search for consistently satisfying reading in mind, every month the authors and editors of Silhouette **Special Edition** aim to offer you a stimulating blend of deep emotions and high romance.

The name Silhouette **Special Edition** and the distinctive arch on the cover represent a commitment—a commitment to bring you six sensitive, substantial novels each month. In the pages of a Silhouette **Special Edition**, compelling true-to-life characters face riveting emotional issues—and come out winners. All the authors in the series strive for depth, vividness and warmth in writing these stories of living and loving in today's world.

The result, we hope, is romance you can believe in. Deeply emotional, richly romantic, infinitely rewarding—that's the Silhouette **Special Edition** experience. Come share it with us—six times a month!

From all the authors and editors of Silhouette **Special Edition**,

Best wishes,

Leslie Kazanjian,
Senior Editor

ELIZABETH BEVARLY
Donovan's Chance

Silhouette Special Edition

Published by Silhouette Books New York

America's Publisher of Contemporary Romance

For Pragna,
the first to read the first

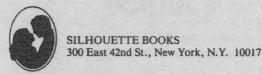

SILHOUETTE BOOKS
300 East 42nd St., New York, N.Y. 10017

ISBN: 0-373-09639-9

First Silhouette Books printing December 1990

Printed in the U.S.A.

Books by Elizabeth Bevarly

Silhouette Special Edition

Destinations South #557
Close Range #590
Donovan's Chance #639

ELIZABETH BEVARLY,

an honors graduate of the University of Louisville, works as a sales associate for a chain of retail clothing stores. At heart, however, she's an avid traveler who once helped sail a friend's thirty-five-foot sailboat across the Bermuda Triangle. "I really love to travel," says this self-avowed beach bum. "To me, it's the best education a person can give herself." Her dream is to one day have her own sailboat, a beautifully renovated older-model forty-two-footer, and to enjoy the total freedom and sense of tranquility it can bring.

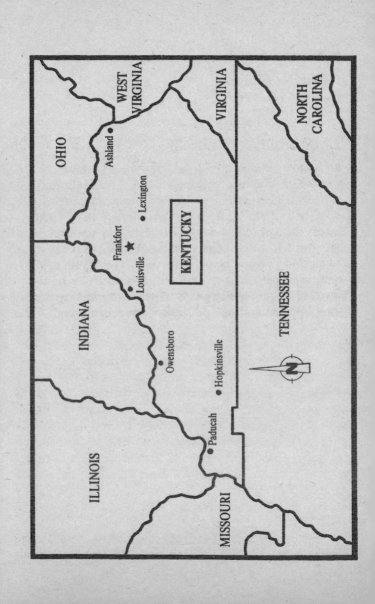

Chapter One

Maximillian Donovan gazed silently and with considerable distraction out the plate-glass picture window of his office into the darkening sky above New York City. Shadowy skyscrapers and thoroughfares began to come alive with the flickering fluorescent lights of dedicated executives working late, and with the car headlamps of those not so dedicated speeding toward the various highways that led to their homes. Maximillian, of course, was effectively already at home here in his office, having spent the majority of his adult life behind his massive chrome and glass desk, cradling a telephone with one hand, shuffling blueprints and building designs with the other. Even when he wasn't in his office, he was somewhere on location, overseeing his latest venture, ensuring that every last detail met with his approval.

At the moment, however, he was restless. Although he received great satisfaction when one of his real-estate deals was completed and construction had begun, an uneasiness inevitably settled over him, and he became inexplicably edgy until he started wheeling and dealing again. Maximillian hated being idle. It made him feel useless. And as ridiculous and unfounded as such a feeling was in a man like Maximillian, it was nonetheless one that was becoming more common and more obvious with each venture he concluded.

Running a big hand through his impeccably cut, dark blond hair, he sighed impatiently and continued to stare out the window, lost in a jumble of thought. When he heard his office door open and the quick clatter of high heels crossing the white tile floor toward him, Maximillian turned abruptly to face his assistant, welcoming the interruption.

"Is everything set to go now with the MetroData Center and Starlight Towers projects?" he shot at her before she had a chance to speak. "You know it's impossible for me to concentrate on a new deal when there's still something left unsettled with an old one. I'd hate to leave for Louisville tomorrow, only to have to interrupt business there when something falls apart here in New York." His voice held a touch of a threat as to what might happen to her if anything went wrong to upset the two biggest real-estate deals of his career.

Adrienne Ellis returned her boss's stare levelly. She certainly wasn't afraid of him, he knew, try as he might to be domineering and forceful. For ten years she had listened to such affected bullying, and he'd realized long ago that she knew it was all bravado. She simply rolled her eyes at him and responded in her usual way when he slipped on that icy facade. She smiled broadly at him, because she knew it made him nervous.

"Everything with the MetroData Center and Starlight Towers projects is just peaches, Maximillian," she assured him without the shadow of a doubt. "All the contracts are signed, sealed and in the bag." She carelessly tossed a sheaf of papers onto his desk so that they fanned across it in an almost perfect pattern. As she continued, she illustrated her words by counting on her fingers. "We've got contractors, we've got electricians, we've got plumbers, we've got building inspectors. We've got advertisers, decorators, and designers that will knock your socks off. We've even got caterers. Trust me, Maximillian, everything is under control."

Maximillian stared with what he hoped was indifference at the statuesque redhead, knowing full well that he could trust her. And he knew he was being unfair, not to mention ineffective, in his attempt to intimidate her just because he was, as usual, worried that he'd missed something in the completion of his latest deal. The fear was groundless, of course. He was the most thorough, cautious developer in the business. Consequently he was also the most successful. His skill, judgment and perception, along with a considerable amount of foresight and good luck, had enabled him to turn over quite a bit of local real estate in the past several years, beginning with that first deal, made almost immediately after he received his M.B.A. from Harvard Business School.

His father and brother had called him crazy to invest in that waterfront swamp on the Hudson. But Maximillian had held on to it, seeing its potential. Using the knowledge he'd gained with his other degrees in architecture and urban planning, he'd proposed a rather massive and ambitious riverfront condominium project, complete with chic boutiques and "happening" nightclubs. With the aid of daring and farsighted investors, he'd seen his dream become reality. After other, similar deals that were touted as insane and worthless by the pros turned to gold in his hands, the real-estate and financial specialists began to see Maximillian

Donovan in a new light. Soon enough, his name was on the tongues of city planners and contractors across the country, and the rest, as they say, was history.

In the past ten years he had turned around more than one waterfront. Large and small communities, along with corporate giants in the private sector, all had sought his services for their own expansion projects. He'd been responsible for everything from shopping malls to subdivisions, from luxury hotels to high-rise corporate centers. His success had been the subject of articles in every major newspaper across the country, and his face had graced the cover of more business and architectural journals than he could name. Maximillian Donovan had become, to put it mildly, a very successful man.

And now another potential project awaited him. He'd never been to Louisville, Kentucky, and had absolutely no idea what to expect. The Houghton Company, who'd hired him to design and build their new corporate headquarters there, had sent him a good deal of statistical information describing the city as a metropolitan area populated by somewhere near one million people, an up-and-coming community that had lately experienced a considerable spurt of growth and development. Along with this practical material, Maximillian had also received an invitation from Steven Houghton himself to come for a visit during the Kentucky Derby Festival that filled up the last week of April and the first week of May. It was a time when the city apparently came alive with parties and parades, with festivities that ranged from craft fairs to steamboat and hot-air balloon races.

Because the moment was opportune, having tied up two successful and smoothly arranged deals in New England, Maximillian decided to go down and see what The Houghton Company had to offer him. If nothing else, there was

Steven Houghton's promise of a multitude of parties given by the city's elite, and Maximillian enjoyed the elegance of parties thrown by people in high places nearly as much as he enjoyed his work.

Thoughts of his job brought him back to the sleek white walls, chrome and glass that formed his office. It was accented with splashes of black and red in the form of abstract paintings and twisted, modernistic sculptures. Maximillian liked things clean and stark and minimal. Clutter made him nervous. His apartment was a repeat of his office, a coolly furnished penthouse that overlooked busy Manhattan on one side, idyllic Central Park on the other. And he really should head home soon, to make sure Edison had packed everything he'd need for his trip, maybe even get some sleep before his early-morning flight, he thought with some distraction.

Adrienne seemed to sense his line of thought. "There's nothing more you need to do, Maximillian," she told him one final time. "Go home, pack your bags and head south. I'll meet you there Saturday like we planned."

Maximillian gazed absently at his assistant. Adrienne was a beautiful, intelligent woman in her early forties. She was quick, creative, infinitely patient and knew as much about the business as he did. He considered her invaluable. He also considered her a great friend.

"All right," he conceded. "I'll go. And I'll see you there Saturday. I'll want your opinion on whatever deal they offer me. But if anything goes wrong between now and then with anything here, you call me and let me know, all right?"

Adrienne shook her head. He was clearly a hopeless case. "You know I will, Maximillian."

He nodded wordlessly. Of course he did. He was just feeling edgy. He had to get something new going, get back to work. It just wasn't in Maximillian's nature to relax and take it easy, not even for a brief time. Perhaps what The Houghton Company had to offer him would be too tempting to pass up. Already excitement began to churn in his blood. He became animated by ideas of real-estate possibilities the way some men got fired up over a football game. All of his interests, all of his hobbies, everything centered on what he did for a living. When he went to parties, he sought out investors. When he went out to eat, it was with the intention of settling a deal. Turning a piece of land into a societal necessity was a passion with him. It was his life.

"Good," he replied finally. "Then I'll be heading out. Have Sonny bring the car around, will you?" He glanced around his office one more time to make certain he wasn't forgetting anything. "So I guess the plan is that I'll go down there, let them chauffeur me around, go to a few parties and see what develops. No pun intended. Then after hearing Houghton's proposal, we can come back here and get on with our business, okay?"

Adrienne frowned at him. "Maximillian, I hope you're taking this invitation seriously. If you're just going down there to be wined and dined and entertained for two weeks, with no intention of accepting their offer, then you're behaving childishly, unfairly, and with a considerable lack of ethics."

Maximillian picked up the papers scattered across his desk and shoveled them into his briefcase, then made a face at his assistant. "Of course I'm going to consider their offer, Adrienne. But I have a lot of other projects brewing, too, you know. Anything can happen."

Adrienne regarded him with clear disapproval. "You know, sometimes you just don't seem to take things seriously enough," she told him. "You treat this business almost as if it were a game to be played. And when that happens, it can only mean one thing, Maximillian. Your life is entirely buried beneath your career, if you have to resort to your work for entertainment. It's true enough that anything can happen down there," she added as he turned to leave. "I only hope it won't be something that will blow up in your face."

"Okay, Rowan, they're just getting ready to start the fourth heat. You're gonna be up in a minute."

Rowan Chance nodded at her best friend, Tara McQuade, as she hopped from foot to foot to limber up before the race. "Oh, Tara, I want to win this so badly, I can taste it."

"You've been in training for weeks now," her dark-eyed, dark-haired friend reminded her. "You've cut your time in half since you started. Your balance is good, you've been pacing yourself, you're in the best shape I've ever seen you in. You're good, kid," she added somberly. "You're a winner."

Rowan smiled a little shakily. "You think so?"

"I know so. Besides, have you taken a good look at the competition? I mean, really."

Rowan looked around her at the other contestants. She'd watched the first three heats of the race, two women's and one men's, and hadn't seen much of a threat to her best time. Still, it was better not to get overly confident. Anything could happen between now and the end of the race. Nervously she smoothed her long, black bangs, then tucked the short strands of her straight, bobbed hair behind her ears while she eyed her competition. Some talked among themselves, absently smoking cigarettes or adjusting their aprons. Those who had completed their heats walked about anxiously with beakers of blush wine. For perhaps the twentieth time, Rowan checked her pocket to make sure she had her corkscrew, checking it again to be certain that it wouldn't jam at the most inopportune moment. It was, after all, the most crucial part of her athletic paraphernalia.

Tara reached up to straighten Rowan's black bow tie as the gun sounded to start the fourth heat. Both women watched with excitement as waiters from several area restaurants began uncorking bottles of wine and turning up six plastic wineglasses on cocktail trays. Most wore their uniforms from the restaurants or bars where they worked, sporting everything from shocking pink, spandex shorts to formal tuxedos. It was The Run for the Rosé, and a trip for two to Walt Disney World was at stake. Rowan and Tara cheered as a tall, lanky waiter from September's, the restaurant where they worked, broke away from the tables first and took the lead. He would have to follow the winding route up Fifth Street and around the grounds of the county courthouse, down Sixth Street and back across the grounds to the finish line. There, his time and the amount of wine left in his glasses would be entered into a computer to calculate his standing in the race.

Rowan applauded furiously as the waiter she knew crossed the line somewhere in the middle of the pack. Butterflies began a raucous party in her stomach as she realized that in a matter of minutes she would be the one competing. She took a tremulous breath; doubt began to take hold of her mind. Gazing at Tara, who was not competing, but acting as her trainer, she was assailed by second thoughts.

"I'm not sure I can do this," she blurted out suddenly.

Tara gave her friend a scolding look. "I don't want to hear any negative talk," she said. "You've put too much into this."

"Why am I doing this?" Rowan muttered to herself.

"Two words," Tara answered. *"Disney World."*

Rowan continued to stare, her usually full lips pulled into a tight line, but said nothing.

"All right," Tara cajoled, "one more word. *Miranda.*"

At the mention of her daughter's name, a warm feeling pushed aside Rowan's anxiety. Miranda had been talking about nothing but Mickey Mouse ever since she found out her mother was going to be competing for the trip. Rowan looked past the ropes that marked the course and into the audience, where another of her friends from September's stood, holding her three-year-old daughter. Miranda was laughing, as usual, squirming in Cathy's arms like a playful kitten. The soft breeze blew her black hair into her face, and the little girl brushed it back with both hands, laughing even harder. When Miranda saw her mother smile and wave, she lifted a tiny hand in response.

What a great kid, Rowan thought. It had been tough trying to raise a baby all alone, and she had been forced to make more than one sacrifice, but she had never once regretted her decision. Miranda's father might have been a completely irresponsible jerk, but if he'd had to leave her, at least he'd left her with something wonderful. She only hoped she could give her daughter all the joy and laughter she herself had known as a child. A trip to Disney World would be an excellent beginning.

"Okay, okay," Rowan mumbled with a smile, returning her attention to Tara. "So I have a great reason to win."

"The best."

"That doesn't mean I'm going to."

"Rowan, your best time is way lower than anybody's had today. If you can even come close to repeating it, you've got this race in the bag."

Rowan began bouncing from foot to foot again to limber up.

"Just don't spill any wine," her friend added.

"Right, Tara, like it's that easy. I don't think they'd consider Glad wrap exactly sporting."

"Just be careful."

Rowan was going to reply with something flip, but the announcer was calling for the runners in the fifth heat. With a final, expressive glance at Tara, she took her place at one of the long tables. When the gun sounded, Rowan uncapped and uncorked her bottle of wine with deft fingers. Quickly, with the skill of someone who'd been waiting tables for over five years, she upturned and filled the six plastic wineglasses, spilling not a drop. She was the first to break away from the tables, the first to head down the sidewalk to Fifth Street, and the first around the course. When she climbed the courthouse steps and rounded the announcer's box, he was pleased to announce to the crowd that number thirty-two, Rowan Chance, had made it halfway through the course, having spilled only a tiny splash of wine. At the base of the courthouse steps, still leading the pack, she had spilled no more.

Rowan felt as light as a feather, as graceful as a swan and as lucky as Luciano. Nothing could stop her now. With six full glasses and no one to pass, she could envision herself and her daughter enjoying the endless wonders of Disney World. Space Mountain. Pirates of the Caribbean. Epcot Center. The new MGM Studios theme park. Mickey and Minnie. Miranda, laughing with delight when the two big rodents shook her tiny hand.

She could sense the end nearing, could taste the triumph and smell the sweet fragrance of victory. When Rowan looked up to get her bearings, she could see the brightly colored plastic pennants that festooned the finish line and the colossal digital clock that displayed her time. It was even better than the best she'd managed in training. However, instead of stepping over the line to win a trip for two to Orlando, Rowan slammed face first into a chest the size of Cleveland that came at her out of nowhere, dousing both the man and herself with what a local wine critic had called a lightly teasing, but very playful and satisfying white zinfandel.

Maximillian Donovan had absolutely no idea what a tuxedoed waitress with a tray full of rosé was doing in the middle of the county courthouse grounds in the center of downtown Louisville. And quite frankly he didn't care. She had, however, spilled that rosé all over his favorite suit, and now he was going to look pretty ridiculous when he met with Steven Houghton and the local city planners. Consequently he was a bit touchy when he spoke.

"What in the hell is the matter with you?" he roared at the woman who stood motionless before him.

He watched as her gaze wandered from the scattered plastic wineglasses and the dark patch of wine that stained the sidewalk to a number of other waiters with trays who passed them to one in particular who crossed the finish line first. Finally her eyes settled on his. With a silent and involuntary intake of breath, Maximillian noted that those eyes were huge and thickly lashed, the color of blue delft china. He'd never seen eyes so blue. Nor had he ever seen eyes so angry. And accusing. And completely full of fight.

"You owe me a trip to Disney World," the woman said simply, but Maximillian sensed she was making a tremendous effort to remain civil.

He was so taken aback by her statement that he could only mutter, "I beg your pardon?"

"I said—"

"I heard what you said," he interrupted her abruptly. "I just don't know what you're talking about." He still held her eyes, unable to look anywhere else, despite the pink stains that were oozing across his silk shirt and tie and down his dark tailored suit, all the way to his designer underwear. "If anyone owes someone something, it's you," he added.

Rowan's eyes widened in surprise, then narrowed as she became even angrier. "Oh, really? And just how do you figure that?"

"I figure you owe me a new suit."

She laughed humorlessly at the tall, sneering man, excusing the erratic beating of her heart as nothing more than her extreme irritation at his clumsiness. "You're out of your mind, guy. You just cost me the first vacation I would have had in over four years. *You* owe *me*."

"Rowan!" she heard Tara's voice call out.

By now the announcer had made it clear to the audience that number thirty-two, Rowan Chance, who had been in the lead until nearly the end of the heat, had met with an unlucky mishap, then had lost all of her glasses and that it was a heartbreaker. Amid aws and ohs, Tara pushed her way through the spectators to the finish line and called to Rowan from the sidelines.

"What happened?" Rowan's friend and trainer asked, raising her hands above her shoulder in a confused shrug.

"I lost," Rowan muttered in defeat, tossing her tray disconsolately onto the grass before crossing her arms across her midsection.

"Look, would somebody please tell me what's going on here?" Maximillian was at a complete loss now. He'd only been in the city for a day and a half, but he'd already begun to think it was a nice place, seemingly full of friendly people and potentially inviting night spots, and if last night's welcoming reception was any indication, hosts and hostesses who really knew how to throw a good party. But this... waiters with glasses of wine in the middle of downtown Louisville... during lunch hour, when they should be serving people... racing for a trip to Disney World...? It was all a bit much, really. Derby Festival or no Derby Festival, this was all too bizarre.

Rowan turned to look once again at the man who had dashed the hopes of her daughter and herself. Wine-stained or not, dressed in his pin-striped, tailored suit, with his dark blond good looks, he seemed to be the type of person who would eat at September's and pay with his gold or platinum credit card, the type to whom things came too easily. She could sense it in the way he kept making demands. Without knowing the man, Rowan found herself disliking him. But then, she'd found herself disliking rich people for a long time now. Why this one should unsettle her more than others was a question she didn't care to examine.

When the woman turned back to him but said nothing, Maximillian became a little uncomfortable. She looked hopeless and helpless, beaten down and tired. As if she'd seen one of her lifelong wishes ground into the dust. For some strange reason he felt as if he should apologize. It didn't make sense. She was the one who'd come crashing into him, even if he had been where he shouldn't be. Yet this woman with eyes the color and clarity of a mountain lake in the spring made him want to apologize, and worse, make amends for some unlucky action that wouldn't be undone, simply because he felt remorseful.

"I'm sorry," he said quietly, still not certain what he had to be sorry for.

Rowan's expression remained the same. "Don't worry about it," she told him coolly, and needlessly, she thought. He'd probably completely forget the incident after he'd related it with considerable complaint to his dry cleaner.

Maximillian continued to watch this walking accident with a bow tie as she strode slowly and with sagging shoulders toward the dark-haired woman by the ropes. After she had recounted what had happened, her friend turned to glare at him with accusation, as if he were the devil himself, come to steal happiness from the world. He found himself taking a step forward, wanting to defend himself, then wondered why he should care. As the black-haired woman with the haunting blue eyes disappeared into the crowd, Maximillian brushed absently at the wine still dampening his shirt, then turned back toward the courthouse to make his meeting. For some reason, though, he suspected it would be a while before he would be able to fully address the issues that would arise during his session with Houghton and the city planners.

Chapter Two

The riverfront Chow Wagon, a popular outdoor Derby Festival fixture and parking lot cum food festival boasting a large variety of home-style cooking and music was bustling with people, especially now during the workday lunch hour. The bright sun beat down on pin-striped executives and blue-jeaned picnickers alike. Children with ice cream ran and squealed among bankers and businessmen, who cut deals while enjoying a loaded bratwurst and plastic cupful of beer. Rowan and her friends from September's Restaurant sat around a picnic table, enjoying the balmy afternoon. An abundance of local fare was offered by the long row of food stalls covered with red-and-white-striped awnings to Rowan's right. To her left the muddy Ohio rippled peacefully southwest, and Rowan lifted her face to the sun, inhaling deeply of the fresh afternoon. The aromas of barbecue and beer, corn dogs and Kentucky burgoo filled her nostrils, and she suddenly found herself craving a slab of barbecued ribs.

"I'm going back for more," she announced to Tara, who was seated across from her.

"Good Lord, Rowan, you've eaten everything in sight already," Tara groaned. "I still don't know where you put that last tiger ear. If it were me, I'd have gained ten pounds, just looking at it."

Cathy, too, looked at Rowan, who held Miranda in her lap, and laughed when the little girl stuffed a fat French fry into her greedy mouth.

"Like mother, like daughter, I'm afraid," Rowan said. "Miranda's eaten more than I have. She especially likes Tara's burgoo." She tweaked her daughter's nose. "Don't you, sweetheart?"

Miranda chuckled and repeated, "Burgoo."

"Of course she likes it," Cathy muttered, tossing her pale blond braid over her shoulder. "It sounds like something a baby named and looks like something a baby would spit up. Personally, I can't abide the stuff. All that slimy okra. Yuck."

Tara dropped the plastic spoon she'd been lifting repeatedly to her lips for the last ten minutes back into her bowl as if the spoon had burned her. "There's okra in there?" she asked ominously.

"Among other things," Rowan told her.

"I hate okra."

"Tara, you're nearly finished with it and you never even noticed," Rowan reminded her. "What's the problem?"

"I just don't understand," Tara began in melodramatic bewilderment, eyeing the bowl of red sauce that harbored numerous spices and vegetables of unknown origin as if it had turned into a vat of worms. "Usually I can tell, you know? Usually there's always a clue of some kind, a sign.

The sliminess Cathy mentioned. Or the hairiness... or the seeds. But this..." She indicated the foam bowl. "It seemed so safe, so harmless. How could I have known it would be filled with..." she gasped "...okra?"

Rowan shook her head and smiled at her friend, while Miranda reached over and dunked a fist into Tara's burgoo. "You're going to be a wonderful actress, Tara," Rowan said. "I just hope you pass all of your finals next week."

"Worry about your own finals, kid," Tara responded. "Have you finished that paper on Dante Gabriel Rossetti yet?"

Rowan's back went up at the reminder of how much she had left to do before the end of the semester, and how little time she had left to finish it. "No, I haven't finished the paper on Dante Gabriel Rossetti," she snapped. "I'm still working on the one about doors for my Victorian Architecture class."

"How's your independent study paper?" Cathy asked, reaching across the table to wipe absently at Miranda's burgoo-filled hands with a paper napkin.

"It's fine," Rowan replied sharply.

"You haven't finished it yet, have you?" Tara's question was delivered more as a statement, and Rowan grew even more defensive at her friends' implications.

"Look, will you guys just lighten up?" she demanded, feeling like a mouse backed into a corner by a group of greedy alley cats. "I've had a lot of work to do down at The Warehouse this month, all right? I'll get my schoolwork done by next week, so just get off my back, okay?"

"Rowan," Cathy said softly, "we're only on your back because we know how important it is to you to graduate this semester."

Before Rowan could open her mouth to defend herself yet again, Tara cut her off. "Yeah, we know you want to get the shop open as soon as possible, but you've got to get your priorities in order. And you've told me over and over that your degree comes first, your business second."

"I know." Rowan sighed in defeat. "But I'm so close, you guys. It's just..." She struggled to find the right words. "Ever since my parents died, I've been searching for something stable, trying to get back on my feet. When I met Joey four years ago, I thought things were really going to start happening right for a change, you know? But then..."

Her eyes wandered to the little girl in her lap, who sat oblivious to the conversation, too wrapped up in devouring what remained of Tara's lunch.

"Well, things didn't exactly turn out as planned," she finished off quickly, giving her daughter a gentle squeeze and an affectionate kiss on the forehead that made Miranda giggle. "And now things are finally back in reach again. It's so frustrating, knowing it's all so close. I want it all right now."

"But you can't have it all right now," Cathy reminded her. Then a new thought seemed to strike her. "You're not in any kind of trouble, are you?" she asked her friend. "Financially, I mean?"

"No, I'm all right," Rowan assured her. "I'm making enough at September's to get by. It's *time* I just don't seem to have enough of. Trying to function on four hours of sleep a night isn't as easy as it used to be," she added, only half joking. "I just want to see the shop opened because... because...just because."

Because I'm beginning to feel like a worthless failure, she said to herself. Because it seemed as if she would never see a time in her life when she wasn't fighting to overcome some obstacle that prevented her from achieving her dreams.

* * *

For the first twenty years of her life, Rowan had led a storybook-perfect existence. She'd grown up in Louisville in a rambling, old Victorian house in the Highlands, the daughter of a carpenter and an artist. Her parents had purchased the house in a state of utter disrepair when she was a baby, and she had spent her childhood amid remodeling and renovation, helping out where she could by toting around tools for her father or by cleaning her mother's paintbrushes. While her mother was teaching classes at the university, she'd help her father fix the stairs. When he was working on a construction site, she helped her mother pull weeds in the garden.

Every evening the three Chances would eat dinner together, always something organic with one or more fresh vegetables from the backyard garden, and every night her parents would take turns reading to her. *The Wind in the Willows* and *Winnie-the-Pooh* had been her mother's favorites, while her father had preferred *The Call of the Wild* and *Treasure Island*. Surrounded by comfortable old furnishings and potted plants, in the constant company of cats and canaries, with her father's big-band albums or her mother's chamber music tapes essential parts of everyday life, Rowan had grown up an extremely well-adjusted, well-educated, well-loved child.

It had all been so wonderful, so perfect. Until that one weekend in August, a week after her twentieth birthday, two weeks before she was to return to college for her junior year. The weekend her parents had spent down at Lake Cumberland to celebrate their twenty-fifth anniversary. They'd been almost home when they were sideswiped by some intoxicated idiot who had raced through a red light at breakneck speed, slamming his luxury sedan into her parents' compact and crumpling it like aluminum foil. An extremely rich and powerful idiot, who had later used his money and influence to have the charges filed against him dropped.

Then Rowan had been left alone. And as loving as her parents had been, they'd neglected to make any provisions for her future, should such a tragedy occur, and Rowan was also left broke. The deaths of her parents affected her more deeply than any of her friends ever really guessed, she knew. With the theft of her happy existence, Rowan became utterly despondent, and began to feel as if life had nothing left to offer beyond constant reminders of what she'd once had, what had been so suddenly and heartlessly ripped away from her. Why bother planning for the future, when the future could never be predicted? she'd reasoned in her depression. What was the point of doing anything worthwhile, when everything could be changed so drastically, without notice? Today was all one could count on. Best make the most of what was at hand.

So Rowan gave up any hope of a future. She decided not to go back to college, and instead took undemanding, dead-end jobs that enabled her to survive, even if deep down she was certain there was nothing to survive for. Eventually she found herself working at September's and part of a social circle that consisted of fun-loving waiters and bartenders, who kept very late hours and partied endlessly. She also found herself making upward of one hundred and fifty dollars a night in tips, and without any prospects for the future, saw little reason to save it. Consequently Rowan became the ultimate party girl.

And she became very good at it. Every night after September's closed, there was a gathering of restaurant workers somewhere in town, and every night Rowan was there. Usually the festivities began around two in the morning and lasted until the sun crept up over the earth. Many were the times Rowan thought of herself as a vampire, sleeping all day, only to come alive at dusk to work her shift and party until dawn. She stopped at the all-night supermarket to buy her groceries, feeling smug because she *never* had to wait in line, and became quite an expert on exceptionally bad, grade-B monster movies that Channel 41 ran all night long.

But the parties had been the best part, and fortunately there had been many of them. Yet even at her most self-indulgent, Rowan never took a drink if she was going to drive. She would never be like the man who had taken her parents away from her. She would never be the one to shatter someone else's life. Under the influence or not, Rowan found the parties provided her with a way to elude the fear and ignore the numbness that always seemed to chill her soul. It was a way to be someone besides her parents' daughter, a way to forget the hopelessness that had been so much a part of life since their death. Always beautiful, always entertaining, chatty and clever, Rowan Chance was very popular at these parties. She dated frequently, but gave her heart to no one. Loving was too dangerous, she knew. Love was so easily lost. But she could have fun for the moment, she decided. After all, moments were abundant in this lifetime. There were virtually thousands of them every day. And who knew what the next one held? She might as well take as many as she could, and make the most out of each of them.

Two years after starting work at September's, she was still living exactly the same way. The night Joey Monaco started bartending there, Rowan had sensed immediately that something was about to change. Joey was darkly handsome, enormously funny, and he always called her Venus. For some reason she trusted him. Somehow she'd even let herself fall in love with him. Maybe because Joey Monaco said all the right things at all the right times, to break through her facade and tear down all of her emotional barriers. He seemed to know exactly what she wanted to hear and made sure she heard the words over and over again. Joey Monaco had made her feel special, even loved, for the first time since her parents' death.

Unfortunately, she'd discovered that Joey Monaco had made a great many women feel that way. And when Rowan had revealed that she was expecting his baby, he'd done something that she had eventually realized was very characteristic of him. Joey took off. Left with the prospect of raising a child alone, Rowan was forced to massively adjust her perspective. Suddenly she did have a future to plan. And not just hers, but her child's, as well. All at once, things began to take shape for her again. Her life began to have meaning once more.

Her late nights and partying came to an end then, and strangely, Rowan didn't even miss the continuous blur of socializing. She sold her parents' house for ten times what they'd paid for it and bought an old, broken-down Victorian only blocks from where she'd grown up, planning to renovate it, as her parents had done so many years before. In an attempt to prepare for the future, she also purchased an equally worn-out warehouse on Main Street and reformulated her precollege plans. She would get her degree in Art History and open up a combination antique and home renovation shop, called simply The Warehouse. And after Miranda's birth, Rowan had gone back to school part-time.

Between her daughter's arrival, the renovation of her house, the restoration and organization of The Warehouse and her studies, the remainder of her finances had been steadily and sufficiently depleted. Working at September's afforded her enough money to provide for herself and Miranda and allowed her the very valuable time to get her life back in order, but every day she felt the demon of economic insecurity clawing more tightly at her throat. Despite what she had said to Cathy, that was the other reason she wanted to get her shop open as soon as possible.

"No, we're all right," she promised her friends once again. "It's just that I'm getting more anxious every day. I'm almost ready to open."

"But you have to get your degree first," Cathy reminded her in a singsong voice. "At least that's what you've been saying you wanted for the last three years."

"I still do." Rowan sighed wearily. "Look, I can handle this, all right? Everything will be just fine." She was almost able to convince herself of the fact. Almost. But the looks on her friends' faces assured her that they weren't so easily swayed. Abruptly she changed the subject. "I'm going back for ribs. Anybody want anything?"

"Will you get me a beer?" Tara asked her, reaching over to steal one of Miranda's French fries.

"If you'll hold my offspring," Rowan agreed, rising. She handed the little girl to Tara, who promptly offered Miranda what was left of her much-maligned burgoo.

Rowan had changed her clothes after the race, and now as she purchased a large slab of thick, wonderfully greasy ribs, she tucked her change into the pocket of her faded jeans, then smiled when the wind tugged playfully at the hem of her red and black bowling shirt as she headed leisurely toward the beer booth. She laughed out loud in delighted surprise when the man serving carded her, and thanked him most graciously when he said, "Man, you sure don't look twenty-six." Shaking her head in disbelief, she picked up the plastic cup filled to the rim with draft beer with one hand, and hoisted the plate of ribs into the other. When she turned to head back toward her friends, someone beside her jostled her elbow, and she felt her burden of barbecue beginning to slip. So preoccupied was she with keeping the plate balanced that she neglected Tara's beer, and too late, felt the cold brew spilling out over her hand.

By the time she pivoted fully around, she was lost in concentration on the struggle to retrieve her lunch. Evidently so was the man she bumped squarely into. At least he had been, until the beer sloshed onto his Hugo Boss suit, and the ribs plopped messily onto his Gucci loafers. For a moment, Rowan couldn't react to what had happened. She was too distracted by the splotches of pink that stained the man's shirt. A sense of foreboding clouded her thinking then, and she raised her face reluctantly to find herself staring into familiar, if furious, hazel eyes.

"Oh, no," she groaned at the man who had cost her a trip to Disney World.

"Oh, yes," Maximillian replied testily, as incredulous as she.

He had all but forgotten the clumsy waitress with the haunting eyes, after explaining his appearance to Houghton's amused group a short time after the mishap. But now when he gazed down into those dark blue eyes again, the same confusing reaction he'd had before came back to him in a rush. He found himself involuntarily placing his hand gently on her upper arm to steady her, despite the fact that, having already spilled her lunch all over him, she no longer needed steadying.

Rowan was immediately aware of his gesture and yanked her arm out of his grasp to take a step away from him. This action resulted in her collision with another man, who promptly spilled his own beer.

"Do you make a habit of this?" Maximillian asked, unable to let his gaze stray from her face for even a moment. "Should I find it reassuring that I'm not your only victim?"

Rowan mumbled her apology to the grumbling man behind her, then turned her attention back to Maximillian.

"No apology for me?" he wanted to know.

When she'd run into him the first time, she'd been so upset by his costing her the race that she hadn't paid much attention to his good looks. Now that she found herself face-to-face with him a second time, she couldn't help but take notice. He was very good-looking, she realized with a frown. Well dressed, polished, confident, apparently intelligent, unquestionably rich. Arrogant, too, she added silently, taking in his menacing stance and the obvious threat he held in his eyes, eyes that flashed from brown to green in the afternoon sun.

"Why should I apologize for something that clearly wasn't my fault?" she retorted sharply. Rowan was usually a very even-tempered person, but something about this man put her back up without giving her a chance to even wonder why.

"Oh, I suppose I'm to blame again. Is that what you're trying to say?" He took a step toward her, then felt the slab of ribs ooze slowly from his shoe onto the pavement and looked down. He'd been so shocked by the sudden splashing of cold beer on his abdomen that he hadn't noticed the glob of pork on his foot until that moment. "Great," he muttered at Rowan when he lifted his eyes back up to her face. "This is just great. It isn't enough that you ruin my shirt and jacket, but you have to go after the rest of my wardrobe, too."

"You should watch where you're going!" she snapped. "You brought this on yourself, you know."

"Oh, no, you don't, sweetheart. You're not going to pin this one on me. Tell me where to send the bill. What's your name and where do you live?"

"You're out of your mind if you think I'm going to tell you where I live. It's bad enough running into you on the street."

"So you admit that *you* ran into *me*!" he announced triumphantly.

"No, I didn't mean it like that," she protested. "I meant—"

"Too late," Maximillian interrupted her, enjoying the fact that now *she* was on the defensive. "I have witnesses, isn't that so, gentlemen?"

"Yes, sir, Mr. Donovan."

"Absolutely, sir."

"Without question, Mr. Donovan."

"Clearly, Mr. Donovan."

For the first time Rowan noted the entourage with whom this man was traveling. All wearing suits, incongruously gripping corn dogs, caramel apples and blue and purple snow cones, the businessmen nodded vigorously their unequivocal support for their leader. Then the name they had uttered struck her like a thunderbolt. Donovan. You didn't have to be a student of art and architecture to know the name Maximillian Donovan. You had only to read the newspaper, look at magazines or watch television. She felt like an idiot for not having recognized him right off. Of course, the photographs she'd seen of him didn't do the man justice. He was much more three-dimensional in real life. In fact, he was almost larger than life. Certainly much larger than Rowan.

She closed her eyes and swallowed with some difficulty. "You're Maximillian Donovan?" she asked softly, already knowing the answer.

"I am," he responded smugly. "And you're...?"

For some reason, the idea of Maximillian Donovan knowing her name terrified Rowan. This was a man who laid claim to whatever struck his fancy, who owned *everything*. She did not want to give him anything that belonged to her, lest he try to consume that, too. "I'm still not to blame for this," she said evasively. "You'll have to take care of your own dry cleaning. Now, if you'll excuse me..."

Still gripping the half-full cup of beer meant for Tara, Rowan tried to push quickly past Maximillian Donovan and escape. Before she could even complete two steps, his hand snaked out to grasp her wrist, tightening its hold when she tried to wrench free. She spun around to glare at him and demanded, "Let go of me."

"Not until I've had that apology," Maximillian said in clipped tones. He couldn't understand why this woman made him so angry, why he had become so antagonistic over such a trivial accident. Maybe it was because she refused to back down and give him what he wanted. Maximillian wasn't used to having people face him down and deny him what he demanded. Especially people of the feminine persuasion.

"I don't owe you an apology," Rowan countered. He saw the glitter of combat flashing in her eyes as she tried unsuccessfully to twist free of his hold on her.

"You owe me more than an apology," he insisted. "But I'll settle for that."

Rowan's heart beat furiously beneath skin she knew must be hot to the touch. She'd had more than one run-in with demanding men, often having to deal with customers who'd had too much to drink or who were simply self-important jerks. But this man... It was like facing down a bulldozer, so steely did he seem, so focused on his purpose. But she would not give in.

"You'll have a long wait," she assured him, giving her arm one final tug to free her wrist, as surprised as he when she succeeded. Before he could say another word, she spun quickly around and headed back to her friends, who must surely be wondering what had happened to her.

Maximillian watched her departure with interest, fascinated by the rhythmic sway of her curvy hips under the long shirttail. Absently he took in the design embroidered on the back of her red shirt, three bowling pins being struck by a ball, and to the side, in black letters, the words Alley Cat. He felt his menacing scowl disappear, replaced by a slow grin. She was a cat, all right, he thought with a soft chuckle. But an alley cat? Probably not. He could still remember the look that had clouded her eyes for only a moment, the one that made her seem so helpless and tired. Behind all of her spitting and hissing, beyond her raised back and extended claws, he could sense a harmless kitten that shivered and shook even as it attacked. A kitten backed into a corner by a pack of wild dogs who had her sputtering and growling in an attempt to be fearless.

But Maximillian wasn't fooled. He only wondered what he'd have to do to see the softer side of this woman. He watched her rejoin her friends at the table, unreasonably grateful that they were all women. Then, with some sense of distraction, he turned back to his colleagues and sighed. All work and no play was making Maximillian a very dull boy. But what else was there?

With one last glance over his shoulder at the blue-eyed black-haired waitress, Maximillian let his mind wander for a moment before getting back to business. "Gentlemen," he began finally, grabbing a handful of napkins from the table at the beer tent to dab at his clothes. "Where were we?"

"I can't believe that was Maximillian Donovan you ran into today," Tara said for perhaps the hundredth time as she and Rowan tucked Miranda into bed for a nap. "Twice, no less."

"Don't remind me," Rowan told her friend on a weary sigh. "It was bad enough when it happened. I don't want to keep reliving it every time you bring it up."

"I'm sorry, but it's just so incredible." Tara ran a hand through her thick brown curls. "Cripes, do you realize how *rich* that guy is?"

"Yes."

"I mean, he can buy *anything* he wants."

"I know."

"*Anytime* he wants."

"I know."

"Just imagine." Tara's voice grew more and more animated. "You want an island? Pick up the phone, bam, you got an island. You want an estate on that island? Bam, a few months later, you got an estate. You want a harem in that estate on that island? No problem! Bam, you got it. You want—"

"Tara, please," Rowan pleaded quietly. "The baby's trying to sleep."

Tara lowered her voice to a whisper. "I was just trying to make a point."

"You've made it. Over and over again. Let's go downstairs."

After retrieving a pitcher of iced tea from the refrigerator, the two women went outside to relax on the back porch. If Miranda was Rowan's joy, then her backyard was her pride. She'd labored many hours to achieve the English garden setting, but every day she admitted that the result had been well worth the effort. Two towering maples and an ancient oak shaded the soft, green grass, fragrant, colorful flowers dotted its sunny patches. Honeysuckle grew in thick vines along the back fence, and red and white roses climbed the trellis along the porch. To their right was a small herb and vegetable garden, and to their left was a multihued and sweet-smelling flower bed. All along the side fences were bushes of lilac and wisteria, and the continuous buzz of bees and hummingbirds was a constant reminder to Rowan that her flowers would be there for Miranda and herself season after season. The thought comforted her a great deal.

She looked over at Tara, who seemed lost in contemplation, absently moving back and forth in the aged, brown wicker rocker. Rowan's wicker chair creaked as she stretched her long legs onto the matching table and lifted her glass to her lips.

"Maximillian Donovan," Tara said again dreamily. "I still can't believe it."

"Believe it, Tara," Rowan muttered after swallowing a mouthful of sweet, minty tea. "And drop it."

"Do you think he'll call you?"

Rowan nearly choked on her next sip. *"Call me?"* she gasped after she stopped hacking. "Why on earth would he call me?"

Tara shrugged lightly, letting her imagination get the better of her. "He's a man, you're a woman...."

Closing her eyes in a silent plea for patience, Rowan shook her head hopelessly. "He's a man who doesn't even know this woman's name."

"You didn't give him your name?"

"Of course not. He's a total stranger."

"He's Maximillian Donovan!" Tara reminded her, aghast.

"A total stranger," Rowan repeated emphatically.

"You're crazy, Rowan," Tara told her. "I would have given the guy my name, address, phone number, Christmas list, dress size, you name it."

"That's because *you* are a woman of easy virtue," Rowan told her friend with a smile.

"I am not," Tara protested. "But I know a good thing when I see it."

"Yeah, right."

Tara eyed her friend with frank speculation. "You know what your problem is?"

Rowan didn't think she was going to like what was coming, but played along anyway. "Oh, please, do tell me."

"You're afraid," Tara said succinctly.

"Of what?"

"Of men. Specifically of *liking* men."

"That's crazy," Rowan denied, but felt her back straighten involuntarily at Tara's analysis. She wasn't afraid of men. Not really. Hey, some of her best friends were men. Sort of.

"Look, Rowan, just because Joey Monaco was a total creep—"

"Joey Monaco has nothing to do with this," Rowan said sharply, indicating that this was not a topic she cared to discuss.

"He has everything to do with it," Tara insisted. "Between your parents' deaths and Joey's desertion, you've gotten pretty gun-shy where relationships are concerned. You're afraid that if you risk loving, or even *liking* someone again, they're going to leave you."

After another shake of her head, Rowan stared at Tara in offended disbelief. "You, my friend, are out of your mind. The two are in no way similar, nor do they have anything to do with Maximillian Donovan. And as far as being afraid to like someone, well, I like you. Usually. And anyway, since when are you such an expert on relationships, you of the monthly, week-long affair?"

"Oh, sure," Tara said stiffly, "just because I haven't met the right guy yet..."

"That's one way of describing it," Rowan mumbled.

Tara's mouth snapped shut. "Fine. Just forget it."

"Gladly."

The two women sat in stilted silence for some minutes, letting animosity charge the air between them.

"You haven't been with anybody since Joey, have you?" Tara asked suddenly. A light of understanding flickered to life in her eyes.

Rowan's eyes widened as she stared at the other woman. "Where did that come from?"

"You haven't, have you?"

For some reason, Rowan was uncomfortable and began to squirm in her chair. "I haven't had much spare time," she stalled. "And I haven't had the opportunity to meet that many men."

Her friend made a rude sound of disbelief. "Ha! Every week some new guy asks you out," she accused Rowan. "And you hardly ever accept."

"That's because most of them are married guys in their fifties, or guys who just want a tumble with a woman who obviously has no morals, because she's had a child out of wedlock," Rowan complained bitterly.

Tara adopted a smug expression of self-righteousness as she analyzed her friend's behavior. "*I* think you've repressed your sexual urges for the last four years because you're scared of being abandoned again. And *I* think you've transferred those sexual urges into anger directed at the male population because of your past experience with Joey. *I* think you need to go out and get laid and free yourself from your sexual prison. That's what *I* think."

Rowan rolled back her eyes and slapped a palm against her forehead. "Oh, thank you, Dr. McQuade. I wasn't aware that you'd received your Ph.D. in Human Sexuality, but thank God you're here. Whatever would have happened to me without your misdirected guidance?''

Ignoring her sarcasm, Tara continued to assess the situation. ''If you don't go in for a radical attitude adjustment soon, Rowan, you're headed for a serious fall. Bitterness can eat you up inside until you don't have a heart left. You mark my words.''

Rowan pushed her long bangs off her forehead and stared at her best friend for several moments through narrowed eyes. After careful contemplation, she spoke slowly and quietly. ''Tara, sometimes I just do not follow the bizarre workings of your mind. I'm not sexually repressed, and I'm not bitter about anything.''

Tara sniffed indignantly and said succinctly, ''Ha.''

''Oh, what would you know about it, anyway?'' Rowan muttered. ''The only tragedies you've ever suffered have involved home perms and press-on nails.''

''Yeah, well at least I reacted to those,'' Tara said in her own defense. ''I cried my eyes out when that body wave came out looking like something from the North Shore. Did you ever shed a tear for your parents?''

''That's enough, Tara. This isn't open for discussion.'' And it wasn't. Her reaction to her parents' death was no one's business but her own. Grief took many forms, she told herself. The fact that she hadn't cried didn't make her feelings of desolation any less painful or significant.

''No, you transferred your grief into anger,'' Tara went on relentlessly. ''And it's been eating you up inside ever since. How can you expect to get over what happened if—''

''I think it's time we started studying, don't you?'' Rowan asked pointedly, clearly indicating that the subject of her parents was closed.

Tara shook her head hopelessly. "Someday, Rowan..." she said quietly, her voice fading off at the warning.

"Well, not today," her friend assured her. "Not today."

For the remainder of the afternoon and evening they did study, hovering over books and notes until their vision blurred. When Tara left, it was well into the next morning, and Rowan remembered they'd both promised Louis September, the restaurant's owner and manager, that they would work the following night at a party September's was catering.

"Can I catch a ride with you to the Simpsons' dinner party tomorrow night?" she asked as she dumped her friend's textbooks into the passenger seat of her car. "I still haven't had a chance to get my car to the shop and have that busted radiator fixed."

It was only a small lie, Rowan reasoned. She'd actually had plenty of chances. But she didn't want to spend the money. She'd gotten so used to taking the bus, she was almost resigned to leave the old heap in the garage indefinitely. But where the Simpsons lived, the buses didn't run. They didn't need to. When everyone in the neighborhood got a Porsche or Corvette for their sixteenth birthday, the idea of needing a bus line was, well, a little silly.

"Okay, I'll pick you up at four-thirty," Tara promised as she got into her car and started the engine. "You know, I worked the Simpsons' Derby party last year."

"So?"

"So they're unbelievably wealthy people."

"No kidding," Rowan said mildly. "People who can afford Louis for a caterer have got to have more money than they know what to do with."

"Yeah, but there were a lot of celebrities there. I got Bob Hope's autograph."

"Do tell. Is this all leading somewhere?"

"I was just thinking that maybe Maximillian Donovan will be there."

"Oh, Tara, will you get off that? You're beginning to sound like a broken record."

"I'm just trying to prepare you," Tara told her.

"Why? So I can get my Christmas list in order?"

"No, so you can work on your footing," the other woman quipped.

"Just pick me up at four-thirty, okay? And leave the dry wit at home."

Tara revved the engine playfully. "The Simpson Derby party," she intoned with mock gravity. "Be there, or be square."

Rowan laughed. "What does being there as cocktail servers make us?"

"Real square," Tara said on a sigh.

"At least we have our health."

"Good health does not guarantee one emeralds and islands," Tara reminded her.

"Well, we may not be rich, but at least we get to sleep late. See you in the afternoon."

Tara brightened visibly at Rowan's philosophy. "Don't forget to iron your penguin suit!" she called out the window as she backed down the driveway.

Rowan smiled and lifted a hand in farewell as her friend drove off into the night, then suddenly frowned in mid-wave. Her penguin suit still had wine stains on it. It would be a while before she could turn in, she realized, hoping fervently that she could get the stains out of the only white shirt she owned. Damn Maximillian Donovan, she thought. Damn, damn, damn!

Chapter Three

The Simpson Derby party was like every other catered "Affaire by Louis" that Rowan had ever worked, and the Simpson house was like every other stately Glenview home. Edgar and Danetta obviously had moldy old money up to their yahoos, Rowan thought, and well, when you've seen one Italian marble ballroom and gilt and crystal dining room to seat eighty, you've seen them all. The female guests sparkled with the aid of gemstones and designer gowns, and the male guests, Rowan discovered, seemed to be unusually preoccupied with the hired help. More than once she found herself dodging fingers and crumpling up business cards with personal phone numbers scribbled on the back.

"Jeez, these guys are unbelievable tonight," Rowan muttered to Tara at one point in the evening as she retreated briefly into the Simpson kitchen to reload her silver tray of champagne. She noted as she splashed the sparkling, pale gold liquid into elegant, crystal flutes that the room was larger than most suburban homes.

"What now?" Tara asked as she impaled hors d'oeuvres with tiny gold swords.

"Oh, everything," Rowan mumbled, waving a hand airily at nothing in particular. "Those guys just think they're so clever and so gorgeous and that the sun should rise and set because they tell it to. Just because they have money."

"I find it very hard to believe that every man out there spoke to you with the specific intent of irritating you, Rowan," Tara said, shaking her head slowly back and forth at her friend.

Rowan made a face at the other woman. "Okay, okay. I admit it. Maybe I have just a teensy-weensy little bit of a negative attitude toward the opposite sex. On occasion."

Tara smiled sweetly. "What did I say yesterday?" Then, adopting her best Sigmund Freud voice, she added, "Now I sink vee are makink progress. Tell me, *Fräulein*, just how long haf you detested half of zee population, und vat haf you been dreamink about lately? Erector sets? Hotdogs und doughnuts? Choo-choo trains goink into tunnels? Hmm?"

"You know, I'm beginning to detest clever waitresses, too," Rowan replied through gritted teeth as she topped off the last champagne flute.

"Rowan! Tara!"

She heard Louis's urgent voice and closed her eyes for a moment, in an effort to make him disappear. It didn't work. The little man waddled up and glared at them with his hands on his ample waist. Rowan noticed that he had used even more hair goo on his thinning black tresses than usual this evening, and he had waxed his handlebar mustache until it looked as though she could reach over and snap a piece off. He must be trying to impress someone tonight, she thought wryly.

"I should think you both have better things to do than mill about gossiping," he told them crisply. "If not, take your conversation outside and I'll mail you your severance checks. Now get back to work!" He clapped his hands twice and made a shooing motion with them.

After sparing one more look to Tara that indicated she detested Louis, too, Rowan lifted her loaded tray onto one shoulder. As she backed out the kitchen door, her thoughts centered on why she'd found herself so suddenly at the top of God's hit list, and why her life lately seemed to be picking up speed as it rolled steadily downhill.

So lost in her thoughts was she, in fact, that as she rounded the sweeping, elegant main stairway to make her entrance into the ballroom, she paid scarce attention to the tall, golden-haired man descending. Not until her small foot connected with his large one at the bottom of the steps and she went tumbling, along with her tray, into his arms.

"Oh, no!" Rowan exclaimed when she realized she was falling. She made a valiant effort to save her expensive burden, but to no avail. At approximately the same time she noted the big hands grasping her arms to catch her, she also noted the expansive chest whose starched, pleated tuxedo shirt was now sopping wet with hundred-dollar-a-bottle champagne. Almost as an afterthought, the silver tray clattered with the flourish of an orchestra cymbal onto the parquetry floor before landing silently on the pricey-looking and champagne-stained Chinese carpet, drawing every eye within a twenty-foot radius. Unfortunately, two of those eyes belonged to Danetta Simpson. Two more belonged to Louis. And the two nearest her were beautiful and thickly lashed with dark gold, glittering with disbelief and humor as they flashed first green, then brown.

By the time he'd seen what was coming, it was too late to stop it. At first Maximillian had been as mad as a wet hornet, but when the waitress who made it a habit to spill things on him had looked up into his eyes, he'd been stopped short, feeling as if someone had just kicked him in the lungs. "Are you all right?" he asked her softly.

She had regained her balance, but for some reason he maintained his gentle hold on her upper arms. She felt so small, so fragile. When her blue eyes had met his, something within them seemed to be begging him not to let go.

When Rowan realized what she had done, she could only stare for a moment, wondering why Maximillian Donovan wasn't tearing into her for ruining his clothes again. To her chagrin, she had to admit that, this time at least, she was at fault, having allowed her mind to wander so far that she hadn't been paying attention to what she was doing. "I can't believe I did that," she muttered quietly. "Not to you, not again. I'm so sorry."

Quickly, and with trembling hands, she stooped to pick up the tray and crystal glasses, many of which had snapped in two at their elegant stems. Louis was going to kill her, and worse, Maximillian Donovan was going to think her an utter fool and complete klutz. It startled her that she should care what he thought of her.

When Maximillian bent to help her clean up, Rowan paused to gaze at him, her surprise evident in her expression. His smile indicated he understood her reaction, but he shrugged and continued replacing the broken glasses on her tray.

"Thanks, Mr. Donovan," she told him, "but you don't have to—"

"My God, Rowan!" Louis swore as he made his appearance on the scene. "This is absolutely the last straw!" he hissed.

Danetta Simpson had also hurried over with cries of "Good heavens, the Aubusson!" and now reached for

Maximillian. "Honestly, Mr. Donovan," she chided him. "It's nice of you to offer, but, please, let the girl handle this. It's her job, after all. Not to mention her fault."

Positioned on the floor, Rowan couldn't stop her temper from rising, but tried not to let it overwhelm her. Ignore them, she told herself. They aren't worth getting angry about.

"I'm sorry, Louis," she said evenly as she picked up the last glass and stood. She met his eyes levelly. "I wasn't watching where I was going. I should have been paying better attention. It was an accident. I'm very sorry."

"This is the third time tonight that I've been forced to speak to you," Louis told her stiffly, as if speaking to his employees, even by necessity, was distasteful. "And for the past several weeks, your mind hasn't been on your work at the restaurant, either."

Rowan remained silent, knowing what he said was true. Between final exams, term papers coming due, and trying to get The Warehouse into shape, her mind had been everywhere except on her job at September's. But stubborn pride prohibited her from pleading with Louis, nor would she make excuses for herself. And when Louis mistook her silence for indifference, he became even angrier.

"Clean up this mess, Rowan. Then you may leave. And since you did not do your job tonight, don't expect to be paid for it. *Do,* however, expect the price of the champagne and broken glasses to come out of your final check. Not to mention the cost of cleaning Mrs. Simpson's carpet and Mr. Donovan's tuxedo."

Rowan shot her boss an incredulous look, but before she could speak, Maximillian stepped in.

"Now wait just a minute," he protested, more than a little angry at all that had just transpired. "It was an accident, for God's sake, as much my fault as hers. I don't think it's necessary to fire her."

"Mr. Donovan," Danetta Simpson interjected, lifting a bejeweled, refined hand to the tasteful silver chignon at her nape. "I don't think it's our place to tell Mr. September how to run his business. If he wants to dismiss the girl . . ."

Maximillian pierced her with a withering glance, then glared down at Louis, who seemed to reconsider.

"I haven't fired her," he amended.

"Could have fooled me," Rowan muttered.

Louis threw her a look that told her she'd better be careful. "We're far too shorthanded at the restaurant this week," he said. "But if you so much as drop a soupspoon on the floor this weekend, you've had it. I mean it, Rowan. I refuse to tolerate any more of your inattention and second-rate service."

About to object again, Maximillian opened his mouth, then felt Rowan's small hand on his lower arm gently restraining him, and he hesitated.

"Thank you, Louis," he heard her say softly, but somewhat stiltedly. "I'm sorry my work hasn't been up to par lately, and I promise not to let it happen again." Then, with a gracefulness and humility Maximillian had to admire, she turned to Mrs. Simpson and added, "I'm very sorry to have disrupted your party, Mrs. Simpson. I hope you and your guests will forgive me." The last was said with a quick, cautious look at Maximillian. "Now, if you'll all excuse me, I'll clean this up and leave, as Louis suggested."

With that she headed back with her tray to the kitchen, where she offered a quick explanation to Tara. When she returned with some towels to wipe up the puddles of champagne that darkened the floor and part of the Aubusson carpet, the crowd had dispersed, except for Maximillian. He still stood at the foot of the stairs, dabbing at his shirt with a silk handkerchief. Rowan slowed her step when she saw him, wondering why he had come to her rescue with Louis, and why he was still hanging around the scene of the crime.

"I really am sorry about that," she apologized again when she reached him, indicating his shirt. She handed him one of the linen towels she held to facilitate his actions. "I swear to you I'm not the clumsy idiot you must think me."

Maximillian smiled briefly, genuinely surprised that he was no longer angry at the fact that this woman had three times inconvenienced him and nearly ruined some of his favorite wardrobe pieces. "Don't worry about it," he said, using her words of the previous day and meaning them. That surprised him, too. Normally he wanted to chew a piece off someone who'd do something like this to him, accident or not. Something about her calmed him before he had a chance to get riled. She seemed so soft, so gentle. She made him feel that way, too. "Here, let me help you," he told her, reaching out for more of the linen towels.

Jerking them out of reach before he could touch them, she snapped, "Are you crazy? If Mrs. Simpson sees you down on your knees helping *the girl* do her job again, she *will* have Louis fire me. And unlike *some* people," she added angrily, still a little frightened by the episode and blaming him unreasonably, "*I* have to *work* for a living. I *need* this job, even if it does seem like something trivial and insignificant to you people."

Maximillian narrowed his eyes, and drew his brows into a frown. "What the hell is that supposed to mean?" he demanded. "You act like I've insulted you. I'm the one who stuck his neck out for you, remember?"

"Stuck his neck out?" she squeaked incredulously. "What on earth did you have to lose by taking my side? It was only fair, you know. You yourself admitted it was your fault as much as mine."

"Why are you so mad at me?" he asked her, unaware that both had raised their voices to a noticeable level.

"Because you nearly cost me my job tonight," she snapped.

"*I* nearly cost you your job?" he retorted. "You're the one who ran into me, remember? Three times!"

"Oh, sure, bring yesterday up, why don't you? That's *another* thing you cost me! A trip to Disney World!"

"*What?*"

"It's true, you big—"

"Rowan!" This time Louis didn't try to hide his threat.

"Oh, great," Rowan mumbled, covering her eyes with one hand, letting the other that held the still-unused towels fall limply to her side.

"Get out," Louis ordered in a hoarse whisper. "Tell Tara to clean this up." Apparently as an afterthought, he added, "If you're so much as one minute late for your shift on Friday, don't bother coming in. Ever."

She was certain that Louis had had every intention of firing her then and there, but one quick glance at Maximillian must have made him reconsider. Rowan was less grateful than resentful that Maximillian wielded enough power to be able to prevent her unemployment; she knew that if left alone, she would have been sacked for good. Without a word, she returned to the kitchen and quickly explained to Tara all that had happened.

"But how will you get home?" her friend asked as she took the towels from Rowan's shaking hands. "It'll be at least another four hours before I'm finished."

"I'll call a cab," Rowan told her.

"All the way back to town? It'll cost a fortune."

"It won't be as expensive as losing my job if I hang around here," she reminded the other woman as she reached for the phone.

The cab service promised a taxi to the Simpson address within twenty minutes. But an hour later, Rowan still sat waiting alone at the end of the Simpsons' quarter-mile-long driveway. When she heard a car coming from the direction of the house, she thought momentarily of hiding behind one of the tall, beautiful bushes that lined the driveway, envisioning Danetta Simpson's expression of stark horror on discovering one of the caterer's employees was loitering around the grounds. At this point, though, she didn't much care what Danetta Simpson thought, nor was she even slightly inclined to make the woman's life simpler by disappearing. Feeling inordinately brave and rebellious, Rowan squared her shoulders and remained seated atop the concrete base of one of the two huge griffins that stood sentry at the entrance to the Simpson estate.

After Rowan's departure, Maximillian's interest in the evening had quickly waned. For some inexplicable reason, he had suddenly felt he had no reason or need to be mingling with the high-society crowd that comprised the Simpson guest list, and none of the conversations in which he'd found himself had appealed to him in any way. Feeling restless and disjointed, he'd excused himself from the festivities, lamely citing a severe headache and an early-morning appointment.

Now as he guided the sleek, black Jaguar down the Simpson driveway toward River Road, he noted with some distraction the small figure sitting at the foot of a massive marble griffin. The woman dangled a small canvas backpack from her fingers and swung her feet nonchalantly. As he drew nearer and braked the car to a stop, he saw that it was the waitress who liked to spill things. Only now she'd made a tremendous effort to deny that persona by sabotaging her previously impeccable tuxedo uniform. The short black jacket was replaced by a tattered and faded denim one boasting numerous antique pins and buttons spouting popular philosophy. She had untied her black bow tie to let it dangle unfettered below a shirt collar that was unbuttoned far enough to reveal a tantalizing glimpse of a creamy lace camisole. On her feet, her shiny black patent oxfords had been replaced by red, high-top sneakers that had seen better days. On the whole she looked like a wayward adolescent, waiting backstage for a peek at her favorite band.

The evening breeze nudged her short, black hair across her eyes as he got out of his car and stood to look at her, and she lifted a hand absently to sweep it back behind one ear.

"Waiting for a ride?" he asked her, not certain what to say, but for some reason wanting to prolong his contact with her.

Rowan nodded slowly but remained silent. She couldn't help the flutter of her heart as she gazed at him. He was so handsome. But normally, men in suits, or worse, tuxedos, were in no way appealing to her. She liked casual men, men who wore blue jeans and sweatshirts and went a couple of days without shaving. Men who drove cars that did not cost as much as a house. Real men. Normal men. Yet something about this Mr. Maximillian Donovan, in his perfect tuxedo—no doubt owned, not rented—standing confidently beside his costly car, looking every bit as faultless and expensive as his possessions, made Rowan's stomach hurt and confused the hell out of her.

Probably a boyfriend was picking her up, Maximillian speculated, wondering why the thought irritated him so much. All the same, their exchange on the stairs had happened over an hour ago, and she was still here waiting. Maybe the boyfriend was just a tad unreliable.

"Do you have much longer to wait?" he asked, then surprised himself by offering, "I could give you a ride somewhere, if you want."

Rowan looked at her watch again, realizing reluctantly that her taxi had probably found a better fare along the way, then glanced back over her shoulder toward the Simpson home. If Danetta Simpson or Louis September caught her still hanging around, it would without question be the end of her job. Especially now that Maximillian Donovan was leaving and couldn't run interference for her anymore. And as crummy and unappealing as working for Louis seemed right now, it was still unfortunately the only job that would pay her enough to support her daughter and herself by working only two or three evenings a week.

"Are you going back toward town?" she heard herself ask him.

Maximillian was amazed that she would accept his offer, but couldn't help noting the obvious unwillingness that edged her voice. "Back to my hotel, yes," he told her.

"Where are you staying?"

"The Houghton Company put me up at The Seelbach."

"Naturally," she muttered, knowing there were few other hotels in Louisville appropriate for a man like Maximillian Donovan.

"I beg your pardon?" he asked.

"Nothing," she said quickly, then rushed on. "Well, if you don't mind my tagging along, I'd appreciate the ride. You can just drop me off at your hotel. I can get a bus the rest of the way."

"I wouldn't have offered if I minded," he told her a little sharply. Did she think him completely heartless? "I'll be happy to drop you at your home, if you'll just tell me how to get back to my hotel afterward."

"That's okay," she said as she leaped gracefully to the ground and hauled her backpack over one shoulder. "It's kind of a long drive. I live on the other side of town, and you'd probably get lost driving back. It's no trouble to take the bus.''

She really doesn't want me to know where she lives, he realized with no small amount of annoyance. She didn't trust him any more than she would some stranger off the street. Of course, to her, he was basically a stranger off the street, even if he was Maximillian Donovan. Still, it put his back up to be treated as one. He found himself frowning as she walked toward the car.

"Nice Jag," she commented when he came around to unlock and open her door for her.

"The city leased it for me," he responded shortly, still put off by her distant posture. "Part of the lure to develop The Houghton Complex in the city." Where was the look he'd seen earlier in her eyes, he wondered? The one that had looked to him for support? That had urged him not to let go? Now she was aloof and defensive. And he didn't know what he'd done to make her that way.

"Good to see my tax dollars going for something important," she said dryly as she eased herself into the plush interior. "I was afraid they might try to shelter some of those homeless people or feed the hungry with it." She jumped when he slammed the door a little too hard behind her.

Maximillian rounded the front of the car, glaring at her through the windshield, and Rowan felt herself shrinking into her seat. When he got into the car and shifted it abruptly into gear, she felt more than a little embarrassed at her rude behavior. Her mother, who had asserted that good manners were the foundation of civilization, would have been ashamed of her.

"Well, considering the kind of revenue, not to mention employment, that a new development in this city could provide, I'd say your tax dollars are going toward an excellent investment in the future," he snapped back.

"I'm sorry," Rowan told him quietly as they turned down River Road. "You're exactly right, of course. You didn't deserve that dig. Especially after helping me out tonight. Twice."

He glanced over at her for a moment, and felt his anger subside. She really was quite lovely, despite her disarrayed clothes and ragged sneakers. She wore only the scantest amount of makeup, and only because she was working, he suspected. Her eyes were a deep, compelling blue, almost overwhelming in the amount of emotion they reflected. Then he noted with a frown that they were shadowed below by faint purple crescents and that she looked very tired.

Nodding briefly in acknowledgment of her apology, he said, "It's Rowan, isn't it?"

"Oh, yes," she replied, realizing he didn't even know her name. "Rowan Chance."

"Unusual name," he observed.

Outside her window, across the wide, brown expanse of the Ohio River, the shallow, green hills of Indiana rose to meet the setting sun. Rowan rolled down the glass so that nothing stood between her and the falling night, allowing in the cool, evening air. The wind blew her hair across her eyes again, and she smiled as she pushed it back once more. "Yes, I guess it is," she said finally. "My mother was an artist and a poet. A rowan tree in our backyard was one of her favorite subjects for both. I think its magical qualities appealed to her."

"Magical qualities?" he prompted.

"It was supposed to ward off witches and evil. I think naming me Rowan was her way of making sure I was well protected from bad things."

"Has it worked?"

"Not really," she told him as she continued to stare out the window.

He waited for a moment, hoping she would elaborate, but she said nothing more. In an effort to keep the conversation going and to learn a little more about her he asked, "So what does your mother do now?"

Rowan's attention snapped angrily toward him, but she remembered abruptly that he had no way of realizing her parents' fate from what she had revealed. All the warmth left her voice as she stated numbly, "She and my father were killed several years ago. A car accident. Drunk driver."

"I'm sorry," he told her genuinely.

"So am I," she said softly. "Do you mind if I turn on the radio?" she added impulsively, wanting to do something, anything, to change the subject.

"No, of course not," Maximillian assured her belatedly, as she had already flipped the dial to an FM jazz station. The car was filled instantly with the soothing sounds of Dave Brubeck jive, and he could sense her tension easing. "Thanks," he told her after a moment.

"For what?" she asked, confused.

"I've been trying to find a decent jazz station on this radio ever since Monday. I was afraid this city didn't have one."

Rowan smiled over at him, grateful that he'd changed the subject. "Despite what some people might think, we have everything here you could ever want in a city. It's just on a slightly smaller scale."

"Oh, really?" Maximillian asked skeptically.

"Really," she promised. "I've lived here all my life, and I'll bet I've done as many things here as you've done in New York."

He looked at her doubtfully.

"Hey, I've been to New York, and I didn't do anything there that I couldn't have done here," she told him. "And the people here are a lot nicer, a lot saner, and a lot less menacing."

"Well, that's certainly true," he agreed.

"Give it a chance, Mr. Donovan, you'll see."

"I'm sure I'll have nothing but chances, and they'll force me to sightsee this week," he muttered.

"The Houghton Complex thing, you mean," she said with an understanding nod. "Well, there's a big movement going on to turn this town into a substantial commercial and industrial community."

"How do you know all about it?" he asked, unable to mask his surprise that she was so well-informed.

"I do read the paper," she replied tartly. "I'm not some completely mindless being, you know. Just because I'm a waitress doesn't mean I surrendered my intellect in exchange for a tip tray."

"I never said—"

"I happen to be a business owner, too," she announced smugly.

"Is that a fact?"

"Yes, it's a fact. At least I will be, when I open." If I open, she amended silently.

"Open what?" Maximillian asked, honestly curious about her business venture.

"I own an old warehouse down on Main Street," Rowan told him. "For the last three years I've been cleaning it up and modifying it, so that I can turn it into an antique shop and home supply center. There's a renewed interest in old houses these days, especially old Victorians, and consequently there's a big demand for old fixtures. I've been all over town, picking through yard sales and flea markets, and scrounging around construction sites where they're tearing down old houses. For the most part, with the help of friends, I cart off the loose pieces—mantels, doors, hinges, sinks, moldings, doorknobs, railings, you name it. Then I clean them up, and I'm going to try and resell them."

"Sounds interesting," he said with an approving nod.

"But it's very difficult to get it all organized, what with my job at September's and getting my degree this semester and—" She was about to add, "and raising my daughter," but Maximillian's question cut her off.

"You're going to school, too?" he asked.

"Yes," she said proudly. "I'll be getting my degree in art history with a focus on Victoriana this semester. That is, if I make it through three finals and four term papers."

Maximillian looked at her intently for a moment, then shifted his attention back to the stretch of road before him. She was trying to start a business, worked who knew how many late nights a week as a waitress, and was going to school this semester. "No wonder you look so tired," he said softly.

"What?" she asked, but she had heard what he'd said, despite his quiet voice, and felt herself growing a little uneasy at the genuine concern his words seemed to carry.

When he turned back to her again, his heart hammered hard in his chest. That look was back in her eyes, the one that seemed to reach out to him for comfort and strength. It struck him like a freight train when he recognized it as loneliness, and terror raced through him when he realized it must mirror his own disquieting feelings of late.

"Nothing." he muttered raggedly, turning back to gaze down the long, black ribbon of road. "Never mind."

They spent the rest of the drive talking about common interests, and discovered to their surprise that they shared many besides jazz music. They detected, however, even more differences in opinion, but it made for lively and articulate conversation, enjoyable despite its halfhearted, sometimes playful, discord.

As they drove through downtown Louisville and neared the Seelbach Hotel, Maximillian discovered with a great deal of surprise that he did not yet want to put an end to his chat with Rowan Chance. He was having a better time with her than he'd had with anyone he could recall in recent memory. And that included more than a few celebrities, politicians and corporate executives. Why should she be so fascinating, where others, who had far more going for them, had left him cold?

"Do you want to have a drink somewhere?" he asked her offhandedly. "Dinner at the Simpsons' left something of a bad taste in my mouth. A cognac sounds pretty attractive right now."

Rowan narrowed her eyes at him suspiciously, not certain what to make of his invitation. He didn't *seem* like the type of man who wanted a quick score with the hired help, but you could never tell. And she hadn't exactly been a perceptive judge of character where men were concerned in the past. Still...

"I don't think so," she said after a moment, knowing it was the wise choice, even if it felt like the wrong one. "I have a lot of studying to do and—"

"Oh, come on, Rowan," he persisted. "My treat."

She felt heat seep through her at the sound of her name on his delicious-looking lips, and faltered for an instant before she spoke again. "No," she told him reluctantly, obviously weakening. "That paper on Dante Gabriel Rossetti really should be completed by this—"

"Please, Rowan?" he entreated, and she'd never known a man could look so solicitous. "Don't make me spend another evening poring over business proposals and annual reports. I hate it." Funny, though, he'd never really hated it before. Yet the thought of working, when he could be spending time with Rowan instead, made him want to shudder.

Rowan smiled at him then and found that she was unable to resist. It had been so long since she'd gone out alone with a man. Why shouldn't she allow herself one evening away from the demands of her life? Between September's and The Warehouse she hadn't really taken a day off for months, and frankly, she was having a surprisingly good time with Maximillian Donovan. Why not go out for a drink with the man? Miranda and her sitter weren't expecting her home until after midnight. She deserved a little fun.

"Your treat, huh?" she asked impetuously.

When Maximillian smiled back at her, Rowan felt her heart pick up speed. "It was my invitation," he told her with a slow nod, "so, yes, it's my treat. But you'll have to suggest a place, because I'm still not that familiar with the local nightlife."

That was going to be a tricky one, Rowan thought, biting her lower lip pensively. He was no doubt used to a considerably different type of watering hole than she. Restaurant workers generally went for the no-frills relief of a late-night pub that boasted beer specials and free nachos. Somehow she couldn't see Maximillian in his perfect tux chugalugging beer and chomping on chips with her rowdy friends. Of course, she was familiar with all the classy, posh places in town. Her friends all worked in them in one capacity or another. But to be in one of them as a customer? Rowan shrugged mentally. Quite an interesting concept.

"Well," she began again tentatively, "I'm not exactly dressed to kill, but I guess we could try Seventh Street. It's pretty eclectic. Theater crowd and all that. Beautiful bar, wonderful ambiance. I also know one of the bartenders," she added parenthetically.

"Do you go there often?" Maximillian asked her, liking the mellow tone her voice had adopted.

"I can't afford it," she told him artlessly. "But you can."

Surprised, Maximillian felt his eyes widen at her bald statement. "You cheeky wench," he said with a laugh. "All right. Seventh Street it is."

Upon entering the restaurant, Maximillian decided immediately that he liked the place. It was elegantly furnished, accented with plush carpets and lots of marble and brass, but at the same time, the atmosphere was relaxed and undemanding. The hostess, a small woman with cropped blond hair, turned at their arrival, her lively dark eyes brightening with recognition when she saw them come in. Maximillian braced himself for the inevitable female gushing that greeted him on such occasions. He'd probably have to smooth Rowan's ruffled feathers, once the hostess finished cooing over him, but he'd consoled more than one woman after such episodes. He was beginning to think he was getting pretty good at it.

"Rowan!" the woman exclaimed. "It's so good to see you!"

"Hi, Lauren," Rowan returned. "What's up?"

"Nothing much new, but gosh, it's so good to see you out again. It's been a while."

Lauren was one of the many restaurant people with whom Rowan had run around before Miranda was born. She supposed it probably was rather a surprise to the other woman to see her out again after so many years. Since Miranda had come along, Rowan's social life had basically become little more than a memory, because she had wanted to spend all of her free time with her daughter. Still, she wished Lauren wouldn't make such a big deal out of it.

"I thought you were working at Jack Fry's," Rowan told the other woman.

"No, I've been here about six months now."

As the petite blonde continued to gaze speculatively at her escort, Rowan rolled her eyes and wondered about the gossip that would be burning up the food-service-industry grapevine the next day. By the weekend, every restaurant worker in Louisville would know that she'd had drinks with Maximillian Donovan.

Maximillian meanwhile found himself stewing for some unfathomable reason, because the unwanted recognition he'd expected hadn't come. Instead it was Rowan who'd been gushed over, and he hadn't even been offered the slightest introduction. Not that he'd wanted one, of course. After all, why should he? He was just having a drink with a waitress he had met. A woman who was far too young and inconsequential to mean anything to him. Why should he care, if she didn't seem to think him important enough to introduce to her friends? What difference did it make to him that she didn't seem to feel the incredible tension burning up the air and tying him in knots? So what if she was indifferent to him? Why should he care?

Because he wanted to matter to her, dammit, he realized irritably. He wanted her to think he was important. And not because he was Maximillian Donovan, real-estate giant, either. But because, maybe, she liked him a little bit.

"Are you here for dinner?" Lauren asked then, looking down at the hostess stand to check the seating chart.

"No, we're just going to have a couple of drinks at the bar," Rowan told her.

"Well, enjoy yourself," the other woman said playfully. Then, turning to ogle Maximillian, she added, "I'm sure you will. It's about time you rejoined the living."

Rowan felt herself coloring and tried her best to act nonchalantly. Why was it such a big deal that she wasn't the so-

cializer she used to be? When had it become such a crime to
be domesticated?

"What was that all about?" Maximillian grumbled as
they left Lauren behind.

"Oh, I just haven't seen her for a while," she mumbled
quickly. Then, with a sheepish smile in his direction, she
took his hand absently in hers and added, "Come on, the
bar's this way."

Rowan wished fervently that Lauren had kept her mouth
shut. For some reason she didn't want Maximillian to know
what kind of person she was in actuality. She wanted him to
think she was glamorous and carefree and went out nightly
with a captivating, enchanting circle of friends. Of course,
she'd already blown it, she realized to her annoyance, because he'd seen her fouling up at work and wearing the least
glamorous things she owned. Gazing down with embarrassment at her red high-tops and her gaudy blue jean
jacket, the incongruity and hopelessness of the situation
suddenly struck her sharply, and she became morose. Rowan Chance having drinks with Maximillian Donovan? It
was all too funny for words. Why then did she feel so much
like crying?

When they took their seats at the long, marble-topped bar
and the bartender approached them with a welcome grin,
Maximillian knew he was in for a repeat of what had transpired with the hostess. You could tell a great deal about a
person by the reception she received from others, he knew,
and judging by the way people responded to Rowan, she was
remarkably well-liked.

As Lauren had done, Dennis fawned over Rowan and
spoke of her obvious disappearance from the restaurant social circuit, expressing his relief that she was out enjoying
herself again. She really wished her friends would stop re-

minding her how long it had been since she'd gone out. Especially in front of Maximillian.

"I'm not actually working this end of the bar," Dennis said. "But when I saw you sit down I asked Fred if I could pick you up."

"I beg your pardon?" Maximillian couldn't sit out silently any longer. He was used to being the center of attention, the one who was recognized, the one who was spoiled. Quite frankly, he didn't like being thrust into the background. He liked even less the familiarity with which the bartender was addressing his date. Friends or not, Rowan was out with him, not Dennis.

Both Rowan and Dennis turned to gaze blankly at Maximillian's question. Finally Dennis broke the silence.

"I meant pick up your places at the bar, Mr. Donovan. I'm sorry, sir. I just haven't seen Rowan for some time. We're old friends."

So, he had been recognized, Maximillian thought. Good. He wanted the other man to know what he was up against where Rowan was concerned, "old friends"—whatever *that* indicated—or not. Then he wondered wildly why it should matter to him what the man's relationship to her was. They were only having a drink, for God's sake, he reminded himself. After tonight he'd probably never see her again.

"Yes, I'll bet you are," Maximillian muttered while glaring at Rowan, unreasonably perturbed.

Rowan was at a loss. She had no idea what to make of Maximillian's behavior. The easygoing rapport they had enjoyed earlier in the evening had suddenly evaporated, and she couldn't imagine what she'd done to make him so upset. In an effort to make amends, she offered up an introduction, even though she knew it was late in coming.

"Uh, Mr. Donovan, this is my friend, Dennis Russell. Dennis, this is Maximillian Donovan."

"No kidding," Dennis mumbled good-naturedly. "If I may say so, Rowan, your taste in men has improved considerably."

"No, you may not say so, Dennis," Rowan told him indignantly, feeling the hint of a blush creep into her cheeks. "But if you'd like to take our drink orders, I'll have a Johnnie Walker Black Label, please. Mist."

Dennis turned to Maximillian then, who glimpsed just the trace of a smile on the other man's lips and wondered what to make of it and his previous comment. "Courvoisier," he told the bartender.

After Dennis left to get their orders, Maximillian gazed steadily at the woman beside him with undisguised and very intent curiosity. Rowan raised her eyes to lock them with his, and felt her heart go haywire with a hundred emotions as she stared back at him.

"What's the matter?" she finally asked him, her voice a soft caress for his troubled thoughts.

Everything, he wanted to say. *All of a sudden my entire perspective on life and living has shifted, and it's all your fault.* Instead, he remained silent for a moment longer, then, snapping out of it, said, "It really isn't necessary to call me Mr. Donovan, you know. You needn't be so formal. Call me Maximillian."

"If you ask me, Maximillian sounds more formal than Mr. Donovan," she told him a little breathlessly. Was the room getting warmer somehow, or was it her? Why was it becoming so difficult to breathe?

"Well, what do you suggest?" he asked as Dennis put their drinks before them and turned to answer a summons from the other end of the bar.

"How about Max?" she suggested with a shrug.

Maximillian shuddered. "I despise the name Max. *No one* calls me Max. I won't allow it."

Rowan smiled again, the big, mischievous smile that Maximillian had seen and loved so many times on their drive back into town. "Okay, Max it is, then," she said with a laugh.

"Rowan, no. I said—"

But Dennis came back then to inquire about the quality of their drinks, and Maximillian was never able to voice his protest. Not that it would have mattered anyway, he decided later. Rowan Chance was a woman who spoke her mind and decided by herself how her world, at least, was going to turn. Throughout their evening conversation, which lasted for hours and ranged from when to plant petunias to how to construct the perfect blueprint, Rowan consistently called him Max, ignoring his objections and laughing at his indignation. Eventually Maximillian surrendered, and by the time they finished their last round and she expressed her need to get home, he hardly noticed her abbreviated use of the name that had belonged to his grandfather before it had been given to him.

"You can pull all the way up to the garage, Max," Rowan told him when he turned the night-colored Jaguar into the driveway beside her house.

"This isn't exactly what I'd call the other side of town," he told her as he pulled the car to a stop. "It only took about ten minutes to get here."

"So I lied," Rowan admitted. "A woman can't be too careful these days about men who try to pick her up."

"I wasn't trying to pick you up," he denied. "Except maybe for that last time when you fell for me."

"Max..." she groaned.

He smiled, then turned his attention to the small garage before them. "Your apartment is over the garage?" he asked, thinking the building far too small to house living quarters.

"No, I live in the *house*," she said stiffly, stung once again that he assumed the worst of her situation. "I happen to *own* the house," she added proudly, then went on to explain her earlier instructions. "But I always use the back door. Practically all the living that goes on in this house goes on in the kitchen. There might as well not be a front door, for all the use it gets."

Noting the clipped tone of her voice, Maximillian's own irritation began to surface. "What's the problem now?" he demanded.

"I don't know what you're talking about," she said, reaching for the door handle.

"The hell you don't." He swiftly reached across her and clamped his hand over hers in an effort to prevent her escape. "Why are you so mad at me again?"

"Why do you insist on thinking the worst of me?" she asked sharply.

"What do you mean?" he shot back.

"Ever since I saw you yesterday, you've acted like I'm some kind of unimportant, bothersome laborer who amounts to nothing in the scheme of things."

"I have not," he denied vehemently. Had he?

"You have, too," she maintained. She clamped her fingers over the big hand that restrained hers and, with a good deal of effort, removed it. That accomplished, she opened her door and hastily gathered up her backpack, then paused before closing the car door behind her. Max had also used the time to escape the confines of the car, and now stood facing her with his hands in his pockets on the other side.

"Rowan, I'm sorry if I've offended you," he told her quietly. "I honestly didn't mean to."

"I'm sorry, too, Max," she mumbled softly. "I didn't mean to snap. You just touched on a sensitive issue."

"What issue?"

"Never mind." She sighed, shaking her head. "Look, thanks for this evening. For the ride home, for the drinks, for the interesting conversation. I had a good time."

"So did I," he told her. Then, his heart pounding with more uncertainty and nervousness than he'd ever felt in his life, Max ventured, "Want to do it again tomorrow night?"

His invitation took Rowan completely by surprise. It was the last thing she'd expected to hear. Maximillian Donovan was a big shot. A very rich, exceptionally well-known, extremely successful, magnificently gorgeous big shot. Had it not been for sheer dumb luck, their paths would never have crossed. What he was suggesting would make their two separate paths one, and it would effectively upset the order of the universe as far as she was concerned. There was absolutely no way that a larger-than-life man such as Max could even begin to fit into her meager existence. Nor did she try to fool herself into thinking that there was a place in his world for her.

"No, I don't think so, Max," she told him, aware that her voice carried more confidence in her decision than she felt.

Max wasn't used to receiving no for an answer, especially where women were concerned. "Why not?" he demanded gruffly before he could stop himself from forming the words.

"Because I have a lot of studying to do," Rowan told him lamely. "My finals are next week, and my papers are due...."

He said nothing, but glared at her, clearly indicating he did not consider her excuse a very good one.

"Max, I can't, okay? Not with you."

"Why not with me?"

Because you'll be wonderful, and we'll have an incredibly good time together, and I'll fall in love with you, she thought. And you'll leave me, because rich, powerful men don't get involved with waitresses or students. And I just couldn't handle being dumped again. Not by you.

As Max waited for her answer, he walked slowly and deliberately around the front of the car, allowing the still open passenger door to remain a barrier between them as she seemed to want it that way. But when he saw her eyes fill once again with that lonely, needful look, he couldn't stand it. Wordlessly he grasped the hands that held on to the car door as if it were the only link to life, and turned them into his own. Then he gently pulled her around the door to face him.

Rowan found herself gazing up into eyes that reflected the deep longing she felt herself. Before she could say a word, Max's lips descended to claim hers in a whisper-soft kiss. While he tenderly rubbed his lips against hers, his hands came up to close gently around her throat, and with his thumbs under her chin, he tipped her face back until he could fully cover her mouth.

At her quietly uttered whimper, Max drew back, staring into her eyes with ravenous intensity, shaking his head in silent denial of the feelings she aroused in him. Once more he pressed his lips to hers, this time kissing her with a raw passion he could not contain. He buried his hands in her silky, black tresses, holding her head still while he plundered her mouth.

Where the first kiss had been Rowan's quiet undoing, the second took her completely by storm. When she felt the tip of Max's tongue circling her lips, insisting on entry, she opened to him willingly, then had to cling to him to keep from losing her balance as her senses went spiraling out of control. It had been so long since a man had made her feel so desirable. So long since a man had cared for her. Or at least seemed to. With a sudden, startling crash, memories of Joey Monaco collided with her present rapture, and Rowan realized that she was behaving like an idiot. She'd promised herself she wouldn't get fooled again, yet here she was, running headlong toward catastrophe.

"No!" she cried, tearing her lips from Max's, taking several unsteady steps back toward her house. When he covered those same steps himself, she held up a hand to stop him. "No, don't," she insisted. "Please, Max, don't." Her hand was trembling and her breathing was ragged. She couldn't deny the enormous effect he had on her, but she could certainly make sure it didn't go any further.

"Rowan, what's wrong?" he asked her evenly, his voice menacingly quiet, his breathing every bit as erratic as hers. "I thought—"

"Good night, Max," she told him as she found her way up the stairs onto the back porch. "Thanks again, but good night. And goodbye."

"Rowan..."

"I can't see you anymore," she said with finality. When he made no move to leave, she added, "Please go."

Max finally accepted the fact that she meant what she said, but he wasn't going to give up that easily. Not when the woman in question made him feel things he'd never experienced before. No way.

"This isn't the end of it, Rowan," he assured her as he returned to his car. "We've barely begun."

Rowan didn't know what to say to make him understand. This had to be the end of it. She simply couldn't let herself get into another relationship that would leave her alone in the end. It had been bad enough with Joey, when she'd been blind to what was coming. But to get involved with Maximillian Donovan, knowing what kind of man he was, realizing that it would come to an end practically as soon as it began, would be more than stupid. It would be suicidal.

She watched in silence as he started his car and pulled away, then fumbled with her house keys. The sitter was sound asleep on the couch in the study, while zombies terrorized Honolulu on TV. As Rowan watched the badly made-up monsters tear the hearts out of helpless Hawaiians, she couldn't prevent her mirthless chuckle. It was a fitting end to what was perhaps the most bizarre day she had ever had. Starting tomorrow, she was going to have to be a lot more careful whom she ran into.

Chapter Four

Late the following afternoon Maximillian found himself parked on the street in front of Rowan's house, inspecting the big Victorian before he got out of his car. It had looked somewhat looming and ominous in the moonlight last night, though something about it had struck an agreeable chord within him. He normally scorned Victorian architecture as too excessive and nonfunctional, yet somehow, Rowan's house appealed to him. And now, with the late-afternoon sun bathing the three-story, turreted structure in glowing warmth, Maximillian felt almost peaceful.

It needed a new roof, he noted with a practiced eye, and some of the gingerbread trim could use repair. The porch sagged in a couple of places, and the driveway was cracked and weathered. But the house had a fresh coat of golden-brown paint, and the yard was exceptionally well kept. Petunias, violets and peonies lined the pathway from the porch to the sidewalk, and ivy crept stealthily throughout the yard toward the house. Baskets of geraniums and Boston fern hung at regular intervals across the wraparound porch, and lace curtains fluttered invitingly from the windows of the first floor. A tricycle with colorful plastic streamers cascading from its handlebars sat neglected at the foot of the front steps, and Maximillian frowned absently at its implication.

Why had he come back? Last night she had made it crystal clear that she didn't want to see him again. And after the heat and taste of their kiss had faded, Maximillian's reasoning faculties had returned. He'd convinced himself that his actions and the newness of feeling she inspired in him were nothing more than a result of too many nights spent behind his desk. What kind of an idiot was he to go back where he was so obviously unwelcome? So she'd left her bow tie in his car, he told himself. So what? She could probably get another one for a couple of bucks. And even if he felt obligated to return it, why hadn't he just dropped it off at the restaurant where she worked? He'd passed it on his way back to his hotel last night. It was only a few blocks from where he was staying, considerably more convenient than this neighborhood in the Highlands, where he had absolutely no business whatsoever.

Maximillian picked up her bow tie from the seat next to him and fingered it gently. It was much smaller than the ties he wore with his own tuxedo. He'd barely be able to tie this thing into a knot around his neck, let alone make a bow. He remembered how she had looked in the Simpsons' driveway the night before, the black tie undone and dangling from her slender neck, its satin sheen paling in comparison to her silky hair, her crisp, white shirt unbuttoned enough to reveal a hint of champagne-colored lace over soft, ivory skin. He recalled how her surprise at his appearance had darkened her blue eyes, and remembered how tired she'd looked.

Wadding up the scrap of satin in his fist, he threw open the car door angrily. Dammit, why had she taken charge of his thoughts this way? So she was a beautiful woman, he agreed with himself as he marched up her driveway to the back door, remembering her statement of the previous evening. Big deal. Millions of women were beautiful. She was nothing special. She was a *waitress* for God's sake! He'd had affairs with models and actresses, stockbrokers and corporate vice presidents, all far more glamorous and with considerably more prospects than Rowan Chance. Yet in all his years of dating, no woman had commanded his attention the way she had managed to do in three short days.

As he lifted a fist to knock on her back door, he heard music coming from her two open windows and paused. He peered through the glass, above curtains patterned with pink and red roses, and saw Rowan standing barefoot before the kitchen sink, wearing baggy, olive drab army fatigues and an oversize, extremely obnoxious, purple and red Hawaiian shirt. She was silently mouthing the words to "Am I Blue?" and seemed to feel every bit as bereft and lonely as Billie Holiday's plaintive voice made the song sound. He knocked abruptly, fearing that she might look over and catch him watching her, worried that she might misinterpret what she saw.

When Rowan heard the loud knocking at her back door she started, dropping the plate she had been washing back into the soapy dishwater with a clatter. She looked up and saw Maximillian Donovan. After the way they had parted last night, she had been more than certain she would never see the man again, regardless of his assurances to the contrary.

For a moment she could only gaze at him, taking in his thick, dark blond hair that would probably be wonderfully unruly if he'd let it grow out beyond the expensive fashion statement it was now, remembering how his beautiful, long-lashed eyes had kept changing from green to brown and back to green again in the dim light of the bar last night. When she walked slowly across the room to answer the door, wiping her hands on a damp dish towel as she went, Rowan got the unreasonable impression that she was being drawn to him almost as if he were pulling her by a string.

"Hello, Rowan," he said, greeting her in that low, confident voice when she pulled the door open.

"Hi," she responded, noting that he wore yet another expensive-looking tailored suit, dark in color, sleek in design. She wondered if he owned any casual clothes. "What are you doing here?"

Well, that's a hell of a welcome, Maximillian thought dryly. Nice to know she was so glad to see him. Might as well just get on with the reason he'd come. Return her damned tie to her and go out to find some real action, with someone who'd be a little more responsive. "You left this in my car last night," he told her, dangling her crumpled tie from his thumb and forefinger as if it were something grotesque. "I was afraid you might need it."

Rowan smiled a little nervously and reached out to take it from him. "I would have tomorrow night," she said. "It's the only one I have. If I'd shown up without it, it would have been just the excuse Louis would need. I'd be eighty-sixed faster than bad avocados." Her eyes met his briefly before she murmured, "Thanks. I appreciate it."

"No problem."

They stood in awkward silence for some moments.

Maximillian tried to convince himself that now that his business with her was completed, he should head back to his hotel, or better yet, to one of the plentiful downtown bars.

Unable to summon up her misgivings of the night before, Rowan was tempted to invite him in for coffee and conversation, but told herself he probably had somewhere important to go. Even if he didn't, she reminded herself, there was no reason to encourage something between them. He was a big-shot developer from New York City, who would only be in town for a short while. She'd had her fill of watching men leave. Why bring heartache on herself intentionally? She wasn't a masochist, after all.

"Well," she began, feeling last night's butterflies doing a lively mambo again in her midsection. "I'm sure you have some place important to be, some meeting or reception or something, so I won't keep you. Thanks again for my tie."

Maximillian looked past Rowan into her large kitchen. The hardwood floor glowed like sunlit honey and was dotted here and there with tattered throw rugs of dark green and rose. The wallpaper was a repeat of the curtain pattern, ending halfway down the room above a wooden border, below which the walls were painted dark green. He could see her dishes and cookware stacked neatly inside glass-paneled cupboards. She had old appliances, the refrigerator door virtually eclipsed by childish watercolor paintings and bright magnets. The walnut table and chairs were pushed conveniently into a breakfast nook on the side, the table covered with a faded, flowered cloth, one of the rush-bottomed chairs the seat of a one-eyed battered teddy bear. It looked like someone's grandmother's kitchen. Surprisingly, Maximillian liked it.

"Um, can I come in?" he asked abruptly.

Rowan hesitated, but said nothing.

Running a hand nervously through his hair, Maximillian rushed on uncertainly, before she could deny him. "You're the first person I've met here who doesn't want to wine and dine me and shove me into the back of a limo to drive me all over town, showing me this city's potential. Last night with you was the first time in months that I've had a conversation centering on something besides real-estate ventures. You're—" He stopped suddenly, appalled at what he had just revealed, disturbed by the desperation he'd heard his words carry. He shoved his hands into his pockets and glanced down at the ground before stepping away from her door. "Look, never mind," he muttered on a hopeless sigh. "I'm sorry I imposed."

His eyes came up to meet hers again, and Rowan almost reached a hand out to him, so stark was the loneliness they reflected.

"It was nice meeting you, Rowan," he went on quietly. "You were wonderful to talk to. Have a great life and all that. Maybe I'll see you around sometime." And with that, Maximillian Donovan spun on his heel and walked silently away.

As he neared the porch steps leading to her driveway, Rowan stepped out into the warm afternoon and shouted, "Max!" He turned back around quickly, the ghost of a smile playing about his lips at her use of the name he'd told her he hated.

She knew she was probably making a very big mistake, but Rowan smiled back anyway and said, "Would you like to stay for dinner? It's nothing fancy, just spaghetti, but somehow I always wind up making enough to feed the whole neighborhood."

Max slowly retraced his steps to stand before her on the porch. Rowan had to tilt her head back substantially to meet his eyes. "Are you going to have garlic bread, too?" he asked hopefully.

"Of course."

"All right. I'll stay."

Rowan laughed at his expression, one that made him look less a high-powered wheeler-dealer and more of a regular guy, relieved to be home again after a brutal day at the office. Of course, this wasn't his home, and Max wasn't exactly the average working man. He was too good-looking, and in far better shape than most of the soft executives she'd seen. As he preceded her into her house, it also occurred to her that whoever his tailor was, he had a wonderful talent for fitting the clothes on the man. Even if he was wearing a suit, Rowan thought, he wore it exceptionally well. She wondered briefly if he looked as good out of it, then mentally slapped herself for even considering such a thing. She'd be better off remembering that the man was only visiting town for a couple of weeks. They could enjoy each other's company for a while, but that was it. She wasn't about to get involved with another man who would only be around for as long as it suited him. The next time she gave herself to a man, it would be because they had something in common. Because they belonged together, period. Forever.

While Rowan opened a bottle of red wine, Max removed his suit jacket and hung it on the back of one of the chairs, then loosened his tie to unbutton the top two buttons of his shirt. When she came close to hand him his glass, she couldn't help but notice the dark golden tufts of hair that peeked out at her from his open collar. She found herself wanting to lift her fingers to his shirt and undo all the rest of the buttons, then push the soft fabric aside to reveal the solid, lightly muscled expanse of his chest. His skin would be warm and inviting, and she could bury her hands in the soft coils of hair that teased her, placing soothing kisses at the hollow of his throat, where her attention settled when he swallowed his wine. Then she could lower her hands to his belt and . . .

"Rowan?" Max asked cautiously. She hadn't yet touched her wine, but stood staring at his chest as if he'd grown a third arm. "Is something wrong?"

His words snapped Rowan's thoughts back to where she knew they should be, and she could feel herself blush. She took a deep swallow of her wine, then looked at him over the rim of her glass. After clearing her throat nervously, she mumbled, "Wrong? Nothing. Nothing's wrong. I was just thinking about something, that's all."

"What exactly were you thinking about?" he persisted, his voice smooth and dangerously suggestive.

Rowan was about to utter some meaningless, bland reply, but was saved by the appearance of her daughter.

"Mommy?" Miranda said sleepily as she padded barefoot into the kitchen, wearing denim overalls and a red T-shirt, trailing a small, tattered quilt behind her. She rubbed her eyes with tiny fists and found her way blindly to her mother.

Max experienced a severe tightening of his stomach and almost choked on his wine when he heard the child's voice. Mommy? Rowan was a *mommy*?

"Hi, sweetheart," Rowan murmured as she picked up the little girl, who'd curled both arms around her mother's legs. "You slept for a long time! Did you have a good nap?"

Miranda nodded at her mother and, still clutching the quilt, wound one arm around Rowan's neck, popping the thumb of her other hand into her mouth. She gazed openly at Max through eyes as big and as blue as her mother's, and he felt as if someone had knocked the wind out of him when he saw the way Rowan's face grew even softer in the child's presence.

"Max, this is my daughter, Miranda," she said by way of introduction, her voice trailing off when she saw the hard look that suddenly entered his eyes.

"Your *daughter*?" he asked gruffly, confused by his angry feelings. "I didn't know you had a *daughter*."

"Yes, my *daughter*," Rowan snapped back through gritted teeth. Why should it matter to him if she had a child? Rowan wondered. Then again, why had she neglected to tell him about Miranda last night? Maybe he didn't like children, in which case she should probably be relieved. It was another reason not to get involved with Max Donovan. Why should she when there was absolutely no future in it?

"Hi," Miranda said in a small voice without removing her thumb.

Max approached them slowly, his eyes meeting Rowan's with a flash of something she thought was annoyance before moving to settle on her daughter. Miranda seemed to sense his displeasure at her presence and tightened her hold around her mother's neck.

When Max saw the little girl's gesture of withdrawal and realized he had frightened her, he felt like a monster. Somewhere deep inside him, a cold, gnawing void opened up, and he took a long, unsteady breath, wondering about why the presence of a child in Rowan Chance's life was of such enormous importance to him. Why should it matter?

"Hello, Miranda," he ventured in a quiet voice, trying to win her over. He hoped his smile, at least, looked gentle. "My name is Maximillian."

Miranda continued to stare at the stranger with eyes so clear and innocent that Max actually felt as if his heart were growing warm. She removed her thumb from her mouth, and a small smile parted her bowed lips. He was ridiculously pleased that he had scored a point with the little girl.

Nervously she tried to pronounce his name. "Ma...Max..." She ducked her head shyly when she failed to complete the task.

Max smiled back at her attempt. "Maximillian," he repeated slowly, but her shy smile only became larger. She plainly knew there was no way she would ever be able to repeat such a long collection of so many strange sounds. He tried again. "Max..." he prompted, drawing the syllable out in an effort to make it a little easier on the child.

"Max..." she mimicked, drawing it out exactly as he had.

"...i..." he continued.

"...i..." she recited.

"...mil..."

"...mil..."

"...yun."

"...yum," Miranda finished with a childish chuckle.

"Maximillian," Max repeated, concluding the lesson, quite confident now that she would have his name down pat.

"Maxyum," Miranda responded triumphantly instead, and Max found himself laughing at her accomplishment.

"Listen, Miranda, why don't you just call me Max like your mommy does, okay?"

"Okay, Max," the little girl agreed, joining her laughter with that of her new friend.

Rowan watched the exchange between Max and her daughter and felt her tension easing away. There was a gentleness in him she hadn't noticed before, but which her daughter's presence had brought to the surface with little difficulty. Slowly her animosity toward him began to fade, and she found herself once again fascinated by the man. There seemed to be more to him than the things she'd read. Maybe Max Donovan wasn't such a bad guy, after all.

Miranda began to squirm in her mother's arms then, and Rowan set her carefully on the floor, smiling when her daughter made a beeline for the raggedy teddy bear at the kitchen table. Without a word, Miranda made her way back through the kitchen door, and Max looked at Rowan with a question in his eyes.

"It's five o'clock," she told him, as if that explained her child's behavior.

"So?"

"So Bugs Bunny is on."

"Miranda already knows how to tell time?" he asked, surprised.

Rowan shrugged. "No, but somehow she knows when to turn the TV on. It's kind of scary sometimes."

"She looks just like you," he said suddenly. "She'll be a heartbreaker someday."

Rowan smiled a little but ignored the compliment. "Yes, I suppose she does resemble me. Same haircut and all. I only hope I can give her as much happiness as I had when I was a child."

"Are you divorced?" he ventured cautiously.

"No, I've never been married," she replied, but said no more.

Max wanted to ask about Miranda's father, but knew it wasn't his place to do so. If Rowan wanted him to know, she'd tell him. Until then he'd have to be satisfied with whatever she wanted to give.

To her great surprise, Max offered to help Rowan with dinner and was remarkably handy to have around. When the table was piled high with spaghetti and garlic bread and salad, she filled their wineglasses once again, and put a small, plastic wineglass of milk at Miranda's place.

"She likes to do grown-up things," Rowan explained to Max when she saw his expression. "The last time I took her shopping for shoes, she cried because they didn't have high heels in her size. God knows where that desire came from. I don't even own a pair of high heels.''

Max smiled, but Rowan berated herself for not having anything more interesting to say to him. Here she was, entertaining a spectacular man in her home, and she had absolutely no idea how to go about it. What had happened to the dazzling party girl? she wondered, gazing down at her Hawaiian shirt and army fatigues. The one who'd had a clever quip for every occasion, who'd broken some poor guy's heart every time she went out? At one point in her life, before she'd had Miranda, Rowan probably could have matched Max story for story and experience for experience, wowing him with her coy flirtation. But her party-girl days had ended the moment her doctor had announced that the rabbit had died. She'd made a one-hundred-and-eighty-degree turn since her early twenties. Her years of stringing along five guys at once, of vacations to unexplored destinations and of parties that went on so late that she picked up the morning paper from her doorstep on her way in were all things of the past.

Now she was lucky to make it past the eleven o'clock news. She had a daughter to raise, a household to run, classes to finish, a business to get off the ground and a job to moonlight in. She didn't have time for parties and vacations. She didn't have time for one date a week, let alone five. Not that there was anyone interested in something beyond a roll in the sack, anyway. And those days were well over, too.

Whom was she kidding, trying to entertain Max Donovan? Was she crazy? Suddenly the insanity of the situation struck her again, and as she ate her dinner and watched Max try to keep her daughter from turning her kitchen into a pasta war zone, Rowan grew more and more depressed.

Some time later, after they'd cleaned up the kitchen, Rowan excused herself to give Miranda a bath and put her to bed. She had rather thought that Max would make his exit then, knowing it would be the perfect opportunity for him to escape, after his unquestionable realization that he'd made a colossal mistake in accepting her invitation. No doubt he now knew he had far better ways to occupy his evening than to spend it doing the most boring things in the world with the most unspectacular of women. It was still early, after all. He still had plenty of time to hit some of the chic bars and restaurants down on Main Street or up on Bardstown Road, where the beautiful people hung out. People who didn't have to worry about cleaning spaghetti off a high chair or washing greasy dishes. People who wore something flashy and revealing, not to mention tasteful. People who had something substantial to offer a man such as Max. Sparkling wit, interesting stories, expert sexual technique, that sort of thing.

It came as a tremendous shock, therefore, when Max asked Rowan if it would be all right to wait for her to finish. If she minded him hanging around for a little while longer. If she might consider showing him the rest of the house.

"I...I'll only be a little while," she told him as he settled into her living-room sofa with his wine.

"Take your time," he assured her quietly.

As had been the case all evening, Max couldn't keep his eyes off her. He watched as she swept her daughter into her arms and gracefully ascended the stairs. When the two of them were out of sight, his attention began to wander around the living room. Again he was surprised to find that he was not put off by the comfortable homeyness of his surroundings. A faded Persian carpet, at one time probably a rich burgundy but now nearly bare in places, covered all but a small border of hardwood floor. The creamy walls were backdrops for oil paintings on one side of the room and antique photographs on the other. On either side of the marble-manteled fireplace, shelves of books rose ceiling high, books about art, architecture, antiques and home renovation. The sofa and two chairs were over-stuffed and sturdy, covered in a deep forest-green damask that had aged to a fine sheen. Throughout the room, on tables and the mantel, between books and on the window-sills, Max observed little niceties that evidently fascinated Rowan—lace doilies and china pitchers, candlesticks and decorated boxes. The fact that a woman who favored bowling shirts and high-top sneakers owned these knickknacks was a revelation. Rowan Chance was a tantalizing enigma.

A big bay window overlooked the front yard, and a bent-wood rocker sat before it, ensconced in the warm circle of light from a brass floor lamp. The scene almost seemed to beckon to him. When he noticed a book lying facedown on the embroidered throw pillow in the seat, Max's curiosity was piqued, and he rose from the couch to wander casually toward it. He picked up an old, yellowed copy of *Winnie-the-Pooh*, smiling at the pen-and-ink drawings on the well-thumbed pages.

A childish squeal, followed by furious splashing and two sets of feminine laughter, made him turn back toward the stairs then, and it struck Max that he was, at that moment, after thirty-five years of life on this planet, experiencing something entirely new. How strange that a man of his elevated status had never taken a moment from life to read *Winnie-the-Pooh* or listen to a child's playful laughter. What else must he be missing out on?

Max was still flipping pages and pondering his last thought when Rowan came back downstairs, led by Miranda, who tugged her mother's hand impatiently. He turned at the sounds the little girl made jumping with both feet from one step to the next, and smiled at the child's complete absorption in the activity. When his eyes shifted to Rowan, he could almost feel them darken dangerously.

When Max smiled warmly at her like that, Rowan's heart caught fire, and she wanted to forget about everything except the way he made her feel. Warning alarms and danger signals erupted wildly in every corner of her brain, but she was far too willing to ignore them.

"You changed clothes," he said softly, indicating the voluminous lilac sweater that spilled down over the faded jeans, which lovingly hugged her long, slender legs.

Rowan shrugged, tugging nervously at the hem of the big sweater. Max thought she looked pretty adorable. "We sort of got into a game of Sink the Bismark upstairs. Miranda got a little carried away with her depth charges. As usual."

"Oh," Max said, not trying to hide his grin.

They stared at each other a few moments longer, until Miranda lifted her hand to place it gingerly in Rowan's and said softly, "Mommy?"

Rowan's attention gradually came back to the present and she gazed blankly down at her daughter, remembering that she was supposed to put her to bed. "Say good night to Max, sweetheart," she instructed the little girl, noting uneasily the breathless quality her voice had adopted.

"'Night, Max," Miranda said to the man who towered over her. She looked at him for some moments, as if weighing an important decision, then abruptly lifted both arms toward him.

Max looked at Rowan questioningly, uncertain about what Miranda's action meant. Rowan's eyes met his, full of genuine surprise.

"What?" Max asked her.

"She wants a hug," Rowan told him.

"A hug?"

She nodded slowly, still obviously amazed at her daughter's demonstration. "She's never asked for a hug from a man in her life."

Now it was Max's turn to be surprised. "Never?"

Rowan shook her head. "Never."

Max didn't know what to do. Children normally made him very nervous and significantly uncomfortable. Yet that hadn't happened tonight with Miranda. She wasn't like the boisterous, obnoxious toddlers he saw so frequently out in public, whose parents always seemed oblivious to their rowdy actions. Miranda was well behaved and calm. Happy. Secure. Perhaps because she was so certain of her mother's love for her. For some reason, Miranda hadn't frightened him the way most children did.

Slowly he bent down on one knee to put himself at the little girl's level. Immediately the child snuggled her tiny body against his and wrapped her arms around his neck with a gentle squeeze. When Max hugged her back, he was stunned at how small and fragile she felt. His hand seemed to span her entire back, and his arms virtually engulfed her. Max had never hugged a child before. It was an odd sensation.

Apparently satisfied that Max was an okay kind of guy, Miranda disengaged herself and turned back to her mother. "I'm ready now," she announced decisively.

"I'll be right back," Rowan told Max as she lifted her daughter once again in her arms.

Max thought about her last statement as he watched them ascend the stairs a second time. He was reliving all the times he'd been in a woman's home, when the words, "I'll be right back," had indicated that she would return in a moment, wearing something silky, sexy and expensive. Yet when Rowan returned from her daughter's room, Max found her jeans and sweater more appealing than the silk and lace he'd seen on so many other women.

"Do you still want to see the house?" she asked him nervously, not sure she liked the fiery look that warmed his eyes.

"Very much," he told her, although his wants at the moment extended far beyond a sight-seeing tour.

"Even after living here for three years, it's far from finished," she cautioned him as they moved through the downstairs study and spare bedroom. "But it's a definite improvement over the sad state it was in when I bought it. I was shocked that anyone would let a house fall into such disrepair."

"Bad, huh?"

She shuddered at the memory. "You can't imagine. I'll show you the before-and-after pictures sometime. But the foundation was sound, and I was able to buy the place for a song. The first floor is basically finished. I'm sort of working from the ground up."

She gestured toward the stairs with a question in her eyes, and Max indicated that she should precede him. When they reached the second floor, she continued to describe her difficulties and triumphs while practically rebuilding her house, minimizing the worst of the trials by making light of her travails. But Max saw past the humor she injected into so many situations and could tell she hadn't had an easy time of it while restoring the big building.

"I won't even bother with the third floor, because it's just a complete mess," she told him as she concluded the tour in her own bedroom. "Eventually I'd like to turn it into an apartment for the extra income it could provide, but that's still a long way off. I haven't even finished the second story yet. The floors still need to be sanded and polyurethaned, there's drywalling and painting I need to do...." Her voice trailed off when she considered the enormity of the task that still awaited her. "I only finished tiling the bathroom last month. That and mine and Miranda's bedrooms are really the only things completely done up here."

Max let his gaze travel openly around her bedroom. The hardwood floor gleamed with a loving polish, covered beside the bed with a cotton dhurrie rug in varying shades of pale blue and white. The white, wrought-iron bed boasted an aged, but beautifully handmade blue and white quilt, and a smaller quilt with a similiar pattern was tossed over the arm of yet another rocking chair, this one a white wicker that was settled peacefully in the big bay window. He suspected she must love to read to Miranda, while the two of them rocked together in the comfortable-looking chairs. The wallpaper in this room had a delicate blue and white stripe, and as in the living room, her furnishings were old, but well cared for, the dresser, nightstand and blanket chest all clearly refinished with skillful, patient hands. Personal touches were scattered throughout the room—photographs of Miranda at various ages, fresh flowers in a blue jar by the window, paperback novels, and a few toys that looked as if they might be left over from her own childhood. Her home told him a great deal about the woman he'd only known for a few days.

Rowan's accomplishment was amazing. And it was all the more impressive to Max when he realized she had hired no professional help from outside to achieve it.

"You did this all by yourself?" he asked, even though she'd already told him she had.

"Between classes and work and getting The Warehouse in shape, yes," she told him, then added with a shrug and a chuckle, "In about three more years it ought to be just about finished, I guess. Hopefully the roof will last another winter or so."

Max shook his head slowly in silent disbelief. Anyone else faced with her past and present obstacles would have dropped dead of exhaustion by now, yet this young slip of a woman, whom he had until recently thought utterly care-free, had managed to juggle work and school, a family and a prospective business, and so far seemed to have succeeded in every area. He ducked his head in self-reproach that he had initially considered her a shallow, insignificant bit of fluff.

"You've had rather a rough time of it, haven't you?" he asked her quietly.

Rowan wasn't sure what to say. After a moment she lifted a shoulder halfheartedly and said, "You have to take what life gives you, Max. I guess I'm one of those people who've learned to play the breaks, you know?"

"You're quite a remarkable woman, Rowan Chance," he said softly, lifting his eyes to meet hers once again.

That heated look of intent was back in them, and Rowan became fearful as old, forbidden sensations came all too quickly to burning life. Her heart picked up the unsteady beat it had pounded out ever since she'd seen Max through her back door, and her stomach knotted around a tight ball of fire. Blood raced to every nerve in her body, sparking the little flames she'd felt in his presence to big, savage bon-fires that threatened to burn out of control.

You cannot allow yourself to be attracted to this man, she tried to tell herself. He's only in town on business for a brief time, and then he'll be gone forever. He's rich and power-ful and can have any woman he wants. Why would he settle for a nobody like you? To start something with Maximil-lian Donovan was certain to bring her heartache, she re-minded herself. And she wasn't about to let that happen again.

Still, she couldn't deny that he was an immensely handsome man, and it was impossible to ignore the fact that his
eyes held the promise of unleashed passion. Tara's declaration of two days before began to ring unbidden in Rowan's clouded mind. Maybe she should try to free herself
from her sexual prison. Maybe a night of blind, feverish
carnality was what she needed right now. There was no reason she had to fall in love with Max, was there? They could
enjoy themselves this night, and part ways in the morning,
feeling a good bit less tense than they were now. Couldn't
they? It had been so long since she had experienced the kind
of emotional high a man such as Max could offer, even if
only for a short time. So long since she had been held and
kissed throughout the night. So long since someone had
touched her and loved her and made her feel special.

"Um, we should go back downstairs," she said suddenly, decisively, after a moment. "We left our wine on the
coffee table." She took several deliberate strides toward her
bedroom door, but Max reached out a hand that softly but
sternly gripped her wrist, and stopped her before she could
make a successful escape.

"You know, I was really disappointed that you didn't invite me in last night," he murmured, seeming not to have
heard her suggestion that they return to the living room. His
voice was deep and mellow, low and seductive.

All of Rowan's convictions about keeping her distance
from this man seemed to crumble at the hypnotic sound of
his quietly uttered words and at the electric heat that shot
through her body as his hand encircled her wrist.

She looked up into his face and met his eyes evenly as she
responded. "If I had invited you in last night, something
tells me you wouldn't have left until this morning."

Max began to trace delicate, maddening circles on her wrist but said nothing, silently concurring with her conjecture as he continued to meet her eyes.

"And for the same reason," she continued halfheartedly, "I probably shouldn't have invited you in tonight."

"I'd like to stay until morning, Rowan," he told her bluntly. The hand on her wrist brought her limp fist to his chest, and his other hand tangled freely in the hair that fell in silky strands to her jaw. "I want very much to make love to you."

At his roughly murmured declaration, almost a whisper on his lips, Rowan's breathing became shallow. She bit her lower lip nervously as she spread her fingers across the sinewy muscle she felt below his shirt. For an instant she closed her eyes and allowed herself a fleeting glimpse of what it would be like to be filled by this man. Then she quickly opened them again, knowing only that she should not let things go any further.

"You can't, Max," she told him quietly.

"Why not?" he demanded just as softly, pulling her reluctant body into his arms so that she could feel every hard plane of him against her, getting a little delirious himself at the softness his fingers encountered as they wandered over her body. Despite her words, her pupils were large with wanting, and he could feel the desire that quickened her pulse.

She really should stop him, she told herself as his hands roamed freely across her back and shoulders. But it felt so good to be held by him. Why not enjoy it for a few minutes more? Then she would end it.

"You're a disruption in my life right now that I just can't afford, Max." Her voice was unsteady, her words breathless as he placed a light kiss first at her temple, then on the soft skin at her neck.

"How do you mean?" His own voice was thick now, the reality of having Rowan in his arms almost overwhelming him with desire.

Another kiss to her neck made her tremble. "You've kept me from my studies for two nights in a row. I'm distracted at work. My daughter is at a very impressionable age, and I don't want her to get the wrong idea about us. But mostly...oh, Max..." Her words trailed off when she felt his tongue tasting the tender skin of her collarbone, where he'd pushed the fabric of her sweater aside.

Max finally raised his head and looked down at her face, loving the wanton desire blazing in her eyes, pleased that he was able to stimulate her as much as she had excited him. He wanted to lift her into his arms and carry her straight to bed, but the reluctance that still lingered in her voice prevented him. He would have Rowan Chance, but he would have her completely willing.

"Mostly?" he prodded, tipping her chin back with his thumb, then lowering his head until only inches separated their mouths.

Rowan shook her head slowly, as if she'd forgotten what she was going to say, trying to summon the willpower to pull away from him. Yet still she hesitated; still she wanted to feel for a few moments longer the heady sensations that he sent firing through her body.

"Max, you're just so much different from any man I've ever dated," she began quietly. "More mature, more intelligent, more focused...." Then she added with a nervous laugh, "You have a good job."

"I didn't hear 'better-looking' in there," he admonished lightly.

"Don't push it," she warned him with a shaky smile.

"So where's all this leading?" he finally asked her, letting his hands travel once again down the expanse of her slender back, then down farther to settle on the curves of her hips.

Rowan took a deep breath to fortify herself before baring her soul to him, as she knew she was about to do. "I'm afraid...oh..." She had planned to follow through by clarifying that she did not want to travel down this road, as she had done that before and it had taken her right over a cliff. But Max had chosen that moment to press her hips intimately against him, and when Rowan felt the stabbing proof of his obvious desire for her, the words got caught in her throat, and all she could say was, "Oh, Max."

"Don't be afraid, Rowan," he whispered softly, misunderstanding her misgivings. He led her in a slow, sensuous dance that found them at the side of her bed. "There will never be a reason to be afraid of me."

"No, Max, you don't understand," she protested. "I—"

"Shh," he murmured coaxingly, placing his finger over her lips to quiet her objections.

He kissed her fully on the mouth then, his tongue lingering on the traces of wine he could taste there. He felt drunk, intoxicated by the look in Rowan's eyes, by the feel of her soft body arching so perfectly against his, by the faint scent of baby powder that must be a remnant of Miranda's bath.

"Just let me love you, Rowan," he rasped out hoarsely. "The way you deserve to be loved."

Chapter Five

Like dry wood takes to fire, Rowan's nerve endings burst into flames everywhere that Max touched her. As they hovered over the side of her bed, Max used every seductive maneuver in his arsenal to assure her surrender. And Rowan in return attempted to call up every logical argument she could find to convince herself that what she was doing was crazy. When he whispered erotic proposals into her ear, she countered by reminding him that some of them, although intriguing, were in actuality physically impossible. When he tasted her ear lightly and told her it reminded him of seashells, she wanted to know when and where he'd had the opportunity to brunch on seashells. And when he told her, between feather-light kisses to her throat that she had the graceful neck of a swan, Rowan sighed and pleaded with him not to make any reference to the story of the Ugly Duckling, as it struck much too close to home.

Finally Max straightened and gazed down steadily into Rowan's eyes. "All right, Rowan," he said softly as he continued to hold her in his arms. "I get the message."

Flustered and too excited to think clearly, Rowan could only mumble, "What message?"

"You don't want to play games, is that it?" he murmured roughly.

"I . . . I don't know what you mean," she denied hesitantly.

"I think you know exactly what I mean," he countered. "So I'll stop saying pretty things and tell you exactly what I want."

With feigned casualness, Max let his hand roam from the small of her back, under her sweater and over the soft cotton fabric of the undershirt that hugged her ribs, pausing just below the swell of one small breast. Rowan's breathing became deeper and more erratic, and her heart rate accelerated to a dangerous pace. The grim line of Max's mouth eased, until his sensuous lips parted slightly into a predatory smile. His eyes gleamed wickedly as his hand fully covered her breast, and Rowan gasped when the hand that remained on her hips pulled her body into intimate contact with his once again.

"I want all of you, Rowan," Max announced quietly. "And I'm going to have you."

Rowan told herself to deny him, that she didn't need or want him. But as Max's hand gently kneaded the flesh he had encountered, as he softly thumbed the peak of her breast to burning life, as he pushed her more eagerly into the cradle of his thighs, she was forced to confess to herself that she wanted Max Donovan more than she'd wanted anything or anyone in her life.

When Rowan's arms encircled Max's neck, he took advantage of the situation to draw her closer still. Lowering his head to hers, Max kissed Rowan the way he'd never kissed a woman before—with a complete loss of control. As he crushed his mouth to hers, he felt all rationality flee his mind, felt all restraint escape from his body. He quickly became a primitive, almost savage being, his sexual urges toward the woman in his arms nearly overwhelming him. It was as if he'd never made love to a woman before. All the excitement and anticipation, all the fear and anxiety of his first time paled in comparison to what he experienced now.

With shaking hands he struggled to rid himself of his necktie, and when his fingers trembled too badly to unbutton his shirt, he simply gripped its sides and ripped it open, unable to tolerate the amount of time that had passed since his hands had touched Rowan. When they found her again, his fingers grasped the hem of her sweater and quickly pulled it over her head, and Max's eyes fastened intently on the small satin bow sewn primly to the neckline of her undershirt. In the pale white light of the bedside lamp, she looked so small, so fragile, her eyes once again harboring that helpless, haunted expression.

My God, she looks so young, he thought suddenly, registering her size and the rise and fall of her chest as she struggled to steady her breathing. "How old are you?" he asked her impulsively.

It wasn't a question Rowan expected to hear, but she replied automatically. "Twenty-six. Why?"

Max shook his head in puzzlement. "I don't know," he told her honestly. "You just . . . you seem so young, Rowan."

"How old are you?" she ventured.

"Thirty-five."

She nodded then and let her fingers leave his shoulders to rake them softly down the exposed skin of his chest, tangling freely in the furry spattering of dark gold hair that covered it. "Maybe to you twenty-six is young," she told him quietly. "But trust me, in my case you couldn't be more wrong."

Her eyes met his again, and Max knew she was telling him more than he could understand, perhaps more than she wanted him to know. Then, despite the sexual tension that was fast burning up the air between them, Rowan placed her palms flat against Max's chest and gently pushed herself away.

"This is wrong, Max," she said simply, then took a few steps away from him, hoping distance would help her regain some semblance of control. She bent to retrieve her sweater from the floor, and after pulling it over her head, she tucked her hair back behind her ears and looked at him. He stood stock-still, but his golden chest rose and fell in response to his still ragged breathing. His eyes were dark and shuttered, and Rowan was unable to discern his thoughts. For a moment neither spoke, but only gazed at each other cautiously.

Finally Max's softly uttered words broke the silence. "Why is it wrong, Rowan? Why is it wrong for us to want to be together?" He ran a big hand impatiently through his hair and expelled an exasperated sigh. "You want me every bit as much as I want you, and we're both consenting adults who know what we're doing." His eyes reflected a naked desperation then, pleading with her to change her mind. "What's so *wrong* about wanting to chase away the loneliness for *just one night*?"

Rowan took a deep, shaky, breath and answered calmly, "Because that's all it would be, Max. One night. And it might chase away the loneliness for a few hours, but it would only enhance it on the nights to follow. You know it as well as I."

"Rowan..." he petitioned as he took a step toward her with his hand outstretched in longing.

"Let's go back downstairs," she suggested again, moving quickly away from him and out the door.

She didn't look back until she had safely escaped to the living room, where she picked up her wineglass to drain it of the last few swallows, hoping the scarlet liquid would steady her nerves and fortify her against the tension she could already feel in the air. When she did turn around, Max was slowly descending the stairs, his shirt fastened only halfway, because of the number of buttons he'd lost in the heat of the moment. There was a raw sexuality about him, an almost menacing determination that she could actually feel as he slowly approached her. He, too, picked up his glass from the table, gripping it so fiercely that Rowan worried he would crush the delicate crystal into his warm flesh, then drank thirstily of the dark wine as his eyes feasted upon her.

He'll leave now, she thought sadly, honestly aching inside because she would never see him again. Oh, why couldn't circumstances be different? If only there wasn't such a chasm between them. If only he was a little less awe inspiring. If only his power and wealth were not the very essence of the man. If only they had *something* in common. If only, if only... If Rowan had a dollar for every *if only* she could cite right now, then she would be as rich as he. She crossed her arms over her abdomen as if subconsciously shielding herself from the pain that would come with his goodbye.

Finally Max replaced his glass none too gently upon the table and spoke. But instead of the farewell she expected, he said, "Would you like another glass of wine while we talk? I would."

Rowan was confused. "But aren't you going to leave?" The question was out of her mouth before she could stop it, and she paled when she realized how rude it must have sounded.

Max's jaw twitched, and his lips thinned in anger, his eyes darkening at the affront. He placed his hands firmly on his lean hips and said in clipped tones, "You know, if it wasn't for the brief little exchange we shared up in your bedroom a few minutes ago, I'd be wondering right now why it is you hate me so much."

In the otherwise silent room, his rough words hit Rowan like a cannon shot, and her eyes widened in surprise. "I don't hate you, Max," she told him on a shallow breath. "Why would you think such a thing?"

"You tell me, Rowan," he challenged. "Ever since our first meeting you've treated me like I'm someone to be avoided. Even when we seem to be enjoying ourselves together, there's still a definite distance between us."

When Rowan said nothing, letting her gaze fall sheepishly to the floor, he continued, moving closer to her as he spoke until only scant inches separated them.

"Last night," he said, "you accused me of thinking you insignificant because you aren't rich. Well, if that's true, then you're just as guilty of treating me like I'm unimportant because I *am*."

"Max, that's ridiculous," she denied diffidently, still unable to meet his eyes, knowing deep down that what he said was true.

"What is it with you and privileged people, Rowan?" he demanded, cupping his hand under her chin to tip her head back, until he could look into her eyes. He knew by the panic he saw in them that he'd hit a nerve. "Just what is that 'sensitive issue' you said I touched on last night?" Then a new thought struck him. "Or is it just the fact that I'm a man that makes you so damned wary?"

Rowan's shoulders dropped as she sighed wearily. "Lord, I feel like I'm talking to Tara again," she mumbled.

"What was that?"

"Nothing, Max," she told him. "Look, despite what everyone seems to think, I do *not* have an attitude problem. Not toward rich people and not toward men." After a moment's contemplation, she added softly, "At least, I don't think I do."

Max took a deep breath and gazed at her levelly. "Something tells me this conversation really started a long time before I came to town," he said quietly.

Rowan looked at him with a masked expression but said nothing. She wandered over to a photograph of her parents that sat on the end of the mantle, lifting her hand to brush her fingertips over her mother's face. When Max followed her movements, he saw the expression of utter and undisguised anguish that pinched Rowan's features, and any other accusation he might have wanted to hurl at her stuck in his throat.

"Your parents?" he asked her softly.

Rowan nodded but remained silent.

"You loved them very much, didn't you?"

"Oh, Max," she whispered brokenly. "You can't imagine how much."

"Do they have something to do with all this?"

Her fingers dropped back to her side as her gaze fell again to the floor. "Yes," she admitted reluctantly.

Max looked at the picture again. Just as Miranda resembled Rowan, Rowan was a mirror image of her own mother. From the length of her father's shaggy, dark hair and mustache, and from the embroidered detailing on her mother's peasant blouse, Max could tell that the photograph was rather an old one, and that Rowan's parents had been what he and his friends in college would have called "organic."

"Do you want to talk about it?" he asked her quietly. He realized with some surprise that he wanted to discover all he could about her, especially the parts of her history that had had such an impact on her present life. He didn't know why it was of vital importance that he learn all he could about someone he would only know for a few days, but something inside him hungered for a glimpse into the soul of this complex woman.

"Not really," she said. When her eyes looked up into his, they were full of a deep and resounding sorrow. "But maybe it will help you understand a little better why I just can't get involved with a man like you."

A man like you. Her words echoed in his heart as if it were no more than a hollow drum. With no small degree of guilt, Max realized the analogy wasn't far from the truth. His heart *had* felt empty of late. Except for the heat and heavy pounding that seemed to have overcome it since the day he'd stumbled, face first, into the woman who stood before him now. "Talk to me, Rowan," he demanded softly. "It'll be good for both of us."

After a moment, Rowan nodded and walked soundlessly to the couch to sit down. Immediately Max followed, instinctively raising his arm to the back of the sofa, as if reaching out toward her.

Although more than two feet of space separated them, Rowan felt as if Max was very close to her. But this time, instead of feeling threatened by his nearness, she was strangely reassured by it.

"I really can't do verbal justice to the amount of love my parents and I felt for one another," she began. "They were extraordinary people, who got so much joy out of simply being alive. They created beautiful things for a living—my mother with her paintings and poetry, and my father with his woodworking and carpentry. I *hate* it that I have so lit-

tle of what they made, Max, of what they left behind." Her
expression softened. "But at the same time, it seems appropriate that other people are able to share the beauty they
created."

"Why don't you have more of what they made?" Max
asked, entranced by the mellow, mesmerizing quality of her
voice when she spoke of her parents.

"I still have my mother's poems to read, but she sold
nearly all of her paintings. That and teaching were how she
made a living. And most of the work my father did was in
other people's homes. He made *beautiful* mantels and
stairways, and the most gorgeous moldings you've ever seen.
I wish I could have kept the house I grew up in. It was
amazing."

"Why didn't you?"

She shrugged slightly. "I had to sell it when I found out I
was pregnant. I didn't have any money to deliver and raise
a baby. After my parents were...after they died... Well, they
didn't have any insurance, and there was very little in sav-
ings. I had a job and everything, but...I was pretty reckless and irresponsible before Miranda came along."

Max wasn't sure what to say, so he only said, "I'm sorry,
Rowan."

She faked a little smile, trying to disguise her crumpling
features. "I got a good price for it," she managed. "Anyway, as I said, I was very close to my parents, doubly so because they were my only relatives. After they died, I was left
totally alone."

"What exactly happened?" Max asked. "I know you said
they were killed by a drunk driver, but—" He stopped
abruptly when he saw her flinch, and let his hand fall to
settle gently on her shoulder. "But I feel like there's a lot
more to it than that."

When Rowan's eyes met his again, the sorrow was joined by bitter rage. "The man who killed my parents went careening through a red light at twenty miles over the speed limit. He was in a monstrous tank of a car, while my parents were nudging along in a compact. They were killed instantly."

Max slowly expelled the breath he had held while she spoke. "And the other driver?" he asked cautiously.

Rowan stared blindly ahead. "Minor injuries. He'd been coherent enough to fasten his seat belt, even if he couldn't distinguish a red light from a green. He suffered a broken leg, a wrenched shoulder, and he had to have four stitches in his cheek, just below his right eye." Her fingertips traced over her own face as if to illustrate. "He has a visible scar there," she added emotionlessly. "I still see him now and then."

"You still see him?" Max asked curiously. "Why?"

"The man who killed my parents was William Evanston," she informed him.

Max's eyebrows lifted in surprise. "*The* William Evanston? Of Evanston Electronics?"

"The very same," Rowan assured him, not surprised he had heard of the prominent city businessman. Even though Evanston Electronics was based locally, they had holdings throughout the country, and William Evanston was widely known in the business and financial communities. "He shows up at a lot of the parties that September's caters. Of course, he doesn't recognize me. I'm sure he's forgotten most of what happened."

"I seem to remember reading some time ago that he was brought up on charges for drunk driving. But they were dropped, weren't they? Nothing ever came of it?"

"Drunk-driving laws then weren't as effective as they are now," Rowan acknowledged, "and William Evanston has more money and power than nearly anyone in town. He has a fleet of brilliant lawyers and can exert a tremendous amount of pressure on just about anyone he wants. I, on the other hand, was an emotionally devastated, utterly confused and completely broke nobody. As soon as the charges were filed, they were dismissed."

She paused for a restless breath, pushing back her bangs with a shaky hand. "God, Max, it was like some horrible nightmare, some terrible movie. When I finally got myself together enough to bring a civil suit against him, my efforts were steamrollered by the sudden disappearance of any evidence indicating Evanston had blown positive on a breathalizer test."

"How is that possible?" Max asked, confused.

"Amazing what money can buy these days, isn't it?" Rowan muttered bitterly, pressing on before Max had a chance to respond. "So William Evanston got off scot-free and went home to his estate in Shelby County. He can still sit in front of the fireplace with an annual report in one hand and a snifter of brandy in the other. So, no, I guess you could say nothing ever came of it."

Rowan took another deep, ragged breath before she continued. "Except that *my* life was left like all the pieces of broken glass and twisted metal scattered across the road." She clenched her fists against the faded damask of the couch and tried to keep her voice level. "William Evanston went right back to making millions of dollars a year. At Thanksgiving and Christmas he was at home with his family and friends, celebrating, and since the accident his business has been thriving like a weed, and he's seen two more lovely grandchildren come into the world.

"I couldn't go back to school that semester because I couldn't pay for it, and quite frankly, I could barely think straight. At Thanksgiving and Christmas I sat alone in front of the TV for ten hours, and then couldn't even remember what I'd seen." She paused for a moment, when her eyes began to fill with tears. "And my parents have a beautiful granddaughter that they'll never even see. Miranda looks so much like my mother, Max. And she loves to draw. Mama would have been so mad about her. Daddy would have loved her like crazy. . . ."

Rowan broke down and began to cry freely then, tears for a tragedy she had been pushing to the back of her mind for six years. All the anguish, all the rage finally came to the surface, and Rowan felt the grief and the anger that had lain so deeply in her soul for so many years finally crawling from her body with each wracking sob.

Max reached over and pulled her close to him, hugging her tightly, uncertain of what he should say or do. He'd never been confronted with the enormous task of comforting someone before, and the depth of Rowan's grief was something he'd never experienced himself. So Max only held her and offered her his handkerchief, stroking her back with soothing motions, murmuring that she shouldn't be afraid to let it all out, assuring her that she didn't have to be alone anymore.

Finally Rowan pulled away, and reluctantly Max let her go as far as she could without his releasing her shoulders. Even after crying she was uncommonly beautiful, he noted, her blue eyes seeming huge and limitless beneath her tears. He smiled encouragingly when she wiped her nose on the square of silk and ducked her head shyly.

"I'm sorry," she mumbled softly. "I didn't mean to fall apart like that. I know I must have made you very uncomfortable, and I apologize." She glanced up at him quickly, then looked back down at her hands as they twisted his handkerchief. "Thank you, though, for not pushing me away."

"Rowan, I..." He what? He was sorry? He wished things could have been different for her? How could anything he might have to say ever begin to ease the pain she must feel? Suddenly Max felt very inadequate and powerless. It was a sensation he'd never experienced before, and one he found very disconcerting. Why did this woman unsettle him so? "I could never push you away," he finally finished. "How could you possibly think that?"

He wanted to tell her that he was there for her if she wanted him, to help ease her pain and make things better in any way he could. He wanted to assure her that he would *always* be there for her, then saw how very ridiculous such an assurance would be. He would be back in New York whenever she needed him. Where was the assurance in that?

"You must think I'm such a basket case," Rowan muttered into the awkward silence, trying to ignore the way her heart was fluttering in response to his last statement. "Just about every time you've seen me I've spilled something on you. Then I invite you in for dinner, and I...uh...I put you in kind of a compromising position, only to say no at the last minute. Then I fall apart, crying all over you and your handkerchief. Honestly, Max, I really am a very stable person. You just met me at something of a bad time."

She saw him smile at the uncertainty she could hear in her voice. "I think I met you at the perfect time," he told her quietly, his voice laced with a tenderness she'd never heard him use. "And just for the record, I'd say I'm the one who was responsible for the compromising position. And for that, *I* apologize."

Rowan glanced back up at him with a quick, shy smile, then let her eyes fall back to the couch. "That's okay," she said softly.

There was still a question he wanted to ask her, but he was uncertain exactly how to phrase it without bringing up a painful subject again. "Rowan," he said carefully, "I appreciate that you told me about your parents, but I'm afraid I still don't know why what happened to them should have any bearing on us, or why that should prevent you from getting involved with—to paraphrase your own statement—a man like me."

Rowan's head snapped up at that, her eyes huge and dark with reawakened melancholy. She rose restlessly and paced the length of the room and back again. Her tone of voice when she answered him indicated that he should already know the answer to his question. "Don't you understand? Every time I look at you, in your expensive clothes, with your high-class manners and friends, knowing you lead a life that hinges on wealth and power... You're just like *him*." Her voice had grown louder and more excited as she spoke, but now she broke off and took a deep, shaky breath. "Every time I look at men like you," she began again more calmly, "all I see is the man who killed my parents."

Max was speechless. He had no idea what he could say that would adequately defend himself or his life-style. It shocked him that Rowan should see him in such a light, that he should be representative of all that she despised and feared. He wasn't William Evanston, and he'd had nothing to do with the tragedies of her past. He realized crazily that he wanted her to see him as a man who could make a difference, who could bring happiness back into her life, the way she had already begun to do for him. With no small amount of surprise, he discovered that he wanted her to see him as her chance for a new start, just as he could see her as his. Rowan Chance. His chance. Somehow it all became so clear to him then.

"Rowan," he began slowly, uncertain what he wanted to say, knowing only that he needed more time to explore and understand all the confusing things that she made him feel.

"I'm not William Evanston. I'm not responsible for what happened to your parents."

Rowan sighed heavily. "I know that, Max. It's just that whenever I'm in the presence of extremely wealthy people like you, I feel very, very uneasy."

"But—"

"It isn't just the constant reminder of William Evanston and what he did that makes me so uncomfortable," she interrupted, "although obviously that's a big part. I just feel ill at ease with all the opulence and excess that goes along with the way you people live. I don't think it's fair, Max, that so few have so much, when there are so many others in the world who have nothing, you know? I learned at an early age that you can be completely happy with a warm home, a loving family and a deep appreciation for the joys that can be found free, right outside our front door, every day. It's a lesson I want Miranda to learn, too."

"Are you saying that if someone handed you ten million dollars, you'd walk away from it?" he asked skeptically.

Rowan sighed again and slumped her shoulders. "No, I'm not. I'd take it in a heartbeat. But I wouldn't buy some huge, obscene mansion and spend fifty grand on a party for a hundred of my closest friends, either."

Max eyed her with speculation. No, he was certain she wouldn't. Neither would he, for that matter. Hosting parties wasn't his strong suit. But he'd attended more than his share of galas that ran at least that much, without ever considering the price tag on the champagne and paté, without ever wondering how many people could live for a year off what it cost to throw one big bash.

"And just what would you spend it on, Rowan?" he wanted to know.

For a moment she didn't answer. It wasn't that she'd never thought about what she would do, if she somehow managed to get her hands on a huge sum of money. Frankly, not a week went by that she didn't. But her feelings on the subject were personal, her goals in that respect were ones she wanted to attain on her own. For some reason, sharing her lifetime dreams with a man like Max, who could realize his own with a telephone call made hers seem like meager, pointless struggles that would go on forever. Finally she looked him squarely in the eye and told him exactly what she'd do.

"First I'd take care of Miranda's education and make sure she got the best I could find. Then I'd get a new roof for the house and stock my shop with as much inventory as it could hold. I'd get a new car—nothing fancy, maybe a Toyota or Chevrolet—and then, whenever we got the desire to, Miranda and I could travel everywhere we've ever wanted to go."

Max smiled at that. "And where has Miranda ever wanted to go?" he asked softly.

Rowan shrugged. "Disney World," she told him simply.

He nodded silently. "That still leaves about nine, nine and a half million," he reminded her. "What would you do with that?"

"Invest some for the future," she said, reluctant to tell him anything more.

"And the rest?" he prodded.

She lifted her chin defensively, lest he think her next idea that of a completely naive idealist. "I'd probably build a shelter or something for battered and abused children," she said quietly. "Or for the ones who have nowhere to turn when their lives have been totally blown apart."

Max looked at Rowan for some moments, carefully weighing everything he knew about her in his mind. He didn't doubt for a second that she would do what she said, and somehow she managed to make him feel a little embarrassed about his self-indulgent way of life. "I suppose you expect me to feel guilty about my life-style," he surmised.

"No, of course I don't," she told him honestly. "People are entitled to live any way they want, as long as they aren't maliciously mistreating others. I'm just saying that *I* wouldn't live your way, even if my financial situation permitted it. And therein lies the essential difference between you and me."

"It doesn't seem to me to be such an insurmountable one," he told her.

"I'm afraid it does to me," she responded evenly, melancholy lacing her softly uttered words. "I don't think we should see each other anymore," she added more quietly.

Max sat motionless in the silent room, telling himself he hadn't heard what Rowan had said. Not see her anymore? How was he supposed to stop seeing a woman who filled his mind with the strangest thoughts and desires he'd ever experienced? Who made him want to dissect and reevaluate every lesson he'd ever learned from life? Who in a few short days had turned his well-ordered existence completely upside down? Stop seeing Rowan? he repeated to himself. She might as well have told him to stop breathing, because that was how vital she had suddenly become to him. He looked at her for a moment before he said quite simply and firmly, "No."

Rowan blinked, her pupils enlarging with confusion when she did so.

"What do you mean, 'No'?" she asked him bluntly, her words coming out on a shallow breath.

Max rose from the sofa and paced the length of the room until a large distance separated them. He looked down at a bare spot on the carpet, then up toward the filigreed light fixture in the center of the ceiling before his eyes settled once again on Rowan's. "No," he repeated resolutely. "I mean I won't stop seeing you."

Rowan's confusion became anger at his intent to bull-doze her, and she turned to face him squarely. "What if you don't have anything to say about it?" she challenged.

"I have as much to say about it as you do, Rowan," he pointed out. "This affects both of us equally."

"No, it doesn't," she countered. "You're just some car-petbagger from New York who's come down here to put up a building. Next week you'll be gone. But this is my home, Mr. Donovan. I grew up here. I don't need to point out that we scarcely know each other, and that it's crazy to start something that's going to end as soon as it begins. Besides which, I don't want to live in your world, and you don't want to live in mine. Why on earth would you want to see me again?"

Despite her belligerent speech and the look of complete antagonism on her beautiful face, Max was drawn to Ro-wan as never before. People, particularly women, rarely challenged him, and he discovered to his surprise that when done correctly, he found it rather exciting. "Because I like you, Rowan," he admitted reluctantly. "I like you a lot."

Rowan could only stare at him dumbfounded. This was not good, she told herself. This was not good at all. How could Maximillian Donovan like her? They had nothing in common. She didn't want him to like her. It wasn't going to help things in the least. Because the problem was, as much as it galled her to realize it, she liked Max, too. She liked him a lot. And now that she knew it was a two-way street, it was going to be much more difficult to navigate.

Max wasn't sure how to interpret her silent reaction to his statement, so, feeling more reckless and carefree than he had in years, he forged ahead with another startling thought that had entered his brain this evening. "And who says I don't want to live in your world? It's kind of nice, really."

Rowan shook her head in silent denial. "Oh, no, you don't," she warned him, putting up a hand as if trying to ward him off. "You're not going to make me believe that you're anything other than what you are."

She saw Max smile and take a few steps toward her.

"And just what am I, Rowan?" he wanted to know.

She tried to take a step back for every step he took forward, but only succeeded in landing with a muffled "Oof" back on the couch. "You're a powerful, millionaire real-estate and development mogul, who has more money than he knows what to do with. And you have far better things to occupy your time than to hang out with a waitress and her three-year-old daughter."

By now Max had rejoined her on the sofa, but instead of leaving a good deal of space between them as he had before, he leaned intimately against her until only a hair-breadth separated them. "You're wrong, Rowan," he told her as he slanted his face across hers, ready to kiss the living daylights out of her.

Rowan gulped inaudibly, aware only of her racing heartbeat and erratic breathing. "You're a *billionaire* real-estate and development mogul?" she asked him lamely.

He shook his head slowly, leaning toward her until her head bumped softly against the arm of the couch. "I'm not a mogul at all," he informed her. "I'm just a man, Rowan, like any other you've ever met."

His words fell against her face like a warm caress, and she shivered at the thoughts that ran rampant through her brain. "Oh, no, you're not, Max," she assured him breathlessly.

"Yes, I am," he countered, still hovering over her with masculine intent. "I have the same wants, the same needs as every other man on earth, and I'm as capable of falling for a beautiful, desirable woman as the next guy.''

Rowan licked her lips nervously, hoping to stall for time. ''I know all the best places in town to meet beautiful, desirable women, Max,'' she offered hastily. ''And I can get you in good with the bartenders, too. Once you're in good with the bartenders, you can meet anybody you want.''

Max smiled at her attempt to break the spell that had fallen over them. It hadn't worked. The heat still hung in the air around them; their hearts still pounded against each other, as if they were about to explode. ''I've already met somebody I want, Rowan. You.''

She thought then that he was going to kiss her, and perhaps, for a moment, Max had intended to do just that. But instead of closing the scant distance between them, he suddenly pulled away. His eyes brightened with something that seemed like enlightenment, and he looked at Rowan speculatively from his position beside her on the couch. Uncomfortable with his scrutiny, Rowan, too, sat up, her heart still pounding erratically as she waited for him to say something.

Max did open his mouth to speak, but then closed it again as if having second thoughts, all the while gazing at her with interest. Rowan crossed her arms over her chest in a self-protective gesture. At last, unable to tolerate the anticipation any longer, she stared back, challenging him to speak.

''What?'' she finally blurted out when it seemed as if he would never speak again.

''I'm just beginning to understand something,'' he said carefully.

''Max, what are you talking about?''

He ventured a small smile, as if he'd unlocked the secrets of the universe and was uncertain what to do with them. ''You've made such a big production since we met, about how shallow and valueless people who have money can be. And because of what happened to your parents, you actually believe that that's the reason you can't let me get too close, why you can't allow yourself to like me."

"Max..." she said, beginning to disagree.

"But that isn't it at all, is it?" he pressed on. "Deep down, you couldn't care less what I'm worth. You're not that superficial."

"Max..."

"It's the fact that I'm a man, isn't it?" he asked her pointedly, taking a real interest in the fact that she paled at his assertion. "It's the most basic thing in the world, Rowan. You're just afraid to get involved with me, because you don't want to get burned again."

For long moments Rowan said nothing, searching her brain frantically for some snappy comeback to shrug off his ridiculous accusation. Unfortunately, her normally clever mind betrayed her, and she couldn't come up with a single reason to contradict him.

"That's it, isn't it?" Max asked her again, unable to keep the note of triumph out of his voice. It was all so clear to him now.

Rowan emitted a single, humorless laugh. "Max, you're crazy," she said hesitantly, praying silently for some divine intervention. Something like a fire storm or alien invasion. "Just what makes you think I've been burned before, anyway? Maybe I've had nothing but satisfying, fulfilling relationships. Maybe I'm involved with someone special right now." Someone besides you, she thought before she could stop it.

Max shook his head. "If you were involved with someone special, you wouldn't be sitting here with me right now. As for past relationships being nothing but satisfying or fulfilling," he continued, "at the risk of sticking my nose in where it doesn't belong, you appear to have a daughter who is ominously fatherless."

Rowan's back went rigid at the turn their conversation had taken. "You're right about one thing, Max. It's none of your business."

"I'm sorry, but I think it's about to become my business," he said mildly.

Her eyes and lips narrowed angrily, drawing her face into an expression that told him in no uncertain terms that this subject matter was off limits. "I'll say it again," she told him levelly. "What happened between me and Miranda's father, between me and any man, for that matter, is none of your business, nor does it have anything to do with what's happening here right now."

Max clenched his fists and relaxed them, then pushed one hand through his hair in a restless motion. "Rowan, it has everything to do with what's happening between us."

"Max, *nothing* is happening between us," she insisted.

"Only because you're trying so hard to fight it," he assured her.

"*What* is there to fight?" She raised her hands palm up in a gesture of impatient inquiry, her eyes wide with exasperation.

Max couldn't let her question go unanswered. With a wickedly mischievous smile, he countered, "What's there to fight? How about this?"

And with that he reached toward her, closing his hands over hers, using them to pull himself nearer and close the small space between them. He brushed his lips against hers with an infinite gentleness and a maddening tenderness, as if he were almost pleading with her to let him kiss her forever. Rowan was helpless to stop him. She'd never felt such a kiss from any man, so full of pleasure and promise, one that asked for a response instead of demanding it. She was intrigued, she told herself, as Max's mouth softly plied her own. She wanted to stay here for a while and find out what was going to happen next.

After a moment, Max lifted his lips from hers and gazed longingly into her eyes. Rowan's pulse quickened again as she watched his expression, fearful that he would try to talk her into doing something she knew would be a mistake. She could see his own pulse throbbing erratically at his throat, could hear how ragged his breathing had become. When he opened his mouth to speak, she closed her eyes involuntarily, hoping to shield herself from the request she knew was forthcoming.

"Let's dance," Max said quietly.

Rowan's eyes fluttered slowly open. Dance? she echoed to herself. Did he say he wanted to *dance*? *Now?* How dare he get her all worked up this way and then suggest that they should dance! As her breathing gradually steadied, Rowan realized the absurdity of her thoughts and tried to tell herself that his recommendation was the wisest she could come up with, short of asking him to leave again. And at the moment she honestly didn't want to see him go. So instead she nodded almost imperceptibly, as if dancing were exactly what she'd had on her mind, too, and said, "Okay."

Slowly and reluctantly Max pulled away from her again, and Rowan pushed herself up from the corner of the sofa. She tugged resolutely at the hem of her sweater and ran her hands nervously through her hair, furiously straightening her bangs when there was really no need to do so.

Max, in the meantime, had made his way over to Rowan's dated and mismatched stereo system and was inspecting her collection of tapes and record albums. He was surprised at the enormous variety he found there, everything from Mozart to Tito Puente to the Everly Brothers. One group of titles in particular caught his eye. "The

Clash?'' he asked skeptically. ''The Ramones? The Psychedelic Furs? The Crass?''

''I, uh, I kind of went through this punk phase in my early twenties,'' Rowan explained.

''I'm glad to see you outgrew *that*,'' he muttered with distaste.

''Who says I outgrew it?'' she asked him blankly. When he turned to her with his eyebrows raised in question, she told him loftily, ''I'll have you know that when I come home from work, feeling angry and annoyed, cranking up 'Eat the Rich' to dangerous levels can be very purging.''

''Uh-huh, I'll bet,'' Max responded dryly. ''And I'll bet the neighbors just love you for letting them share the experience, too.''

''I use the headphones.''

''Well, that's something, I suppose.'' Then, turning his attention to the tape deck, he asked, ''What have you got in there now?''

Rowan bent over to inspect the tape, too. ''Rick Bartlett,'' she said. ''He's local. He does the *Star of Louisville* cruises.''

''Does he have a purple and green mohawk?''

She laughed. ''No, of course not. He does old standards. He's wonderful.''

''Sounds like just the ticket.'' Max pressed the Rewind until the tape was at the beginning, then punched the Play button. After a few seconds, a smooth, rich voice began a mellow, piano-accompanied rendition of ''You Call It Madness, and I call It Love.'' ''Perfect,'' Max said.

He straightened casually and reached his arms out toward Rowan, silently encouraging her to dance with him. For a moment she almost panicked, not certain what she should do. She hadn't slow-danced with a man since her senior prom. Somehow she knew dancing with Max would be a far cry from dancing with the seventeen-year-old president of the math club. Hesitantly she stepped into the circle of his arms.

But not before he noticed her reluctance to do so.

"It's just a dance, Rowan," he told her as she settled her head against his shoulder. "Nothing more. All I ask is that we spend a little time together, that we give ourselves a chance to see what develops between us. I only know that as long as I'm in the same town with you, I want to be with you as much as I can."

"Max—"

"Shh," he said, cutting her off. "Don't say anything. Let's just enjoy ourselves for as long as we're able, all right?"

Rowan nodded silently, but somehow she knew she should be saying no instead. Because the more time she spent with Max, the more she was certain to fall for him. He was disproving all of the theories about rich men that she had spent so many years nurturing. Instead of being callous and obsessed with his wealth, he was turning out to be sensitive, even thoughtful. Instead of looking at her daughter as if she were an annoying aspect of Rowan's life that he'd have to tolerate, he seemed to honestly like Miranda. And despite Rowan's assertions to the contrary, they did share many interests and goals. In short, Max Donovan was turning out to be a nice, decent, unobtrusive kind of guy. The kind of guy she'd been hoping to find someday for her daughter and herself. A man who would fit comfortably and easily into their lives and care for them with a deep and abiding devotion. A man with whom she could fall utterly and irrevocably in love. And the fact that Max Donovan might turn out to be that kind of man was enough to scare the hell out of Rowan right now.

Chapter Six

The only thing Rowan felt good about by the end of the afternoon on Friday was that she had finally managed to finish her independent-study paper. The handwritten version of it, anyway, she amended, feeling her optimism begin to slip. Unfortunately, she was still going to have to scrounge up some spare time from somewhere so that she could get the damned thing typed up, all forty-five pages of it. Not including the end notes. And the bibliography. And title page. Rowan looked morosely at the seemingly endless mountain range of notebooks, legal pads, textbooks and class notes piled precariously across her aged, mahogany dining-room table and sighed. The last time she'd seen her decrepit, timeworn manual typewriter, it had been lying in a crumpled heap at the bottom of her basement steps. She had heaved it there at the end of the fall semester, when it had jammed up on page three of her thirty-two-page term paper on the Pre-Raphaelites.

"I hate school," she muttered to no one in particular.

Glancing down at her watch, she realized she was going to have to hurry if she wanted to make it to work on time, but then wondered why today should be different from any other. Leaving the tangle of study aids on the table, she quickly threw together a baloney sandwich, then hastily consumed it with a glass of milk as she dressed in her tuxedo uniform. She heard Debbie, the baby-sitter, rap quickly on the back door at the same time she registered the *beep-beep* of Tara's little car. With a swift kiss for her daughter, she snatched up her backpack and was gone for the night.

Tara was as chatty as usual during the short drive to September's, describing in vivid, nauseating detail the disastrous date she'd had the night before, complaining about everything from the man's dental hygiene, or lack thereof, to his taste in music, or lack thereof.

"I mean, really," the other woman went on relentlessly, her eyes never leaving the road, "when was the last time you met anyone over thirty—cripes, over *fifty* for that matter—who listens exclusively to the Ray Conniff Singers? My *parents* gave up that stuff in 1978, and they're the squarest people I know! This guy was *unreal*. He wanted to take me *dancing* at the Budget Inn *Swan Room*, can you believe it?"

Rowan blinked absently and looked at her friend. "It couldn't have been that bad, Tara."

Tara glanced quickly over and frowned. "Great. My cousin Enid fixes me up with a blind date from hell, and you can't be bothered to commiserate with me."

Rowan smiled. "I'm sorry," she said. "But hasn't your cousin Enid done this to you before? I seem to remember some guy who kept asking if he could lick your shoes."

"Roger." Tara said the man's name on a groan, wrinkling her nose in disgust. "He was so creepy."

"I remember you made him drop you off at September's, so you could get a ride home with me." Rowan laughed. "You didn't want him to know where you live."

"He still found out, though," Tara said with a chuckle. "He sent me a pair of espadrilles on my birthday." After a moment, she added, "Why can't I be as lucky as you?"

Surprised, Rowan turned to face her. "Lucky? Me? How do you figure that?"

"Why couldn't *I* have been the lucky one to spill something memorable on Maximillian Donovan?" Tara lamented.

Rowan looked away quickly. "What difference does it make, Tara?" she asked hastily. "Nothing came of it."

"Oh, no?"

At Tara's puzzling comment, Rowan turned again. "What's that supposed to mean?" she demanded.

Tara smiled wickedly. "Just that I came by your house last night. I was going to have Milton—"

"Milton?"

"Yeah, Milton. I was going to have him drop me off at your house—I, uh, I didn't want him to know where I live, either—but there was this black Jaguar parked out front. So I asked myself, 'Gee, who could Rowan *possibly* know that might drive around in a black Jag?' And then it hit me."

"Yeah, probably like a big bag of dirt," Rowan mumbled.

"Maximillian Donovan," Tara concluded triumphantly, ignoring her friend's comment.

Rowan glared at Tara as they pulled into a parking lot across the street from the restaurant, but didn't say a word.

"So?" Tara pressed. "What gives? He was at your house last night, wasn't he?"

"Yes," Rowan responded reluctantly.

"For how long?"

"I don't know. Six hours, maybe."

"Six hours?" Tara was fairly licking her chops at the news.

"Nothing happened," Rowan assured her quickly.

"You were alone with that hunk of male perfection for six hours, and nothing happened?" Tara was incredulous. "What's the matter with you?"

"Miranda was there," Rowan reminded her friend.

"Ooh." Tara nodded in understanding. "Bummer."

Not the way Rowan saw it. She and Max had danced for a long time, Max taking advantage of their closeness during lapses in the quiet conversation by treating her to soft, tender, seemingly innocent kisses. Innocent at first, anyway, she remembered. Until he'd gradually escalated them into what could have become a heavy necking session on the couch. Rowan squeezed her eyes shut now, recalling with embarrassment how she had capitulated to him a second time after telling him they shouldn't see each other anymore. Fortunately for her, Miranda had wakened with a slight tummy ache from all the evening's excitement and had called downstairs for her mommy. Max had been up and off her and the couch like a cannon shot at the sound of the tiny voice, and Rowan had been endlessly grateful when he'd said he had to leave, after finding out her daughter was going to be all right.

At work that night, though, Rowan was far too busy to be preoccupied with worries and doubts about Max Donovan, and by the time she turned in her bank and finished her back work, she and Tara were ready to meet with some of the other waiters from September's for a much-needed beer before heading home. The two women were walking down the alley behind the restaurant toward Broadway when Rowan first saw the front end of a black Jaguar peeking around the corner of the big, brick building beside them, and she halted in midstride.

"Uh-oh," she said ominously under her breath.

"What is it?" Tara asked, concern lacing her voice.

"Bad news," Rowan told her. "Or maybe good news, I'm not sure."

"What?" the other woman whispered anxiously, twisting her head around to look behind them. "Are we gonna get jumped here, or what?"

The bizarre appropriateness of Tara's phrasing raced fleetingly through Rowan's mind, and for a moment she was afraid she was going to break into a fit of uncontrollable giggles. "Not you, Tara," she said cryptically. "But I may be in for a spot of trouble."

The two started walking again, and when they rounded the corner onto Broadway, Rowan almost emitted a helpless, adolescent sigh at the sight that met her eyes. Max was there with his car, in another of his well-cut, dark suits, leaning against the driver's side of the Jaguar with utter and relaxed confidence. His arms were folded over his ample chest, his lean legs were crossed at the ankles. His dark blond hair looked almost silver in the harsh, white light of the street lamp, and the cool, evening breeze ruffled it lovingly as he gazed hungrily right at her. It was as if he'd sensed her walking toward him long ago and knew exactly where to watch for her arrival. Inanely, she thought he looked like a magazine ad for expensive scotch, and she stared back at him as her heart began to go wild.

"Oh, wow," Tara mumbled under her breath. "He looks *great*."

"Yeah," Rowan concurred quickly, feeling her heart come skidding to a halt.

"Guess you won't be needing a ride home tonight."

"Guess not."

It was almost scary how everything seemed to click then, Rowan thought. All at once, the idea of being alone with Max, of coming out of work to find him waiting for her, of going home to spend the evening together felt so perfect, so right. It was as if they did this every evening and would continue to do so until the end of time. Rowan wasn't sure when it had happened last night, but sometime between dinner and dancing, despite her efforts to keep things simple and against her wishes that Max be kept at a distance, some subtle, irreversible event had taken place. At some point in the evening, Max Donovan had become important to her. And now she was going to have to deal with things a little differently.

Her mouth went dry, and her head began to spin at the realization. Then her heart finally kicked in again, but at a very unsteady pace. She squeezed her eyes tightly together for a moment and tried to squelch a disturbing thought that announced itself loudly from the corner of her mind. No. She would not for a minute believe that she was falling in love with Maximillian Donovan. It was too soon, too dumb and too impossible. There was no way it could ever work out.

"Hello, Rowan." Max interrupted her troubled thoughts with his soothing, deeply resonant voice.

"Hi, Max," she replied quietly. When had the sidewalk dropped away? When had the cool, evening air become so steamy and close?

"Max?" Tara squeaked beside her. "You call him *Max*?"

Quickly Rowan gathered her thoughts, and her words came out in a rush. "Uh, Max, this is my friend, Tara McQuade. Tara, this is Max Donovan."

"Duh," Tara said sarcastically to her friend, then turned to greet the man standing elegantly before them. "Mr.

Donovan," she murmured sweetly. "It's *so* nice to meet you."

This was the woman who had glared at him so ferociously his first day in town, Max realized as the other woman spoke, the day that he and Rowan had had their initial mishap. She was certainly looking at him differently now. "Ms. McQuade," he greeted her warmly, but his eyes only left Rowan's for a moment during the exchange.

She had sabotaged her uniform again, he noted with an appreciative grin, letting his gaze flicker down her slender neck to settle on the creamy lace of her camisole that once again peeked out at him from where she'd unbuttoned her shirt. He was suddenly grateful that there were still some things in life that a man could count on.

"Could I interest you ladies in a bite to eat?" He extended the invitation to both, but his gaze never left Rowan's face.

"We, uh, we were just going to go to HPB&L to grab a beer," Rowan told him.

Max shrugged, undaunted. "Mind if I join you?"

Rowan laughed out loud a little nervously, seeing humor in the incongruity of a man of Max's stature seated in the tiny, neighborhood hole-in-the-wall pub. "Gee, Max, for some reason I have difficulty picturing you in a bar with a big, pink neon sign that says Ladies Invited blinking on and off in the front window."

Tara laughed, too, but said tactfully, "Look, why don't you two kids run along home, and I'll tell the others that Rowan had a better offer?"

"Well, if you insist," Max said quickly, the eyes that held Rowan's growing warm with promise.

Tara looked from Max to Rowan and back again, then shook her head in amusement. "Good night, you two," she said quietly.

After watching to make sure her friend made it safely to her car across the street, Rowan turned to look at Max again and smiled. "It's almost midnight. What are you doing here?"

He opened his arms and spread them wide. "Isn't that obvious?"

"Tell me, anyway," she requested shyly.

Max dropped his arms to his sides, uncrossed his ankles and walked silently toward her. Lifting his hands to frame her face, he buried his fingers in the dark, silky strands of her hair and gently tipped her head back to gaze into her eyes. "I can't get you out of my thoughts," he told her bluntly. "All day long I've been staring off into space, missing the conversations going on around me, forgetting to eat, forgetting to breathe.... I can't concentrate on anything, Rowan. And the people I'm doing business with here are beginning to think I'm an idiot." He took a step closer until his body was flush with hers. "All I could think about all day was this."

He lowered his face to hers and tasted her lips softly. Rowan was helpless to prevent the whimper of surrender that came from her very soul. At that quietly uttered request, Max deepened the kiss, covering her mouth fully with his, letting his tongue tangle aimlessly with hers. It was a kiss of both promise and entreaty, a kiss that told Rowan exactly how much he had missed her during the long day.

She slipped her arms possessively around his waist and kissed him back, hoping to convey the same sense of happiness at seeing him as she received from his embrace. Her kiss was gentle and tentative, as she was still unsure what was happening between them, still a little wary of letting things go too far. She only knew that at the moment the world was a perfect place and she didn't want anything to change the sense of well-being that pervaded every cell in her body.

"Max," she whispered, finally pulling away when she remembered they were standing on a downtown street corner in the middle of the night. She laughed quietly and not a little nervously. "Um, I don't think it's a good idea to be hanging around out here."

He looked around curiously, noting for the first time the light traffic and limited number of passersby. "What's wrong? Isn't it safe in this part of town?"

"It's safe enough if crime is your concern," she told him with a smile. "What I meant was, I gave up necking in public after I graduated from high school."

Max smiled back, a smile shining with a predatory gleam. "I have to admit that public displays of affection aren't something I normally engage in, either, but hey...sometimes a man's gotta do what a man's gotta do."

"Well, maybe he should do it in more private surroundings," she proposed, unaware of how suggestive her statement was until she saw his lips turn up in a seductive leer. "That's not what I meant," she stammered quickly as she felt color creep into her face. She'd never blushed around anyone the way she did around Max. "I meant maybe we should go home."

"What an excellent idea," Max murmured, pulling her close again for one more kiss. It struck him as strangely appropriate that the concept of returning with Rowan to her house was the equivalent of "going home." He was as uncertain as she about what was happening between them. But whatever it was, he decided firmly that it was very nice, and very welcome.

After they arrived at the big, rambling Victorian and dismissed the sitter, Rowan offered Max a glass of wine before going to change clothes. "I feel like I'm covered with vinaigrette and béarnaise," she told him with a shrug.

"I think you look wonderful," Max replied.

Her heart trip-hammered in her rib cage at the heated look he sent her way. She said a little breathlessly, "I'll only be a minute."

Max smiled and sipped his wine, looking about her living room thoughtfully. His eyes fell upon the collection of oil paintings on one wall, and he ambled slowly toward them. From the limited knowledge of art he had gained thanks to museum openings and gallery exhibits, he identified them as done in the American Primitive style, not one he'd ever considered especially impressive, when he gave much thought to art at all. But for some reason, these paintings appealed to him greatly, struck some chord at the center of his heart.

One in particular drew his attention and held it, one of a large, turreted Victorian house, similar to Rowan's though with more color and life. Standing before the house, in a green yard dotted with blossoms of red, yellow and blue, were three people arranged according to height: one man with a shaggy, brown mustache, one woman with a long, black braid, and one small child clutching a doll and smiling mischievously. There were two cats and a big, spotted dog in the yard, and birds singing in every tree, along with a yellow canary on the front porch. Max couldn't help but smile at the scene, feeling a warmth and satisfaction, a sense of utter peacefulness, settle over him like a well-worn blanket. Of course, this *was* Rowan's house, the one she'd known as a child, and the people standing beside her in the painting were her parents.

"You like it?" Rowan asked quietly from behind him.

"Very much," he said as he turned around to look at her with a smile. She'd put on a pair of baggy, khaki trousers and a long, cream-colored cotton sweater. Her cheeks were pink—from her heightened awareness of the electricity burning up the air between them?—and she clutched her wine in both hands, as if it were trying to get away from her. "Did your mother paint these?"

Rowan nodded and crossed the room nervously to stand beside him. "These six on the wall are the only ones she didn't sell. They were her favorites. The one you're looking at now is *my* very favorite."

Max turned back to consider it again. "What happened to all the animals?" he asked, curious that Rowan didn't have any pets when she seemed like the perfect candidate to harbor small creatures.

Rowan gazed lovingly at the picture as she explained. "Foley, that's the dog, was pretty old at the time this was painted. A few years later he was gone. Gus and Andrew, the two cats in the yard, eventually wandered off, each on his own. The canary, Dante, died when I was in junior high school. My mother had another one at the time of the accident named Sinatra, but I gave him to Mrs. Stanley, our next-door neighbor. She was elderly and was always visiting just so she could listen to him sing. Afterward, every time I heard Sinatra singing, it just reminded me of my mother, so I didn't really want him around, anyway. The bird, I mean, not Frank."

Max waited for her to respond to the memories that must be crowding into her brain right now, prepared for a repeat of last night's tears. When no such reaction occurred, he was puzzled, worried that she might be suppressing her feelings because of his presence.

As if sensing his line of thought, Rowan glanced over at him and shrugged. "I don't know, Max," she told him quietly. "The pain doesn't seem to be as bad now as it was before. Maybe finally letting it all out last night was the beginning of letting it all go. It still hurts, but it's more of a melancholy feeling now, not the crippling, inconsolable sense of helplessness I used to experience.'' Silently she added to herself that maybe that was because she didn't feel as if she was facing it alone anymore.

Max felt his features relax at her statement, relieved that she felt that way, inexplicably glad that he'd been somehow responsible for her newfound hopefulness. He smiled at her reassuringly and took her hand.

''I would like to get another pet, though,'' she told him, ''someday. I think that Miranda would like it, too, although I want to wait until she's old enough to understand and respect the needs of one. I think it would be good for her to learn about the responsibility that goes along with caring for a life, to learn that all living things have to rely on one another to thrive and stay alive. Nothing can really survive all by itself, can it?'' she added. ''It goes against the laws of nature.''

Max looked at her thoughtfully, wondering if she was trying to imply more than what her words stated. When she looked back at him with an open expression, her features clear of any subterfuge, Max mentally shook himself. This was Rowan, he reminded himself unnecessarily, and she was in no way superficial or calculating like so many other people of his acquaintance. It wasn't necessary for her to convince him that he needed her in his life, because he already knew for a fact that he did. The problem was, she didn't seem to understand that she needed someone in her life, too, someone like him. But what good was he going to do her if he would be leaving in another week? he asked himself. And how could he keep her in his life, when she would undoubtedly want to remain here?

As quickly as the annoying realization entered his mind, Max pushed it unceremoniously away. At the moment, nothing seemed more right than for him to be here with Rowan, in her house, with her daughter sleeping peacefully upstairs. He took a distracted and restless sip of his wine then, and for lack of anything better to say, remarked, "Well, you certainly know how to choose wine. This is really quite excellent. So was what we had last night."

Rowan smiled at him, feeling relaxed and warm in the comfortable aura that seemed to have settled over them. "Yes, well, Miranda's father was a bartender whose hobby was wine, so if nothing else, at least I learned a lot about—" She stopped abruptly when she realized how her comment was going to upset the tranquillity they had been trying to establish. "I'm sorry, Max," she added quickly, looking up at him apprehensively. "I didn't mean to—"

"It's all right, Rowan," he said honestly, taking her chin in his hand. "I told you last night that I wanted to hear what happened between you and Miranda's father. I wasn't under the impression that she was the result of immaculate conception or parthenogenesis, you know."

Rowan's tentative smile told him she wasn't quite certain that he was okay with the situation. It surprised him, too, that he was. Things felt so right with Rowan now for some reason. He didn't feel threatened by any man, even one from her past.

She shrugged. "A lot of guys would get kind of upset if—"

"I'm not a lot of guys," he reminded her.

Her smile became more confident as she replied, "That's certainly true."

"I really would like to talk about it," he told her, pausing before he added, "if you want to."

Rowan's eyes reflected her surprise and gratitude. "Thanks, Max. I think I would like to."

He was glad that she felt that way. He wanted her to share her most important experiences with him. He wanted to know about everything that had ever affected her and made her the woman she was now. And he wanted her to realize that, too. With a sweeping gesture, he indicated the couch with a question in his eyes, and Rowan nodded.

As they seated themselves on the sofa in their positions of the previous evening, it puzzled Rowan that Max should be curious about her past. Before she could stop herself, she voiced her doubt out loud. "I honestly don't understand why you'd want to hear about all this, though."

Max started to tell her that he wasn't sure why, either, that he only knew it was somehow vitally important to learn everything he could about her. He started to tell her that, then thought differently, unwilling to acknowledge the depth of his feelings for this woman he'd known only a short time, so he only smiled and shook his head noncommittally.

When Max didn't respond, Rowan sighed and said, "Joey Monaco. He was from Philadelphia and began working as a bartender at September's about two years after I started working there. I guess in his own way, Joey really did care for me, but he cared for a lot of other women, too. Most women, in fact."

"He was unfaithful to you?"

Rowan emitted a humorless chuckle. "To put it mildly. After I found out I was pregnant, I also discovered that Joey had been with about half the other waitresses at September's. But what was worse, all of them knew about each other and it was no big deal to them. I was the only one who thought I had a monogamous relationship with him. I felt like such an idiot after that."

"If you ask me, he's the one who was an idiot," Max told her. Any man who'd go after another woman when he already had Rowan Chance was more than an idiot.

Rowan smiled and placed her hand lightly over his. "Thanks, Max. Unfortunately, Joey was one of those guys who just can't make a commitment. After I told him I was pregnant, he kind of chose to ignore me altogether." She paused to take a sip of her wine, remembering how painful it had been to watch Joey making dates with other women, to suffer the blank looks he offered her when they wound up working the same shift. "That really hurt," she added quietly.

Max wished he knew where Joey Monaco was now, so he could strangle the little bastard.

"Anyway," Rowan continued, "thanks to the uniform's cummerbund, I was able to hide my condition and keep working until I was many months along. Then Louis pretty much insisted that I take a leave of absence until the baby was born, because he thought a pregnant waitress might give the restaurant a bad image. Good ol' Louis. So I was unemployed for a while."

"Couldn't Joey have helped you out?" Max asked, curling his lips back in distaste when he pronounced the other man's name.

"By the time I came back to work, Joey was gone," Rowan explained. "Someone told me he went to Chicago to work, but since then I've heard he went on to Los Angeles. Besides, I didn't want any help from Joey. Miranda was, is and always will be *my* responsibility. I don't need anything from Joey or anybody else. I've done just fine all by myself."

Her last sentiment was delivered with less conviction than she'd hoped to convey, and her eyes had fallen from Max's face to her glass before she'd expressed what she felt.

Max lifted her hand to his lips and kissed her knuckles softly. "Are you so sure of that, Rowan?" he asked her quietly.

When her eyes met his, he could see clearly that she was not. Still, she mumbled softly, "Yes. Of course I am."

And she had been, she told herself. Until Max Donovan had come along and messed things up. Why, all of a sudden, did it feel as if she had someone to lean on, someone to share in her daily troubles and celebrations? Why did she fear she wouldn't be able to fully enjoy life when he was back in New York? Why had he become so important to her? And how would she be able to handle it when he was gone?

"Rowan?" Max ventured carefully when he could see that she was lost in thought.

"Yes?" she responded, returning her attention to him.

This time it was Max who let his gaze fall to his glass as he spoke. "Did you, uh...that is, were you in love with Miranda's father?" He was almost afraid to hear her answer. He wasn't sure if he wanted to know whether she still carried a torch for the jerk who'd abandoned her and her daughter.

Rowan considered his question carefully before responding. "By the time Joey came into my life, things were totally out of control," she told him. "After my parents died, I went a little crazy. I got kind of self-destructive, experienced a significant loss of self-worth." She shrugged in light confusion before she returned her eyes to meet his. "I don't know. Maybe subconsciously I was hoping that my folks would come back if they saw how badly I was behaving without them, how desperately I needed them to keep me in line. Or maybe I was just trying to forget they'd ever existed. I went out all the time, did nothing but party every night, closed every bar in town." She rolled her eyes and expelled an incredulous sigh as she remembered. "I didn't even drink, Max, but every bartender in the city knew my name, because my friends and I had become such barflies. It's embarrassing now to realize it.''

"You were only doing what a million other young, single, carefree people do every night," Max told her. "Don't be so hard on yourself.''

"But that's just the point, Max. I was never like that before. I was always this quiet, studious, unobtrusive kid who loved peace and harmony. After my parents died, things just blew apart. I could never get my music loud enough, my car wouldn't go fast enough. Even in a crowded bar or at a huge party, there were never enough people around. No matter where I was or what I was doing, I always, *always* felt desperate. And that's how I was when Joey met me. He said the thing that drew him to me, the reason he liked me, was precisely because I seemed so angry, so intense. I guess I carried that anger a lot longer than I thought.''

"And you liked him?" Max prompted. "Loved him?''

Rowan let her eyes fall once again as she said, "At the time, I thought I was in love with him, but I think even then I knew he wasn't a very stable guy. But I needed *something* permanent to keep me from throwing myself totally over the edge, and I tried to hang on to him, because he was the closest thing to it I had. But he let go, and I had to hang on to myself. Fortunately, when the smoke cleared, there was Miranda." For the first time since she'd started to talk about her past, Rowan found herself smiling with genuine pleasure. "And she provided me with all the stability I needed then.''

"And now?" Max asked her.

She gazed at him blankly. "What do you mean?''

"Is Miranda enough for you now?" he clarified.

"Miranda is everything to me," Rowan told him.

His eyes held hers for some moments, then he nodded slowly before releasing her hand, not sure he was content with her response. Somehow he knew that despite the joy and stability Rowan's daughter brought to her, it simply wasn't enough. She needed and deserved so much more, and Max found himself wanting to be the man who provided her with everything she would ever demand or desire, who would make certain that she never lacked anything again. The only problem was, *could* he be that man? Was there any way he could insinuate himself into her life like that? And did he have the right? It troubled him greatly that he was unable to find answers for his questions.

Chapter Seven

Max and Rowan stayed up quite late that night talking, and when Max expressed an interest in seeing what she'd done with her warehouse, Rowan was surprised and pleased, and promised to show it to him the following day. They made plans to go downtown together with Miranda in the morning, and after seeing Rowan's shop, Max insisted, he wanted her to give him a complete tour of the city, this time from a citizen's point of view, instead of from the back seat of a limo, while local businessmen showed him what they thought he'd want to see.

"And I want to go to the Kentucky Derby next Saturday, too," he announced with a smile.

Rowan grinned at his enthusiasm. "All right, but I'm not so sure you're going to like the infield," she warned. "It can get pretty crazy."

"What's so bad about the infield?" Max asked.

She tented her fingertips thoughtfully and said, "Imagine a cross between the Indy 500, Mardi Gras, a lunar expedition and that movie, *It's a Mad, Mad, Mad, Mad World*. And then put the result in a bourbon distillery."

Max raised his eyebrows. "Okay. Never mind. Isn't there a clubhouse or something like that? I heard someone mention something called Millionaire's Row."

"Forget it," she said, waving him off decisively with her hand. "Not unless you're filthy, stinking ri—" She stopped suddenly and cocked her head to one side. "On second thought, maybe we *could* swing it."

Although he was delighted, Max was reluctant to point out that not only had Rowan just been agreeable about the fact that he was wealthy, she had also just indirectly suggested that he use said wealth, along with his social standing, to obtain something she wouldn't normally be able to get on her own. Instead he smiled, loving the way his heart became lighter as a result of her words, and said, "I'll see what I can do about tickets."

Rowan looked at him sheepishly, as if she, too, understood exactly what she had just done, but like Max, she remained silent. So he had money, she thought. So he could throw his weight around, if he wanted to. So what? He'd never once made an issue of his wealth and social prominence. With no small amount of embarrassment, she forced herself to realize that it was *she* who always made such a big deal about it, not Max. For the first time, she felt herself admitting that maybe economic differences really did have nothing to do with her reasons for shying away from him.

"We, uh," she stammered, still reeling a little from her observation, "we could go to some of the other events, if you want to. They're pretty fun. Miranda loved them last year."

"Like what?" Max asked, knowing she only had to say the word and he would follow her anywhere.

"Oh, like the Pegasus Parade," Rowan said slowly, uncertain about the fiery look in Max's eyes. "Or the steamboat race or balloon race."

"Balloon race?" Max murmured as he lifted her palm to his lips, so that he could tickle it with feathery kisses.

"Oh, yeah," Rowan whispered on a shaky breath. "That's a real favorite."

"Oh?" he prompted, closing the small gap of space between them.

Rowan's heart began to hammer hard in her chest, while little explosions of heat torpedoed her stomach and set fires that spread to every nerve ending. "Uh-huh," she mumbled softly, all too aware that the air surrounding them had begun to sizzle. "It's supposed to be tomorrow morning, but now they're predicting rain, so they'll probably postpone it. It seems to happen that way every year."

"Does it?" Max asked as he raised a hand to gently cup her jaw.

Rowan nodded almost imperceptibly. "It's almost a Derby tradition now," she whispered into the silence that had settled around them.

Max looked intently into her dark blue eyes, feeling at once lost forever and rescued from certain destruction. For long moments he gazed at her, wondering why it was that she made him feel so complete, where others had left him wanting so much more. "You're very beautiful," he murmured.

Rowan caught her breath at his words. She'd always shrugged off any compliment from a man as a way for him to get what he wanted. But there was something in Max's voice she'd never heard from others, something that assured her he wasn't interested in feeding her lines. "Thank you," she finally managed to utter in response.

"I mean it, Rowan," he told her anxiously. "It's not just... I mean...it's more than..." *Dammit,* what had happened to his vocabulary? He sighed impatiently before trying again. "There's something about you that's so different from other people, but I don't know what it is."

The hand on her jaw traveled up to tangle in her hair, and Rowan closed her fingers gently around Max's wrist. "I think I know what you mean, Max," she told him quietly.

"Do you?" he asked desperately. "Because I'm not sure I do."

Rowan smiled in encouragement and nodded again. "Because there's something about you, too, Max. Something I don't understand. Something that makes me—" She stopped herself before she could blurt out the words, "love you," because she was afraid of voicing them. Every time she'd told people she loved them, they'd somehow disappeared from her life. So instead she quickly finished, "That makes me find you so much more attractive than other men."

"You do know that I care for you, don't you?" he asked softly.

After a small hesitation, Rowan said slowly, "Yes."

"Then promise me you won't say anything more about how we should stop seeing each other."

"I promise," she vowed softly.

He seemed to relax at her assurance, then took a deep breath before asserting, "Because as long as I'm here, I want to be with you, Rowan. And after that..."

She held her breath, almost afraid to hear what he was going to say.

The hand tangled in her hair settled at her nape, and Max drew Rowan gently toward him, so that her forehead was pressed against his own. "After that, I don't know," he told her honestly.

"That's okay, Max," she said as she pulled back to look into his eyes. "You've just given what we have as much chance as anything else in the world. Fifty-fifty."

His smile was gentle and almost sad. "And that's all right with you?"

"Those are my favorite odds."

"Ah, Rowan."

He said her name softly, his quiet words sounding ominous in the otherwise silent room. Circling her wrist gently with his other hand, he tugged her toward him as he lay on the couch, snuggling her body flush atop his. Leisurely and lovingly he ran his hands over her back, so that they could simply enjoy each other's nearness. Things had happened too quickly last night, and this time Max wanted everything to go slowly.

His fingers at her nape tangled once more in her hair, and Max pulled her face down to his to capture her mouth gently, running his lips along the line of her jaw and neck. Rowan could only sigh and murmur his name, could only circle an arm around his neck and run her fingers through his thick golden hair. For long moments they lay holding each other, exploring and caressing, touching and tasting, loving the feel of having each other so close. Max groaned when Rowan kissed him deeply and ran her hand urgently down the length of his muscular abdomen, then brought it back up to spread open across his chest. He arched her eagerly against him, pressing her more intimately against the cradle of his thighs. When Rowan felt his rapidly rising arousal against her, their kisses became more fierce and furious, and she feverishly worked at the knot in his tie. After she pulled the long length of silk from beneath his collar to let it fall silently to the floor, she unfastened the pearly buttons of his shirt, so that she could bury her fingers in the mat of springy gold beneath.

Finally Max tore his lips away from hers and gazed frantically up into her eyes. "Rowan, Rowan," he rasped out. "Are we doing what I think we're doing?"

Rowan's rapid respiration was as irregular as his, her chest rising to his as they gasped for breath. She counseled herself that she should stop what was happening before things went any further, warning herself that she was about to make a colossally stupid mistake. But the words and embraces she and Max shared tonight had sparked a small flicker of hope in the darkest, coldest corner of Rowan's heart, gradually warming parts of her that she'd thought long dead. Maybe it was careless, but as she let the flame brighten and jump higher, she suddenly felt more hopeful than she had in years that her future held something promising. She knew she was in love with Max, and couldn't quite squelch the thought that maybe, just maybe, he could fall in love with her, too.

"Yes, Max," she whispered uncertainly. "I think we are."

Her softly uttered confirmation was apparently all he needed to hear. With the grace and determination of a silver-screen idol, Max swept Rowan up into his arms and carried her up the stairs to her room. Her bedside lamp with the silk, fringed shade provided the only lighting in the room. He carefully set her on her feet beside the bed and looked down at her, as if she were a beautiful gift to be opened slowly and cherished forever.

"You know, I've dreamed about this since that first night I brought you home," he confessed. "Fantasized about how you would look and feel, wondered about what would turn you on...."

"Oh, Max, stop," she urged him with a nervous chuckle, lifting her fingers to his lips to halt the flow of words. "I'll never be able to live up to a fantasy."

He kissed her fingertips and murmured quietly, "Rowan, you *are* a fantasy. I just can't believe how lucky I am that you became real for me."

He kissed her then, and the world began to spin out of her control. Rowan felt as if every cell in her body had burst into flame, boiling her blood and singeing every nerve. She caught her fingers in his dark golden hair, loving its softness as she mussed it the way she had wanted to do since she'd first met him.

"As much as I hate to admit it," she said after a moment, "I must confess that I've fantasized about you, too."

Max smiled broadly and seemed delighted by her revelation. "You have?"

She nodded slowly, letting one hand creep to the back of his neck and dip into his shirt collar.

"Just what *exactly* did your fantasies involve?" he wanted to know. "Please feel free to use me as a model," he added, further encouraging her.

Rowan shrugged noncommittally, then smiled a mysterious and suggestive smile. But she remained silent after that and smoothed her hands across his chest, pushing open the fabric of his shirt with maddening slowness. When her hands palmed the satiny-warm skin of his shoulders, the shirt fell silently to the floor, and Rowan's thoughts became jumbled at the sight of such a magnificent man standing bare-chested in her bedroom.

When she leaned forward to place a kiss at the base of Max's throat, he groaned almost painfully, then went a little wild as she put her mouth over one flat nipple to taste him. But when her hands fell to the buckle of his belt and unfastened it and the button of his trousers, he caught up her wrists to prevent her from going any further.

"You first," he said, when she looked up at him, bewildered. He lifted her hands to his lips, kissing her palms and sucking on her fingertips until she thought she would melt away. He gripped her long sweater by the hem and pulled it over her head, only to discard it blindly as he gazed at the small breasts that rose and fell with her erratic breathing beneath her lacy ivory camisole. Then, placing her arms once again around his neck, Max went to work on her pants with a quick, well-maneuvered strategy. After the buttons were unfastened and the zipper lowered, he dipped both hands inside to slide them down over her panties and cup her soft derriere, shucking the worn, khaki fabric as he went. A deep, satisfied rumble rose from his chest as he lowered his body down with her pants, and when Rowan stepped out of the khaki pooled around her ankles, Max tossed her trousers aside to join her sweater and his shirt on the floor. Then, gripping her hips, he pulled her body toward him, pressing his lips hotly against the soft, creamy satin that covered the most intimate part of her.

"Oh, God, Max," Rowan groaned.

He allowed his tongue the leisurely pleasure of tasting her there through her panties, then straightened again to gaze down at her face. Without a word, he pulled her camisole over her head and saw Rowan's arms rise instinctively to cross over her nakedness.

"No, don't," Max urged quietly as he gently pulled her arms away. "I want to look at you, Rowan. You're very beautiful."

Rowan felt the heat of a blush that started in her heart and crept into her cheeks. "So are you," she responded somewhat shyly, unable to meet his gaze.

Max grinned. "I don't think anyone's ever called me beautiful before," he said as he drew her close, loving the feel of her silky skin against the coarse hair of his chest.

"Then you've been spending your time with a lot of unperceptive people," she told him, sighing with pleasure at the strength and power that emanated from his big body.

He rested his chin on top of her head and admitted reluctantly, "Now that I've met you, I'm inclined to agree."

"Max—" she began, but he interrupted.

"Listen, Miranda isn't going to wake up, is she? I mean . . . well, you know."

Rowan smiled at his concern. "No, she's always been a sound sleeper. But it might not hurt to close and lock the door. Just in case."

"But will you be able to hear her if she calls you? What if she needs you during the night? What if she has a bad dream or another stomachache or something?"

Rowan came up on tiptoe to kiss him lightly at the corner of his mouth. "Don't worry. If she needs me, I'll know. I'll be able to hear."

"You're sure?"

"I'm sure."

After a moment he nodded, seemingly satisfied by her reassurances. While he took care of her bedroom door, Rowan pulled back the quilt that covered her bed. Max turned, to find her seated on blue-flowered sheets with her legs crossed and drawn up in front of her, her arms hugging her knees. It occurred to him then that she looked a little dazed and more than a little frightened—just the way he felt himself. Max was aware that for the first time in his life, he was about to make love to a woman not only because he wanted her, but because he needed her, too. A woman whose acceptance of him was absolutely vital to his very happiness.

A woman who could somehow make all the difference in the world.

This is it, Rowan thought as she watched Max approach her with slow, deliberate strides. He removed his shoes casually, and then his movements were silent as he neared her, stopping only inches away from where she sat. Her eyes became fixed on the long fingers that slowly lowered the zipper of his trousers, fascinated by the light sprinkling of golden hair on the backs of his big hands. When he stood before her, clad only in skimpy briefs, Rowan almost passed out at the sight of him. He was incredible.

"Rowan, look at me," he murmured huskily.

She heard his rough voice from what seemed like a million miles away, and her eyes wandered slowly up the length of his body, her heart pounding with more irregularity as she took in the glorious perfection of him. Her brain screamed at her that she was way out of her league, that what she was about to do was completely insane, but when her eyes finally fell on Max's face, when she saw the longing and need he was unable to disguise, she opened her arms to him, and he came to her eagerly.

For a moment they only lay holding each other, listening to their hearts beat, breathing in each other's fragrance, touching tentatively for the first time. Then as their explorations grew more daring and dangerous, they became lost in sensual encounters. When Max rolled Rowan onto her back to receive his kiss, she willingly complied, tangling her fingers in his hair as his tongue traced her lips and penetrated the dark recesses of her mouth. He kissed her everywhere—her nose, her cheek, her jaw, her neck—then after a momentary pause, he lowered his head to place a lengthy kiss over her heart. With one hand he gently held her breast, while his lips wreaked havoc on the extended peak, tasting and teasing, suckling and sighing. When his other hand began a leisurely journey down the length of her abdomen, Rowan nearly purred, then gasped as his fingers settled over her panties at the juncture of her thighs.

She cried out loud when he pressed against her, and she writhed in open ecstasy when he cupped her in his palm. Rowan's own fingers tightened in Max's hair, then relaxed and fell to his shoulders before sliding lower to grip his firm biceps. When she lost control of her breathing and her head rolled deliriously back and forth on the pillow, Max knew he couldn't wait any longer. He left her long enough to shed his briefs and help her out of hers, then returned to multiply his ministrations.

Just when Rowan thought she would explode from her desires Max raised himself on his elbows above her, positioning himself with intent between her legs. Then, with one last look into her eyes, he entered her deeply, both of them crying out at the exquisite delight that the union brought to their tensed bodies and lonely spirits.

At their joining two lost souls found each other and became one. For a brief instant, both were overcome with an inner tranquillity neither had ever known. But before their peace could be consciously acknowledged, a physical demand such as neither expected began to carry them far away from normal reality. As Max set a rhythm that drove them deeper into ecstasy, Rowan responded with movements that made the trip indescribable. Just before they reached the peak, they relived that initial second of serenity, then with an explosive frenzy, tumbled into an abyss of luxurious rapture.

For long moments afterward they could only lie spent, entangled in each other's sweat-streaked bodies, gasping for breath, groping for coherent thought. All Rowan could think was that sex must have changed in the four years she'd been away from it, because she had never, ever felt as wonderfully euphoric as she felt now. Surely some book must have appeared in stores that she had missed, but that Max had undoubtedly memorized from cover to cover. He'd made her aware of parts of her body she would have sworn were incapable of feeling anything. He also seemed to have jump-started her heart again, after it had lain sputtering and rusty for years.

Beside her, Max felt pleasantly exhausted and thoroughly sated, as if he'd finally succeeded, after striving for years, in attaining some elusive, unidentifiable goal. He lay on his stomach with one arm draped possessively across Rowan's midsection, marveling again at the way he had responded to her, not just physically, but emotionally and spiritually, as well. It was crazy, the way she had literally come into his life out of nowhere, and had caught him so completely off guard. But what was truly madness was that now he never wanted to let her go.

"Rowan?" he said softly to the woman who lay beside him, breathing deeply, with her eyes closed.

At the sound of his voice, Rowan smiled and opened her eyes, turning her head to face him. Max had to smile back at the unmasked contentment that greeted him in her expression. Utter happiness had replaced the lost, lonely look in her eyes.

"Are you okay?" he asked her with a conspiratorial grin, although he could see the answer on her face.

Rowan drew in a deep, unsteady breath, then turned on her side to place a warm hand against his cheek. "I think 'okay' is just a little bit of an understatement," she told him. "Frankly, I feel like breaking into song."

"C'mere, you." He gathered her into his arms and held her close, kissing her lips, her cheek, her hair, feeling more at ease than he'd felt in years. Rowan Chance had done something wonderful to him, and for the life of him he wasn't sure what. He only knew he didn't want to lose it. Not ever.

As she held Max in her arms, Rowan thought that nothing in her life had ever felt as right as that moment did. Even when her parents were alive, she'd never felt the kind of closeness with them that she'd just experienced with Max. When her thoughts began to include reminders that he might only be in her life temporarily, she pushed them away, instead thinking about what would fill the days they did spend together.

When Max reached over and switched off the bedside lamp, the blue-tinged light of a street lamp outside found its way into the dark corners of Rowan's room, outlining her furnishings and distorting their shapes. After a moment, Rowan heard Max rise from her bed and move to look outside from her big bay window. In the semidarkness he seemed pensive and unsettled, and she padded slowly and silently across the room to stand beside him. For a moment he seemed not to notice her, then suddenly and yet gently, he draped an arm across her shoulders and pulled her close to hug her.

"It's so quiet here," he murmured softly as he continued to gaze over her head into the night. "I'm so used to city sounds, sirens and car alarms and traffic. But I don't think I've heard a single car pass by all night. Just crickets, and the wind rustling through the trees. And look, there are actually fireflies out there."

Rowan smiled at the tranquil tone that she heard in his voice. "Lightning bugs," she said quietly.

"What?"

"We always called them lightning bugs when I was little."

"Oh."

For a few more moments they held each other silently, both loving, but not mentioning, the contentment and sense of security that comes with holding someone after years of loneliness.

Finally Max broke through the quiet aura that surrounded them.

"I like your house, Rowan."

She lifted her head from its resting place against his chest and turned her face to his. "I'm glad, Max."

"I like your daughter, too."

A small pain stung Rowan's heart at the reminder. She really should have thought about how tonight might affect Miranda before jumping in with both feet. But instead of voicing her misgivings, she told him, "And Miranda is crazy about you."

"And her mother?" Max held his breath as he awaited Rowan's answer, silently pleading with her to take his inquiry very seriously.

Rowan took a moment to respond, caught between saying something flip and flirtatious or telling him the truth. Finally she whispered honestly, "Her mother is pretty crazy about you, too, Max."

With her admission, Max felt his spirits become lighter. His smile broadened; his pulse quickened; his heart lifted. Rowan liked him. Because he was Max.

"I like you, too, Rowan," he added, so quietly she was afraid she might have imagined it. "A lot."

Before she could respond, Max lowered his head and pressed his lips tenderly against hers. For a moment the kiss was a gentle caress, but as each began to recall their recent journey into delirium, the embrace grew hungrier and more intense, their demands for satisfaction more insistent. Eventually they found their way back to bed, and as the moon rose higher into the night sky, so did their passion climb once again to cosmic heights. Throughout the night they partook of earthly joys and heavenly delights, each lost in ecstasy and amazed at the newness of their feelings.

Rowan had never felt so cherished, so... loved. Hope flared within her again, and she almost allowed herself to envision something substantial, something—dare she say it?—permanent with Max.

Almost.

Until morning came creeping rudely into her bedroom, and Rowan awoke, pleasantly lethargic and startlingly alone.

Chapter Eight

Well, not quite alone, not exactly. There was a Post-it note, imprinted with the initials M.D., stuck dispassionately to the pillow beside her. The pillow that still held an impression from the golden-haired man who'd lain there, the man who'd made her feel so exquisite just hours before, who was making her feel really quite foolish now. The small square of yellow paper, upon which were a few hastily scribbled lines, effectively shattered the first sense of hope Rowan had felt toward the future in a very long time and completely doused the small flame of hope that had ignited in her heart the night before.

Rowan— I didn't want to wake you as you were sleeping so soundly. I can't tell you how sorry I am, but I just remembered an early meeting that I simply can't afford to miss. I'll call you this afternoon.

Max

I can't tell you how sorry I am.... Rowan read those words over and over until her vision began to blur. He was sorry. He had a meeting. Gazing blindly at her bedroom, she crumpled up and palmed the note until it was a compact ball of lint in her fist. It was Saturday morning, she told herself blandly. Who in their right minds would be having a meeting on Saturday morning? Even businessmen of Maximillian Donovan's caliber weren't *that* conscientious about their work. He hadn't wanted to see her long enough to say goodbye.

With a small sigh, Rowan rolled onto her back to stare thoughtfully at the ceiling, contemplating her situation to determine the degree of mental shaking she should give herself. She'd been down this road before, she realized. More than once. She remembered the morning she'd wakened to discover that her parents hadn't arrived home during the night, as they'd said they would. And she remembered all the mornings following, when she'd been forced to greet the day alone. She also recalled the night she'd told Joey she was pregnant. He'd told her everything was going to be all right, had stayed long enough to make love to her, and in the morning he'd been gone, too. Of course, Joey hadn't bothered to leave a note, but all in all, the outcome and the implication were the same. Max was gone. And not just for this morning, either, Rowan assured herself. Any frivolous little visions she might have enjoyed about sharing coffee and croissants in bed evaporated into a thin mist that made the ceiling look fuzzy.

How could she have been so stupid and gullible? How could she have let herself believe that this time with Max was going to be different? Hadn't he told her last night that he'd fantasized about making love to her since the first time he'd brought her home? she further berated herself. Why hadn't she seen that that was *all* he'd wanted from her? Now that he'd gotten what he wanted, he would doubtlessly go on to bigger game. She should have realized from the start that the two of them had nothing in common but a sexual attraction, should have seen clearly that Max had no reason to be interested in her otherwise. Of course, she *had* seen that from the beginning, she reminded herself, but like an idiot, she'd chosen to ignore it. And for that she would have to live with herself.

It surprised her that all she felt right now was emptiness. She wanted to be insulted and mad. Mad at Max for appearing to be such a decent, caring man, madder still that he had said the tender, seemingly heartfelt things he'd said. Mad because he'd known exactly which buttons to press to make her fall in love with him. Instead she was only sad and disheartened. Deep down it was as if she had expected this, as if her gloomy prediction had simply come true. And for that reason Rowan became angry with herself. But her anger was for having succumbed so easily to simple human weakness. It hadn't been stupidity that had made her feel so hopeful last night; it had been poor judgment. And even if she regretted everything else that had happened, at least talking to Max had helped her understand herself a little better, had helped her to confront some old ghosts and unhealed wounds. Therefore she couldn't really be mad. Could she?

"Dammit," she muttered quietly, giving in to feelings of defeat. Halfheartedly she hurled the offensive little wad of yellow paper at the wall, but it missed by a good two feet. Sure he was going to call her, she thought sardonically. Right. She might have been foolish last night, but as the harsh, white light of dawn illuminated the reality of her situation, she wasn't about to believe that a man who'd sneaked away from her without even saying goodbye this morning was going to give her a call this afternoon. Somehow she knew without question that she had seen the last of Max Donovan.

Boy, he'd been a terrific actor, though, she thought with a sinking heart as she pulled on a faded, navy-blue T-shirt and jeans. She'd have to give him credit for a class-A performance. No wonder she'd fallen so hard, so fast. He'd actually had her believing he cared for her. Had she really been thinking he looked lonely? Emitting a long sigh as she ran a comb through her hair, Rowan laughed humorlessly. Maximillian Donovan *lonely*? He probably had women everywhere clamoring all over him. He could take his pick. He'd no doubt had dozens of lovers in his life and would certainly have dozens more.

The thought that she was one in a continuous string of women depressed Rowan more than any of the other disturbing notions that plagued her that morning. How could she have meant nothing to him, when he'd made her feel so incredibly special? He would go on now to partake of the charms of numerous other women, but Rowan knew without doubt that she'd never be able to give that much of herself to another man. In just a short time Max had claimed a major part of her, and he had taken it with him when he'd left. It was a part of her she'd never known existed until last night, a part she'd never be able to recover now. How could she have let this happen?

She padded quietly into Miranda's pale pink and yellow nursery, pausing beside her sleeping daughter. Miranda lay on her stomach with one hand curled into an open fist beside her face, the one-eyed teddy bear that had once belonged to Rowan snuggled against her side. She's getting so big, Rowan thought, her heart swelling with emotion at the sight of her child slumbering so innocently, oblivious to the turmoil she felt herself. She wished there were some way she might protect her daughter from all of life's hurts and injustices. The fact that she was helpless to do so made Rowan feel inadequate as a parent and only added to the melancholy her other troubled thoughts had brought on.

After rousing and dressing Miranda, she made them both breakfast, a task she had to complete twice, because the first time she burned the bacon and dumped too much salt into the eggs. Later, as she sliced onions to add to the meat loaf in the Crockpot, she sliced into rather a large portion of her index finger, crying frustrated tears as she held it under the faucet. Then, with a hastily bandaged finger, she bundled up her daughter and her backpack and headed out to meet Tara at the library. Leaving Miranda in the children's section for story hour and a movie, she headed for the reference room to find Tara, only to be inundated by her friend's pointed questions about Max, questions Rowan did not want to answer.

"So? So?" Tara asked eagerly before even saying hello. When the reference librarian shot them a warning look, she lowered her voice to an anxious whisper. "What happened with you and the exceptionally attractive Mr. Donovan? And don't spare me. I'm a big girl now. I can handle *all* the gory details."

"Oh, hi, Tara, I'm fine, thanks. How are you?" Rowan replied in a bland whisper, opening her folder to retrieve her notes for the Rossetti paper that was due Tuesday.

"Come on," Tara prodded good-naturedly. "I always tell you every little detail about my love life."

"Yeah, whether I want to hear them or not," Rowan chastised her friend, looking up from her array of notebooks, still unable to find what she needed.

"Rowan." Tara drew out her friend's name on an exasperated sigh.

Rowan took a deep breath and said quickly, "No offense, Tara, but what happened last night is a subject I don't care to discuss right now."

"Miranda was there again, huh?"

Rowan's momentary pause before she answered apparently told Tara as much as her words did. "I'm not going to be seeing Max anymore," she informed the other woman as she began searching again for her Rossetti notes.

"Why not?" Tara wanted to know.

"We'll discuss it later," Rowan said absently, growing more desperate in her search.

"When?" Tara was insistent.

"December 1996," Rowan replied adamantly. Again she shuffled frantically through her papers, and when she realized she had left her crucial notes at home, she muttered angrily, "Dammit!"

"What's wrong?" Tara asked, clearly concerned about the fury with which her friend was tossing about and scattering her notebooks and folders.

With a final, angry heaving of her notebooks across the table, Rowan looked up at Tara, her eyes dark and vacant.

"Rowan?" Tara ventured quietly, cautiously setting down her pencil. When Rowan still said nothing and maintained her catatonic pose, Tara placed her hand before her friend's eyes and waved it slowly back and forth. "Rowan?" she repeated. "Are you all right?"

Finally Rowan's eyes began to come alive again, and she focused quickly on Tara. "Did you ever have one of those days when it just seems like all hell is breaking loose?"

"Days?" Tara rolled her eyes. "Try *years*. Back in 1984, every time there was a holiday, something bad happened to me. On New Year's Day, the front wheel of my car fell off. Valentine's Day, the guy I was out with went to the men's room and didn't come back. Saint Patty's Day, my goldfish died. Easter, two flat tires. Mother's Day, well, never mind Mother's Day.... Hey, Rowan, are you listening?''

Rowan was staring blankly again. ''What?'' she said when her friend stopped talking.

Tara narrowed her eyes suspiciously. ''Rowan, are you okay?'' she asked. ''You seem kind of distracted. Just what happened between you and Max last night?''

With a deep sigh, Rowan threw back her head and stared at the pinholes in the library ceiling. ''Yeah, I'm okay,'' she said softly, ignoring Tara's second question. ''Just, sometimes it seems like the gods get bored and try to see how much stuff they can dump on you before you become a stark, raving lunatic. You know what I mean?''

''Tell me about it,'' Tara muttered dryly. ''Look, are you sure there isn't anything you want to talk about?''

It would probably help her to talk about what had happened between Max and herself with Tara, Rowan thought as she lowered her gaze back to her notebooks. But her emotions toward him were still too raw, her memories still too fresh and painful. Tara would probably take what had happened the wrong way, and frankly, Rowan just didn't want to go into it all right now. Her shoulders slumped a little as she said, ''I'm just tired, that's all. There's so much I have left to get done for school, and so little time to finish it.''

''Well, that's what we're here for, isn't it?'' Tara pointed out.

Opening her textbook to stare absently at a photograph of a Rossetti painting, Rowan sighed again. ''That's what we're here for,'' she repeated quietly.

The two women used up most of the afternoon studying and adding to term papers, then collected Miranda from a showing of *The Velveteen Rabbit* and rushed back to Rowan's house to wolf down dinner and change for work.

Debbie, the sitter, was fifteen minutes late, and Tara nearly killed both Rowan and herself, speeding to work in an effort to make it on time. They clocked in with thirty seconds to spare, but Rowan couldn't shake the edgy feeling that comes with rushing around.

She was exhausted from a lack of sleep and an excess of lovemaking, worried about the incompleteness of her schoolwork, frazzled from the hurry to be on time, and still stinging and depressed by Max's rejection. As a result, her concentration that evening was virtually nonexistent, and she continuously dropped silverware and china, confused orders and spilled drinks at the bar. All the while Louis's threats earlier in the week of firing her paraded through her mind, making her efforts to right herself next to impossible.

As she stood at the service bar, waiting for a drink order, and saw the hostess leading Max Donovan and a leggy, more than beautiful redhead to one of her tables, it was absolutely the last straw. How dare he? she thought with a strangled sob. How damned *dare* he? What kind of sick mind did the man have? Wasn't it insult and injury enough to have used her and dumped her with a Post-it note? Why did he have to reinforce the message by showing up here tonight with a woman who made her look like a junior-high-school geek?

Seeing Tara pass by, Rowan reached out to grab her shoulder and said desperately, "You've got to pick up table fourteen for me."

Tara nearly dropped her tray, but at the note of panic in her friend's voice she said, "Why?"

"Look who's sitting at it."

Tara craned her neck around the service bar and smiled. "Maximillian Donovan," she murmured. "I don't know what's going on between the two of you, but here's your chance to fix it. Go for it."

"No way," Rowan told her. "Look, you're hot for the guy, you take him."

"Can't. I'm in the weeds big time. I picked up one of George's tables, and I've got my hands full. Besides, get a load of his date. He wouldn't notice me if I walked up there stark naked with a duck on my head."

"Why don't you try it and see?" Rowan suggested hopefully.

"Can't," Tara repeated. "The people at table nineteen ordered Moët. You know how long it takes me when I have to do wine service. Especially champagne. They'll probably end up opening it themselves. Sorry."

Rowan's body sagged in resignation. "That's okay. Thanks, anyway."

"Just be careful, and don't spill anything this time," Tara added with a smile. Then, as an afterthought, went on, "Unless you aim for his date."

"Very funny," Rowan muttered as she collected her order from the bar. It was going to be a long night.

Max's day had been nearly as bad as Rowan's. When he'd wakened that morning before dawn, it had been with a remarkable feeling of well-being. At first he hadn't understood why he felt so wonderfully relaxed. But when he'd turned to see the woman still slumbering beside him, he'd remembered where he was and what he'd spent the night doing, and an even greater warmth and calmness had washed over him. At that moment he'd experienced a peaceful state of mind such as none he'd ever known. For long moments he'd simply gazed at Rowan while she slept, recalling her responsiveness to his lovemaking, marveling that she looked even more beautiful and vulnerable in sleep, amazed at how much he wanted to be with her. Then, like a bolt of lightning, he was struck by the reminder that Adrienne was coming in that morning on an early flight, and that the two of them were to meet with some local contractors in an adjacent county.

He'd wanted to wake Rowan then and explain the situation, to apologize for reneging on their plans to spend the day together. But she'd looked so tired all week, and they'd stayed up so late enjoying each other. As he'd watched her sleeping, he'd thought about how peaceful she looked then and about how badly she needed to rest. He'd known that leaving a note was a cold method of communication, but surely, after all that they had shared last night, Rowan would understand his reasons for letting her sleep.

After dressing hastily he'd allowed himself a few final moments of observing Rowan as she slept. She'd lain on her stomach with one delicate arm resting on the pillow above her head, the other stretched across the mattress to cover the spot where he'd been sleeping. One silky, black strand of her hair had fallen onto her soft cheek, and Max hadn't been able to resist bending to tuck it back behind her ear, leaving a feather-light kiss in its place. Rowan had been sleeping so deeply that she hadn't stirred at his gentle caress, but Max could have sworn she'd emitted a satisfied little sigh at the gesture.

He'd rushed back to his hotel to change, only to discover that Adrienne hadn't yet arrived. Several calls to the airport had revealed that her plane hadn't even left New York, and Max's mood had grown black when he realized he could have enjoyed more precious time with Rowan.

After meeting with the contractors alone, he'd gone to the airport to pick up Adrienne himself and had wound up waiting around for nearly two hours until she'd finally arrived. By that point, both Max and his assistant had developed wicked, mean moods, and had argued extensively all day over trivial, insignificant things.

But most irritating and maddening of all was the fact that each time Max had telephoned Rowan throughout the morning and afternoon, not once had she been home to answer. Why hadn't she been there, when he'd told her he would call? Where had she been all day? And with whom?

Now as he and Adrienne sat down at the table he'd requested, his spirits began to lift at the prospect of seeing Rowan again. Surely there was a good reason she hadn't been home to receive his calls. After last night, she couldn't possibly be trying to avoid him. Could she?

"Okay, Maximillian," Adrienne began as they took their seats. "Here we are at this fab restaurant you've been talking about all day, and I don't see why it's such a big deal." She glanced around, raising a beautifully manicured hand to straighten the lapel of her ivory suit jacket and finger the delicate pearls around her throat. "Catchy name," she added negligently, "reasonably attractive patrons, tasteful decor. Although the carpeting isn't what I would have chosen. So why were you so insistent that we come here? What was the problem with that Afro-German Tea Room the bellboy recommended?"

"There's someone here I want you to meet," Max said with a smile.

"Another business meeting?" Adrienne groaned. "Have you done nothing but work all week? Can't you even let one meal go by without it concerning—?"

"A woman," Max interrupted.

"What?" Adrienne asked suspiciously through narrowed eyes.

"I want to introduce you to a woman I met this week."

"What woman?"

"Someone . . . special," he clarified.

The beginnings of a smile played about Adrienne's lips. "Maximillian," she said, delight evident in her voice. "You've been holding out on me."

Max grinned proudly at his assistant but said nothing.

"Where did you meet her?" Adrienne wanted to know.

"It's kind of a long story. We finally, uh, connected at a party given by a member of the local society."

"That's wonderful," Adrienne declared, her smile brightening. "Does she feel the same way about you that you evidently feel about her?"

Max found himself grinning as he puffed out his chest and said proudly, "Let's just say that after last night, well, I think she's as taken with me as I am with her."

Adrienne laughed out loud at his expression. "Well, I for one have never seen you look happier or more satisfied, and I couldn't be more delighted for you. What does she do? Is she meeting us here tonight?"

"She's—" Max's statement was cut short by the arrival of their server.

"Hello, how are you all this evening? I'm Rowan and I'll be taking your orders tonight. Would you like something from the bar while you're looking at your menus?"

At first Max was surprised by Rowan's cool distance, but then decided that since she'd approached their table from behind him and had filled their water goblets as she spoke, she must not have realized that it was him, Max, sitting at her table. "Hello, Rowan," he greeted her softly.

Rowan had promised herself she wouldn't look at him directly or acknowledge in any way the turmoil his presence made her feel. But at the sound of his deep, brandy-smooth voice, she was unable to help herself. Slowly she lifted her gaze from the heavy crystal pitcher she held until her eyes locked with his. Immediately, images of their lovemaking assailed her, and she felt her whole body grow warm as she realized that his thoughts mirrored her own. She took a deep, strengthening breath, then tried to speak civilly and evenly when she said, "Hello, Mr. Donovan. Would you and your date care for a drink?"

Max felt his smile fall at her formal address. Then her question registered in his brain, and he realized she misunderstood the presence of his assistant.

"Rowan, this is Adrienne Ellis," he informed her. "She's not my date. She's my assistant."

Rowan's eyes traveled quickly over the woman seated across from Max, taking in the fashion-model perfection of her hair, face and clothes. Adrienne's eyes held intelligence and perception, but there was no way Rowan was going to believe she was Max's assistant. Not in any professional capacity, anyway.

"Of course she is," Rowan said indulgently, unable to prevent the ripple of jealousy that straightened her spine. "And what will you and your, ah, *assistant* be drinking tonight?"

"Rowan—" Max began, his own temper beginning to rise.

"I'll have a gin and tonic," Adrienne cut him off quickly, clearly uncertain about what was going on, but trying to maintain some semblance of courtesy. "And I'm sure Maximillian will have a dry vodka martini, won't you, Maximillian?"

"I guess you'd know," Rowan muttered mildly before Max could respond. Mentally jotting down their orders, she told them, "I'll be right back," then made her escape.

"She's a waitress. Is that what you were about to say?" Adrienne asked dryly after Rowan's abrupt departure.

"What the hell is the matter with her?" Max asked the question more of himself than of his assistant.

"That must have been some impression you made last night," Adrienne added mildly in reference to his earlier statement.

Max's attention came back to his assistant. "Something is seriously wrong here, Adrienne, because last night everything was so... We were both... We said things that... And I felt like..."

Adrienne gazed at her boss with frank speculation. "I don't think I've ever seen you at a loss for words before, Maximillian. She must be something special."

"She is," Max assured her. "She is."

When Rowan returned with their drinks and set them on the table, she straightened and began to recite her usual menu suggestions to the two diners. Unfortunately, because of the day's continuous heaping of misfortunes onto her shoulders, and because of the nightmarish overtones of her current situation, Rowan's speech came out a little differently for Max and Adrienne than it had at her other tables that evening.

"Hank the cook says the meat loaf's pretty good tonight, and the gravy isn't as lumpy as usual. The house burgundy isn't too bad, if you're into drinking paint thinner, and I don't think the mushrooms came from the same supplier as those leeks that made Mrs. Masterson sick last week. Just to be safe, though, you might want to stick with a salad. For your information, the vinaigrette's fresher than the creamy Italian dressing, but it has a tendency to be pretty oily. Kind of like Louis. All in all, it might be wise to try The Afro-German Tea Room. They have a great spread for dinner. Would you like me to call and make a reservation for you?"

Rowan saw Max and Adrienne look first at each other and then at her, their surprise and curiosity obvious. She remained poised and silent, quite serious in her suggestion that they try a different restaurant.

"Well?" she prodded hopefully. "I know one of the hostesses there. She owes me a favor. I can probably get you in with a minimal wait."

"Rowan," Max began slowly. "Is this what you suggest to the other diners?"

"Oh, gee, no, Max," she assured him mildly. "To them I say, 'Chef Henri has prepared tonight a scrumptious chateaubriand with a delicate herb and garlic wine sauce.' Then I suggest the Château Lafite '45, because most of the people who eat here have more dollars than sense, present company excluded, of course. Then I tell them, 'The vinaigrette is a wonderful collection of the finest spices and lightest Italian olive oil,' because Louis always buys too much of it and we have to get rid of it somehow. But, hey, you're a smart guy, Max. Why would I try to sway you, not to mention your lovely assistant here, with some meaningless sales pitch, hmm?"

"We'll have the chateaubriand," Max said tightly, continuing to stare daggers at her as he snapped his menu shut viciously. "*And* the Château Lafite '45," he added maliciously. "*And* the vinaigrette on our salads." He didn't know what kind of game Rowan was playing, but he inexplicably felt the need to be defiant. Tearing his gaze away from Rowan to focus on his assistant, he added, "Is that all right with you, Adrienne?"

Adrienne closed her menu cautiously and said deferentially, "Sure, Maximillian. You know how I love a good chateaubriand." After Rowan's departure she added, "Well, I can see why you're so taken with her. She's charming."

Max ignored the comment but vowed, "I'll get to the bottom of this before the night's finished."

Much of the remainder of the evening was lost on Rowan. Little by little, reality seemed to crumble before her very eyes, and nothing she could say or do would reestablish what meager control she'd once had. It was as if the angry gods who'd spent the day hurling misery down upon her had become bored with that game, and were now sending human emissaries to wreak havoc on her in a more personal way. Every unreasonable person in the city must be out tonight, she thought at one point, and they were all taking turns sitting at her tables. Every group of diners offered her new ways and reasons to feel small and inadequate, and every time she turned around, she saw Max and Adrienne caught up in apparently animated and meaningful conversation.

The people at one table in particular gave Rowan fits throughout their meal, demanding a good portion of her time and attention, only to belittle her at every opportunity. Rowan smiled grimly at the group, reminding herself that their final check would be in excess of three hundred and fifty dollars and that since she'd provided them with impeccable service, her tip would probably wind up being enough to buy groceries for a week. When the leader of the group waved his platinum card at her, she speedily brought the check, smiling and wishing them a good evening after he'd signed the credit voucher, delighted to see them leave.

Max had hoped to have a few words with Rowan while she worked. He wanted to discover why she was so distant, but realized with some annoyance that she was far too busy for conversation, especially after the arrival of a boisterous trio of couples at the next table. He had watched with growing anger the manner in which the other diners had behaved toward Rowan, frequently wanting to approach them and point out their unnecessary rudeness. He felt better when they left, and was finally able to enjoy his coffee and cognac after his meal. As he sipped the rich, fragrant brew, he followed Rowan carefully with his eyes, growing alarmed when he saw her pick up her tip tray from the other table, only to slump into one of the recently vacated chairs, slowly shaking her head as if in disbelief.

"Maximillian, what is it?" Adrienne asked him. "What's wrong?"

"Excuse me a minute, would you, Adrienne?" he asked her with some distraction.

Adrienne opened her mouth to speak again, but never had the chance as Max quickly rose and strode past her.

As he approached Rowan and pulled up the chair beside her to sit down, he grew more worried. She was mumbling incoherently, clutching the credit card voucher in one fist, clearly oblivious to his presence. Finally he placed one hand on her shoulder and said tentatively, "Rowan? What's happened?"

At the sound of her name Rowan looked up, but her eyes were still vacant, and she gave no indication that she even recognized Max. "He stiffed me," she said in utter disbelief. "A three-hundred-and-seventy-five-dollar check, and the little creep tipped me a buck."

"He did what?" Max asked, as incredulous as she.

Rowan didn't seem to hear him, but continued to mutter, "And here's the kicker. Three percent of my sales go into a tip pool for the bartenders and busboys. Not only did I get stiffed, but I have to pay out more than ten dollars from my other tips to cover this check."

"Rowan, are you okay?" Max asked her. He didn't like the high-pitched quality her voice had taken on.

Rowan laughed mirthlessly. Getting stiffed after being treated with such indignity was the perfect, bitter icing on an already bad-tasting cake. It was just the thing necessary to snap her tenuous grasp on reality. Suddenly she sensed an idea taking root in her exhausted, disoriented, overwrought mind. A wonderfully wicked, maliciously vengeful, highly illegal idea. Still gazing at Max, she began to describe her plan in a trembling voice.

"I'll get even, though," she promised, looking down at the credit voucher she still clutched in her hand. "I've got everything I need right here. Name, Preston F. Garwood. Credit card number, expiration date.... Look, the idiot even filled in his address and phone number."

Max didn't like the delirious tone her voice had adopted. He liked even less the way her eyes glazed over as she continued with her plot for revenge.

"So tonight," she went on, "when I'm watching late movies on Channel 41... You know how they have all those commercials for Ginsu knives and Pocket Fishermen and Garden Weasels and Time-Life Books? Imagine Mr. Preston F. Garwood's surprise when fifteen Fishin' Magicians show up on his doorstep. And the next day, when twenty-five Veg-o-matics follow. And then magazine subscriptions! And Craft-matic adjustable beds! Oh, I just remembered something!" she added with a triumphant grin. "Tara's got cable! The Home Shopping Club! This is gonna be great!"

"That does it," Max announced finally, hoping Preston F. Garwood would appreciate what he was about to do, knowing, though, that the man probably deserved what Rowan had planned.

He pried the credit voucher from her reluctant fingers and smoothed it out on the table. The fact that Rowan continued with her retaliatory tirade and didn't seem to notice he'd taken away her ammunition disturbed Max to the point that he no longer cared for appearances. Amid the gasps and shocked looks from the other diners, he hefted Rowan into his arms and stood.

By now she was completely lost in her plan to financially ruin Mr. Garwood and didn't resist Max's actions, feeling instead as if her position in his arms were the most natural place in the world for her to be. Suddenly she was more tired than she'd ever been in her life, and surrendered to the lethargy that made her limbs feel so heavy. She rested her head on his strong, broad shoulder and wrapped her arms lovingly around his neck. As she closed her eyes, Rowan thought she'd never felt so wonderful. Just before unconsciousness overcame her, she wondered what cologne Max wore to make him smell so delicious.

Max hugged the limp Rowan to his chest and hurried back to his table to quickly explain things to Adrienne.

"She's completely exhausted," he told his assistant. "I'm going to take her home and put her to bed. Can you take care of the check on the company credit card?"

"Of course, Maximillian," Adrienne told him. "Is she going to be all right?"

Max gazed down at the woman in his arms, thinking that she seemed more fragile than ever before. "I think so," he ground out a little hoarsely, unable to mask his worry for Rowan. "She's been trying to do too much. She just needs to rest." Then a new thought struck him. "Listen, Adrienne, she could lose her job for this. Her boss is kind of a jerk."

As if mentioning him conjured up the little man, Louis September burst through the doors of the kitchen with Rowan's friend, Tara, right on his heels. By the woman's quickly running mouth and wildly gesturing hands, Max could tell that the other waitress was fast pleading Rowan's case. He admired her spunk, but knew it was going to take a much more persuasive person than Tara to convince Louis not to fire Rowan.

"Uh, Adrienne," Max began, his anxiousness to be gone from the restaurant growing more demanding with every step Louis took.

"Yes, Max." Adrienne's voice was flat with resignation, having seen where Max's gaze was headed and anticipating what was to come.

"Could you use your more than ample feminine charms to calm Mr. September down?"

"It won't be pleasant," she told him with a grimace.

"I'll make it up to you," Max promised.

Adrienne sighed. "All right. But my Christmas bonus better include a couple of tickets to Tahiti," she warned. "And a big, gorgeous, overdeveloped, conspicuously silent man to accompany me."

Max smiled. "I'll do my best."

"Oh, get out of here," Adrienne told him, standing to meet the whirling dervish that was Louis September. "I've got work to do."

"I'll call you at the hotel later," Max shot over his shoulder as he beat a hasty retreat with his sleeping captive.

Rowan was still dozing when he pulled his car into her driveway fifteen minutes later. Good God, he thought, what had she been doing to make her collapse that way? He'd known she was probably overextending herself after everything she'd told him she was doing, but this... Just how hard had she been driving herself, and for how long? And more important, what could he do to help alleviate some of her burdens? It amazed him how seemingly overnight her troubles had become his, and now he felt almost obligated to take some of the heat off, if he could. Yet it was an obligation that was strangely welcome.

Carefully, so as not to wake her, he removed her sagging body from the car and carried her to the back door. The sitter Max had met the previous evening opened it and stood dumbfounded to the side as he entered the kitchen with the sleeping Rowan.

"My gosh, Mr. Donovan, what happened to Rowan? Is she all right?"

"She's exhausted," he explained. "She collapsed at work, but she'll be okay. Where's Miranda?"

"She's in the den playing," Debbie told him.

"I don't want her to see her mother like this," Max said. "It might frighten her. Go keep her occupied while I put Rowan to bed."

Nodding briefly, Debbie left the kitchen, and Max followed some moments later, climbing the stairs toward Rowan's bedroom. Once there, he placed her gently on the bed, then sat down cautiously beside her. His heart still pounded with fear and concern, but as he watched her breathe in slow, steady breaths, his tension began to ebb. She seemed at once both unconquerable and defeated, indomitable yet delicate. The spitting kitten had finally taken on more junkyard dogs than she could handle, and now Max wanted to see to it personally that she'd never have to fight alone again.

When he raised an unsteady hand to brush back the black satin of her bangs, she sighed. The small sound made Max smile. Gently he undid the bow tie at her throat and unbuttoned the two, pearly shirt buttons closest to her chin. That accomplished, he carefully removed her shoes and placed them on the floor at the foot of the bed. Freed from her bonds, Rowan contentedly muttered something in her sleep and turned on her side to snuggle deeper into her pillow. Max stole silently across the room to retrieve the quilt tossed over the wicker rocking chair, then returned to cover Rowan's sleeping form with it. After kissing the downy, cool softness of her cheek, he straightened and forced himself to leave her alone. Pulling the bedroom door closed behind him, he took a few moments to convince himself that Rowan would be just fine for the time being without him.

Chapter Nine

Max paused for a minute at the entrance to the den, taking in the strangeness of the sight before him. Like every other room in the house, Rowan had filled this one with books and old furniture, accenting it with an abundance of plants and personal belongings, the predominant colors those of an autumn day. In the soft yellow glow of an old, battered, brass floor lamp, he viewed Debbie, sprawled like the teenager she was, across the pale gold sofa, reading a popular fashion magazine while chomping furiously on a mouthful of gum. Miranda squatted on the floor beside her in that peculiar, flat-footed way that only children seem to manage. Her well-loved teddy bear was perched against one leg of the coffee table, and a coloring book was spread open at her feet, surrounded by a scattering of colorful crayons.

The scene was so blatantly domestic it should have had Max screaming in horror and running for his life. Instead, he found himself strangely drawn to it, wanting desperately to be a part of it. His cool, clean, sparsely furnished apartment in New York seemed a million miles away.

"Hi, Miranda," he called out quietly to the little girl.

When she looked up at him, surprise and delight filled Miranda's expression. "Max!" she cried in her tiny voice, then jumped up to run toward him.

Max's smile broadened when she skidded to a stop at his feet and gazed up at him with wide, blue eyes. She wore pale blue, footed pajamas, and when he bent down to her for a hug, he inhaled the sweet scent of baby shampoo and powder that surrounded her.

Miranda laughed as Max gave her a gentle squeeze, then disengaged herself to ask, "Where's Mommy?"

"She's upstairs, sleeping," Max informed the child. "Looks like it's just you and me, kid."

The little girl smiled and said, "Goody."

After learning from Debbie that Miranda should be put to bed no later than nine-thirty, Max paid and dismissed the sitter, promising to take care of everything. Faced with the prospect of more than an hour alone with a three-year-old, Max was understandably somewhat intimidated by the small child. But when he sat down restlessly on the sofa, Miranda climbed up after him, dragging behind her an old, hardback volume of children's stories that looked as if it weighed nearly as much as she.

"This one," the little girl said simply, opening the book to a story in the middle.

She seemed too young to be able to read, so Max tested her. "What's the name of the story?" he asked.

"'The Cat That Walked By Himself,'" she told him correctly.

"Miranda," he began, surprised at her knowledge, "can you read?"

"Not yet," she told him almost ruefully. "But Mommy's going to teach me soon."

"How did you know this was the story you wanted?"

Miranda rolled her eyes at Max, as if he were the silliest person she'd ever met. "Because of the pitcher of the kitty-cat," she told him, pointing to the illustration above the title.

"Oh." Max realized there was a great deal he had to learn about children, much of it probably the most obvious stuff in the world. He began to read the Kipling tale to Miranda, refusing to question the surprising ease with which he slipped into the role of baby-sitter and storyteller. And when Miranda finally fell asleep with her dark head snuggled against his quietly beating heart, Max made a point not to ponder the new, unfamiliar feeling that spread through him like hard-packed winter snow, melting slowly away in the sun-warmed spring. Instead, he carefully lifted the sleeping child into his arms and carried her up to her room to tuck her in, just as he had done with her mother a short time before. And just as he had watched Rowan, he also observed Miranda's peaceful slumber, noting with a smile how similar the two were in sleep.

After checking on Rowan one last time, Max returned to the den to call Adrienne. He asked her to send over some of his things, and apologized again for the abrupt end to their dinner. He also told her that he was going to have to bow out on a rather important social function he'd planned to attend the following evening and asked Adrienne if she'd go as his representative in his place.

"What's in it for me?" his assistant asked him bluntly. "Aside from those tickets to Tahiti, I mean."

Max smiled, but knowing Adrienne as he did, he'd already anticipated such a reaction and offered a variety of bribes. "It promises to be a very nice party, Adrienne," he told her.

"And?"

"Great food, expensive champagne, the works."

"And?"

"And I want you to keep an appointment I made to meet there with a man named Michael Canadian. He owns one of the construction companies we'll be using, if we accept this deal."

"Oh, come on, Maximillian. You call that a *bribe*?" Adrienne's disappointment was audible.

"You haven't seen Michael Canadian," Max cooed.

"Oh, yeah?" Adrienne's interest seemed to be returning.

"I need to get out of that party, Adrienne," Max told her. "I promise, come Monday, it'll be business as usual."

"No problem, Maximillian," Adrienne assured him. "It isn't like you to make a habit of this. Just keep in touch, okay?"

"You know I will. Thanks."

"I'll send over everything you've asked for," she promised.

"See you Monday morning," he said before settling the telephone receiver back into its cradle. He hoped with unbusinesslike passion that Monday morning would never arrive.

When Rowan opened her dry, bleary eyes in the morning, she had to wonder for a moment where she was. She remembered seeing Max come into September's with an unspeakably attractive woman, then recalled how an obnoxious group of diners had had the audacity to stiff her on one of the biggest bills she'd ever seen. The rest of the evening, unfortunately, was still pretty blurry. Looking down at the crumpled uniform that still clothed her body, she assumed Tara must have brought her home and put her to bed, and made a mental note to call her friend before she went to work again, to find out if she still had a job.

Still half-asleep, Rowan shed the tuxedo and left it in a heap on her floor, then changed into blue jeans and a bright red, Louisville Cardinals sweatshirt, before starting automatically downstairs to fix breakfast. As she descended the stairs, however, her nose lifted involuntarily into the air, and she inhaled the familiar fragrances of brewing coffee and frying bacon. When she strode warily across the living room, she heard unexplainable sounds coming from her kitchen—metal clanking against metal, then a male voice calling out, "Here we go!" followed by her daughter's squeals of delight and irregular applause. When Rowan pushed open the door that linked the dining room and kitchen, she was helpless to stop the cry of shock that erupted from her lips.

"Aah!" she exclaimed, and saw Max and Miranda turn to her in surprise. A golden-brown pancake seemed to hang suspended in the air for a split second, then plummeted with a soft *splat* onto the hardwood floor. All eyes followed it there until Miranda drew their attention away with her excited chatter.

"Mommy! Do you know what Max can do? He can make pancakes! And he can throw them way far in the air and catch them when they come down. Well, sometimes. And he reads real good, too!"

Rowan looked dumbly at the handsome man who held her cast-iron skillet in two hands that were covered with pink oven mitts, his sexy lips twisted into a sheepish grin. Max wore faded, form-fitting blue jeans and a taupe-colored sweater that somehow made his eyes seem brighter than usual. His dark golden hair was wonderfully mussed from sleep, and he was barefoot. Rowan closed her eyes briefly, then cautiously opened them again. But it did no good. He was still there. Maximillian Donovan was standing barefoot in her kitchen, wearing regular clothes, with unruly hair, flipping pancakes with her three-year-old daughter. No question about it. She had finally and completely lost her mind.

"Mommy?" Miranda prodded, pulling at Rowan's fingers with both hands. "Max made breakfast for us."

"I'm not sure how palatable it will be," he warned her when she continued to stare with huge, disbelieving eyes and remained silent. "It's been a while since I've cooked breakfast. Usually I just grab a bagel or something on the way to work. But back at Harvard, I was pretty famous at the dorm for my Sunday brunches."

Rowan choked back the urge to break into hysterial laughter only by clapping a hand viciously over her mouth, a motion which managed to limit her outburst to a single, nervous chuckle. After clearing her throat, she took a few tentative steps into the kitchen, then experimentally removed her hand, muttering, "You, uh, you came as a bit of a shock to me."

Max's smile grew warm, his eyes glittering with some unknown fire as he replied, "No more of a shock than you were to me, lady."

"What are you doing here?" she asked him almost breathlessly, trying to ignore the way her heart seemed to want to leap into her throat at his roughly murmured words. "And where did you—?" Her eyes fell to the small child, who glanced from her to her companion and back again. "Where did you s-l-e-e-p?"

"I brought you home last night and s-l-e-p-t in the s-p-a-r-e r-o-o-m. Don't you remember?"

"Not really," she confessed with a shrug. "It's kind of blurry. Do I still have a job?"

"Adrienne convinced Louis he'd be better off keeping you on than letting you go," Max told her.

At the mention of his assistant, Rowan straightened her back and stared disconsolately down at her stubby fingernails. "Ah, yes. Your *assistant*," she muttered distastefully. "How can she trust you spending the night with another woman, Max? My goodness, she must be very understanding."

"You have absolutely no reason to be jealous," Max assured her, turning back to the stove so she wouldn't see the smug grin of satisfaction that he knew stretched across his face.

"*Jealous?*" Rowan squeaked. "Me? Jealous? I've never been jealous of anyone in my life."

"Oh, really?" Max countered skeptically as he poured more batter into the skillet.

"Mommy, what does 'jealous' mean?" Miranda asked.

"See there? My daughter doesn't even know the meaning of the word," Rowan pointed out proudly to illustrate her claim.

Max rolled his eyes at her and got down on one knee to face Miranda. Very carefully he explained, "Jealous is what happens to a person when she sees the boy she likes out with a girl she doesn't know and she's afraid the boy won't like her anymore."

"The boy she likes?" Rowan sputtered. "Now wait just a minute—"

"But of course, that's silly," Max plunged on, "because the boy is always going to like her."

Miranda nodded as Rowan stood narrow-eyed and gaping, contemplating Max's statement as studiously as her daughter did. "I like Dustin Sheffield," the little girl announced. "He's four. He lives across the street. Mommy won't let me cross the street alone, so Dustin always plays with Megan. I don't like Megan. Is that jealous?"

"Sounds like it to me," Max told her before he straightened to flip the pancake, this time with less flourish than before. "But you know, Miranda," he added, pointing down at her with the spatula, "it's not good to be jealous, because a boy can like one girl one way and another girl another way. Maybe Dustin likes to play with Megan sometimes, but he can still like you, too. Maybe someday he'll even grow up and want to marry you."

"I don't want to get married," Miranda announced, shaking her head with such determination that Max wanted to laugh.

"Why not?" he asked her.

"It's yucky. Mommy said so."

Max lifted his eyebrows in surprise and looked at a flustered, embarrased Rowan. "Did you tell your daughter that marriage was yucky?" he demanded.

Rowan tugged at the hem of her sweatshirt in a gesture that Max was beginning to realize meant she was very nervous. "No, I...uh...Actually, Tara and I were discussing it one day on the back porch, while Miranda was coloring. I didn't think she was paying attention. I guess she's more, ah, perceptive than I thought."

"Why would you be opposed to marriage, Rowan?" Max asked more quietly, loving the way she lost her normal composure when she was put on the spot.

"I'm not exactly opposed to it," she said defensively. "My mother and father had a wonderful marriage. I just, uh, I'm not sure it's for me, that's all."

"Why not?" he asked pointedly, feigning nonchalance as he turned his attention back to the pancakes. He didn't want her to know how important he considered her answer.

Rowan dropped her eyes as she responded. "I don't know," she hedged. "It's just not something I've ever really envisioned in my future, I guess." *Not until the other night, anyway,* she added to herself, before she could stop the thought from coming.

Max surprised himself with his decision that he might have to do something to change Rowan's view of the future, but all he said out loud was, "I see. Well, this is about done. Everyone ready for breakfast?"

"Yeah!" Miranda chirped. "Look, Mommy, I set the table."

Rowan took in the mismatched plates and silverware and smiled. "Boy, you did a great job, too," she said enthusiastically to the little girl.

Miranda beamed. "I did it all by myself."

"I'm so proud of you," Rowan added, sweeping her daughter up for a hug. Miranda giggled and squirmed, but finally let herself be hugged, and then threw her arms around her mother in response.

Max took in the scene with mixed emotions. In a sense he felt close to them both, but to each separately, in different ways. When he saw the two of them together like this, he was a little overwhelmed by the depth of emotion that ran between mother and daughter. They were so very much alike, and each depended on the other for so many things. Could he ever hope to share in what they had created for themselves? Did he have a right to intrude? Was there any chance at all they might include him in their lives? And why, dammit, was it so utterly important to him that they should?

In just a few short days, Rowan Chance had managed to turn Max's life completely upside down and inside out. Was it really such a short time ago that he'd had total control of his life and a firm focus on his future, that he'd been so definitely certain of what that future involved, right down to the last detail? Not long ago he'd had his business and social calendars memorized minute by minute for the upcoming month. Right now he could scarcely remember where he was supposed to be at eight o'clock Monday morning. And what was worse, he didn't care. He knew where he wanted to be then, though, and where he wanted to be every morning, afternoon and evening following. He wanted to be with Rowan. He didn't care where or under what circumstances, he only knew he wanted her to be a part of whatever he was doing. And that realization terrified him more than anything in the world.

"Max?" Rowan asked when she saw that he was lost deep in thought. "What are you thinking about?"

His attention snapped back to the present, and for a moment he feared he might drown in the two sets of blue eyes that fixed with his. Trying to shake the feeling that a part of him was already lost to the two Chance women, he pulled out a chair and mumbled, "Nothing. Just that the food's going to get cold if we don't dig in."

Rowan was delighted to discover that Max was a very good chef. By the end of the meal she was substantially more awake and coherent, and the fuzzy, almost dreamy feeling that had enveloped her upon seeing him in her kitchen finally seemed to subside.

"So what do you want to do today?" Max asked her after he'd dried the last stoneware coffee mug and placed it inside the proper cupboard. Miranda was in the den, watching cartoons, so he had Rowan all to himself. He tossed the damp dish towel onto the counter and pulled a surprised and unprepared Rowan into his arms.

"Max, what are you doing?" Rowan protested, placing her hands ineffectually against his chest in a halfhearted effort to stop him.

Max smiled playfully at the gesture and pulled her even closer. "I'm going to kiss you, Rowan," he announced. "It's something I've been thinking about doing since I woke up beside you yesterday morning."

"Max, don't," she told him, mentally willing him not to mention the madness that had overcome them the other night, remembering what a fool she'd been to have allowed it to happen in the first place. She pushed against his chest insistently in an attempt to free herself from his possessive embrace, trying not to think how wonderful it felt to be held by him once again.

But Max ignored her slight struggle. With one arm roped boldly around her waist, he let his other hand wander leisurely up the length of her spine, over her shoulder until he could caress the soft skin of her neck. Rowan's insides caught fire at the feel of his coarse fingertips brushing over the sensitive skin at her nape, and she was helpless to prevent an audible little whimper when he tangled his fingers in her silky hair and pulled her head back to look more fully upon her face.

"You don't want me to mention the fact that we made love the other night, do you?" he guessed in a rough whisper.

Rowan said nothing in response, but Max could see by the pain-filled expression that darkened her eyes that he had surmised correctly.

"Well, that's too bad," he informed her. "Because no matter how often and how adamantly you deny it, Rowan, we did make love that night." His hazel eyes warmed with golden fire as he added, "More than once, if you recall."

"Max . . ." Rowan pleaded.

But he pressed on relentlessly, gripping her head firmly in his hand as he spoke, bringing his face down to hers until only a breath of space separated their lips. "And it was a night I'm not likely to forget, either."

Rowan could feel the scintillating warmth of his softly murmured words against her mouth, and her body became electrified by his insistently kneading fingers on her scalp and waist. She closed her eyes so she could concentrate more fully on the sensations penetrating her brain and body.

"Remember, Rowan?" Max asked as he rubbed his lips against hers. "Remember how I made you crazy? How I touched you here . . . ?" The hand on her waist had crept up under her sweatshirt until it settled fully over her bare breast. "How you came to life when I did this . . . ?"

Rowan moaned almost in pain when he took her nipple between the V of his index and middle fingers and closed them tightly over her. All the while he placed breathless, feather-light kisses along her jaw and neck.

"And remember when I touched you here, Rowan?" he demanded, his voice having dropped to a low, gravelly pitch. The hand at her nape had traveled slowly down her back and now hovered over the faded denim covering her derriere, then ventured farther down, between her thighs. Rowan cried out loud when his long fingers caressed her through her jeans.

"Max, please . . ." she gasped out her protest.

He smiled ferally. "Please what?" he asked leisurely. "Please go on? Please do it again?" He caressed her once again, as if she had answered in the affirmative, and with a softly uttered moan, Rowan rolled her head back in involuntary surrender. Max took advantage of her offering, lowering his head once more to taste and nip at the creamy skin of her throat.

"Are you remembering, Rowan?" he asked her between kisses, demanding that she should recall every coaxing caress of their night together, wanting her to become as delirious and tormented by the memories as he. "Because I want you to remember that night and this morning for the rest of your life. Just like I want you to remember every erotic moment we spend together from here on." He turned her until her back was against the counter, then crowded his big body even closer to hers, all the while touching her with intimate, demanding familiarity.

For a short time Rowan let herself forget who and where she was, returning Max's kisses and caresses as eagerly as they were offered. When his lips took hers with insistent demand, she countered by tangling her tongue possessively with his. Her fingers threaded urgently through his hair, and she pulled his head down to hers, so that she could gain even deeper access to his mouth. She vaguely heard his breathing become as labored and irregular as hers, felt the groan of need that rumbled up from his throat when she finally pulled her lips away.

"I want you, Rowan," Max growled against her throat, shaken by the absolute loss of control he experienced whenever she came near him. "And don't try to convince me that you don't want me, too, because it just isn't going to wash."

"Max—" she began, but he cut her off.

"Look, I don't know what was going on last night at the restaurant, why you were so mad at me, but I apologize for whatever I did to make you angry."

"Max—"

"I just want to be with you, Rowan. I want us to spend time together, to be together. Like we should be."

Rowan noticed he didn't put a time frame on his wish that they spend time together. Did he mean today? This week? Until he got tired of her? What? But she remained silent, biting her lower lip. "Is Adrienne really your assistant?" she asked him.

Max smiled at her uncertainty. "Has been for ten years," he told her.

Rowan sighed heavily. Why was she having so much trouble where Max was concerned? Why did her thoughts seem to tumble so ceaselessly and incoherently through her head whenever he was around? She felt that small flame of hope in her heart flicker to life again and mentally tried to throw water on it. It sputtered and hissed for a moment, then came raging back to life like a torch. She did not want to be his temporary, on-site lover, nor did she want him to view her as such. Yet she just didn't quite have it in her to lay her cards upon the table and demand he do likewise. Frankly, she still wasn't sure what kind of hand she held, and she'd never been any good at bluffing.

With a shaky breath, Rowan pushed herself away from Max and nearly scrambled free until he appeared to realize what she was doing. But he caught her wrist before she could flee entirely, and with a gentle tug, brought her back into the circle of his embrace. He seemed to sense her troubled thoughts, though, for this time there were no passionate kisses or intimate touches. This time he only held her to his heart and tucked her head under his chin. Rowan gave in to the need to be close to him then and looped her arms about his waist, loving the feel of hard muscle that her touch encountered, entranced by the gentle thumping of his heart below her ear.

Max could tell there was something bothering Rowan besides her concern about Adrienne but consciously chose not to investigate what it might be, lest she again try to push him away. Instead he repeated his question of some moments before, hoping to steer their conversation into more agreeable waters. "What would you like to do today?"

Rowan wasn't content to change the subject when she felt so much was left unsaid and unsettled, but was even less willing to pursue her line of questioning when she wasn't sure what his answers would be. So she decided to take the coward's way out and cross her bridges when she came to them, praying she'd have the foresight not to burn them behind her after she did so. With a resigned sigh she told him, "Sundays are my days with Miranda. I always try to keep them free, so that she and I can spend time together. But I still have so much homework to finish...." Her voice trailed off at the realization.

"I could keep Miranda occupied today," Max offered, "if you still have a lot to do."

Rowan smiled at his generosity. "Oh, Max, that's sweet of you, but I couldn't intrude on your time like that."

"Intrude?" he asked incredulously. "*Intrude?* How can you possibly think spending time with Miranda would be an intrusion? She's such a wonderful child."

"But, Max—"

"And you said yourself that she likes me," he pointed out.

"She does, but—"

"I'd like to do it, Rowan," he said in quiet earnestness. "I really would." Then, knowing she was about to give in, he added, "Just how much homework do you have left, anyway?"

"Too much," Rowan muttered. "If I never see another Rossetti painting as long as I live, I'll die a happy woman, so how do you feel about zoos?"

"Zoos?" His expression indicated his confusion at the change of subject.

"Miranda loves the zoo," Rowan told him, smiling at the warm, relieved expression that came over his face when he realized she was okaying him as a baby-sitter.

"I haven't been to the zoo since I was about six years old," he told her wistfully.

"What was your favorite animal?" she asked him, loving the childlike interest he seemed to take in the upcoming excursion.

"The lions, of course," he replied without hesitation. "The kings."

"Naturally," Rowan remarked dryly. "Well, prepare yourself. Miranda likes the snakes."

Max's lips curled down in visible disgust. "I hate snakes."

Rowan laughed. "You two should have an interesting day, then."

Actually, the two of them did have a good time together, Max acknowledged later, as he and Miranda shared an ice-cream cone at the end of their hike through the zoo. He'd found himself smiling throughout the day, laughing as Miranda preceded him from one exhibit to another, tugging impatiently at his hand as she chattered about the different animals, misidentifying them with names like bassoons, libras and cheetos instead of baboons, zebras and cheetahs. All in all, Max found it a delightful change of pace to spend the day with a three-year-old, and discovered that his view of the universe was left slightly, but pleasantly askew as a result of the encounter.

Listening to Miranda's laughter as he chased a dribble of chocolate ice cream down the side of his cone with his tongue, Max experienced the startling realization that he was fast beginning to fall hopelessly and irrevocably in love with the two Chance women. The thought so disturbed him that for a moment he could only stare blindly at the brown river of chocolate that overran his cone and puddled in the juncture of his thumb and index finger. Love? he asked himself tentatively. It was a word that was scarcely present in his vocabulary. But what else could it be? How else could he explain the weirdness that had come over him since his very first encounter with Rowan? As he noisily slurped up the chocolate mess on his hand, much to Miranda's childish delight, Max couldn't help but grin. He was in love for the first time in his life, and he'd be damned if he knew what to do about it. He thought about that startling fact through the ride home.

Miranda was nearly out of the car before it stopped in the driveway. She shouted excitedly to her mother about the sights they had seen before Rowan even had the back door open. Max took a more leisurely approach to their arrival, fiddling about with things in the car that needed no fiddling with, nervously jingling his keys in his jacket pocket as he sauntered toward the back porch. He suddenly felt awkward around Rowan, was uncertain how he should behave. He wanted to tell her about his startling realization over the ice-cream cone, but was reluctant to do so yet, lest the confession make her skittish. Whether she admitted it or not, she was still smarting from rejections and losses she'd suffered years ago. How would she react to his avowal of love for her? Would she even believe him? And if she did, would she become fearful that entering a serious, loving relationship with him would ultimately lead to another rejection or loss?

Max felt justified in keeping his feelings to himself for now. They still needed time to get used to each other's presence in their lives, still needed time to accept the fact that they never had to be alone again. Rowan seemed a little wary yet of getting too close to him, and it would probably be best to go slow with her. He still had a week before things had to be decided definitely for them, a week that he could use to bring her around to his way of thinking.

As he climbed the stairs to her back porch, Max saw Rowan holding an excited Miranda, the two of them framed by the house on one side and the rose-covered trellis on the other. Behind them the sun, huge and red, hung low in the sky, and as he inhaled deeply the spicy aroma of roast and baking bread, the very air around him seemed to become warm and glowing with welcome. Approaching the pair who stood in the doorway, awaiting his arrival, Max felt like a real human being for the first time in a long time. Her house felt like his home. And it occurred to Max, as he lowered his lips to Rowan's for a brief hello kiss, that nothing else in his life had ever felt more like coming home.

The evening was growing late by the time Max and Rowan put a reluctant Miranda to bed, and once the feat was accomplished, Rowan began to feel inexplicably edgy around Max. Maybe it was because of the comfortable way the three of them had felt all evening, or maybe it was because of the secretive, little, satisfied smiles that had stretched across Max's face ever since he and Miranda had returned from the zoo. Rowan wasn't sure. She did acknowledge one thing, though, that was definitely making her nervous. Max had offered no indication that he intended to leave tonight, nor did she want him to assume that he would be spending the night again with her. Yet it was a subject that she didn't know how to address. Finally Max saved her the trouble by broaching it himself.

"Rowan, would you mind if I don't stay here tonight?" he asked her pointedly as they finished up the last of the supper dishes.

She was so surprised by his question that she only stammered, "What?"

Max plowed ahead, as if unaware of her surprise. "As much as I'd like to stay here, I really should go back to my hotel this evening. Now that Adrienne's here, we're going to have a lot of work to see to and quite a few meetings to attend. You don't mind, do you?"

What was going on? Rowan asked herself, feeling the thin veil of domesticity that had surrounded them all evening disappear. Why was he suddenly pulling away from her? "No, of course I don't mind," she told him, unable to thoroughly disguise her puzzlement. "Why would I mind?"

Maybe because you love me and can't live without me? he wanted to ask. But instead, at the note of uncertainty in her voice, he pulled her gently into his arms to explain. "I just don't want to rush you into anything, Rowan. I don't want you to feel pressured or unsure about us." He smiled when he saw the relief that flooded into her eyes. "I want to *date* you. At least once or twice."

She laughed when she, too, realized they had yet to go out on a real, prearranged date. "Gee, what a concept," she said with a chuckle.

"So what do you say?" he asked her. "You busy tomorrow night?"

Her smile vanished when she remembered that she still wasn't finished with all of her homework. The dreaded typing still loomed ominously before her like a death sentence. "Actually, I am," she said ruefully.

This time Max's smile vanished, too. "Who is he?" he damanded playfully. "I'll have his legs broken."

Rowan's smile returned. "I have a date with someone at the library. A little, short guy with a lot of teeth."

"All right, I'll have his teeth broken," Max declared. "What's his name?"

"Smith-Corona," Rowan supplied.

"A typewriter," Max guessed brilliantly.

"A typewriter," she confirmed.

Max thought quickly and was rewarded with an excellent idea. "Houghton's given me access to a steno," he offered. "Give me your paper, and I'll have it typed up by one of the secretaries, and they can put it on my bill."

"Max, I can't let you do that," Rowan told him.

"Why not?"

She shrugged a little. "Because."

"Because why?"

"Because it wouldn't be right," she explained lamely.

"Oh, come on, Rowan," he cajoled. "Of course it would. You know you want to. All you'd have left to do then would be study for your finals. Wouldn't that be great?"

Rowan's conviction began to sway. "It *would* be great...." she said slowly.

"Then it's settled," Max concluded hastily. "Now, where do you want to go tomorrow night? Do what you will with me."

She raised her eyebrows at that, but didn't voice the erotic thoughts that paraded through her mind at his suggestion. Instead she forced herself to think seriously about his question. It had been so long since Rowan had been out on a date that she'd almost forgotten what her choices were. "Dinner?" she asked experimentally.

"We can do that." Max nodded agreeably. "What else?"

Rowan thought some more. "Dancing?" she asked after a moment.

Again, Max nodded eagerly.

Slowly a smile spread across Rowan's face. "And a river cruise," she added decisively.

"Sounds like we've got plans," Max surmised with a grin.

"The Star of Louisville," she announced. "It'll be fun. I've never been before."

"Sounds good to me," he conceded.

"We can hear Rick Bartlett," Rowan added, bringing up memories of dancing in the living room some nights before.

"Sounds perfect," he agreed. "Looks like we've got ourselves a date."

Chapter Ten

In fact, Rowan and Max went on several dates, and their courtship moved along quite beautifully that week, for the most part. They went out every night, enjoying everything from the river cruise and a play festival at Actor's Theatre to an orchestra performance at the Center for the Arts. Every night Max brought Rowan home, and after sharing cognac or coffee with quiet conversation, he kissed her good-night, kisses full of passion and promise, and then returned to his hotel. Together they took Miranda to the balloon race on Tuesday and the steamboat race on Wednesday. Now it was Thursday as the three of them sat on rickety bleachers to watch the Pegasus Parade go by, and Rowan realized she had yet another reason to feel festive. She'd taken her last final that morning and was more than optimistic that within a matter of days, she would be a college graduate.

On the whole, Rowan felt very good about the way things were going, but for some reason she just couldn't quite shake the feeling that something, she wasn't sure what, wasn't right. Certainly Max had given her no indication that he was uncomfortable about their current situation, and Miranda had blossomed considerably during the time the three of them spent together. Therefore, Rowan concluded, whatever was bothering her was of her own making. She only wished the edgy feeling would go away.

It was the party, she decided after searching deep inside herself. The party that Max wanted her to attend with him the following evening. He had signed a contract with The Houghton Company to develop the riverfront complex they wanted, and to celebrate and announce the deal, Steven Houghton had invited Max to a gala Derby party his company was throwing at The Brown Hotel tomorrow night. Naturally he had invited Rowan to accompany him, and of course, once she'd found someone to cover her shift at work, she had accepted, thinking it would be fun.

But now as she watched the band from her former high school parade before them, performing a questionable rendition of "Sweet Georgia Brown," Rowan began to have doubts. They'd spent the week moving in her world, doing what was familiar to her. Frequently Miranda had been with them, and at Max's insistence, Rowan had always called the shots, had chosen where they'd go and what they'd do.

The party tomorrow night, however, would be hosted and attended by the city's wealthiest, most prominent, most elite citizens, all people who were Max's social and economic equals. Rowan suspected that the only other waitresses there would be serving food and drinks. She would be moving outside her normal sphere of experience, would be at a complete loss as to what exactly was expected of her. Certainly her mother had raised her not to be a social embarrassment, and she read Miss Manners's column in the paper often enough to know the basic principles of etiquette. Too, she had worked enough "Affaires by Louis" to know what to expect. But this time she wouldn't be observing the festivities silently from the other side of a silver tray, making mental remarks, eavesdropping on conversations. No, this time she would have to take part in those conversations, would have to at least pretend that she belonged there.

Could she do that? she wondered. Or, more specifically, did she *want* to? She wasn't sure. She only knew that she was dreading tomorrow night, was fearful of what was going to happen when she appeared at Max's side. But if they were to have any hope of a future together, this was going to be a big test, maybe even the final exam. And it was one Rowan wanted to pass with flying colors, as much for herself as for Max. There was a great deal riding on tomorrow night. She only hoped she was making a bet that was going to pay off. With a sick feeling in her stomach, Rowan remembered then that she'd always been a lousy gambler.

When Rowan stood before her cheval mirror the following evening, inspecting the outcome of the afternoon's labors, she couldn't make up her mind whether she was pleased or disappointed. Tilting her head to one side to catch the last light of the sun on her face, she had to admit that Tara had done a good job on her makeup before she'd left a half hour ago. And the manicure her friend had given her through nonstop chatter about how lucky Rowan was, did give her small hands a very elegant look. And despite the fact that there was only so much she could do with her short, straight, blunt-cut hair, it still looked nice, swept behind one ear that way. It gave her a Roaring Twenties kind of look.

Maybe it was the dress. And the jewelry, or rather the lack of it. The only dress Rowan owned that was appropriate for such an affair was the one she'd worn to her senior prom nine years ago, and which had originally belonged to her mother. When she'd anxiously admitted that to Max, afraid he'd balk at her choice of attire, he had only smiled and told her he couldn't wait to see it. She loved the slim lines and simple cut of the black velvet, strapless formal. Coupled with the pearl choker and earrings, which had also been her mother's, Rowan thought she looked very nice. But then, what did she know about such things? She thought she looked nice in her bowling shirt.

Her uncertainty about her appearance tugged at something deep inside her, an insecurity born long ago in adolescence that had been reinforced over the years by loss and rejection. Normally Rowan would swear that such an insecurity didn't exist in her. But at times such as these, she had to admit that she was only human, and right now she felt like an awkward thirteen-year-old with brand-new braces, who was going to her first boy-girl dance. Oh, well, at least these days she didn't have to worry about getting a pimple. She hoped.

When Debbie called up to her that Max was here, Rowan suddenly felt nauseous. She could almost hear the sigh in her baby-sitter's voice and knew that he must look incredible. Then she remembered she'd seen him in a tux before. And he had looked incredible. Her spirits sank even lower at the prospect of being outshone by her date. This test was getting harder and harder by the minute, she thought. She really wished she was better prepared to take it. With one final perusal of her appearance in the mirror, Rowan picked up her small clutch bag and wrap from the bed and readied herself to meet Max.

Downstairs in the living room, Max paced anxiously back and forth, swinging a huge bouquet of red, red roses as if they were a baseball bat. He couldn't believe he was this nervous, couldn't believe he felt like an awkward kid again. But tonight was going to be a special night, momentous even. He wanted everything to go just right. He would be returning to New York tomorrow, but before he left, he wanted, needed, to discuss some things with Rowan. Big things. Important things. Things that could change their lives forever. He just wasn't quite sure how to broach the subject, and as a result his thoughts were in a jumble.

A small sound behind him made him turn, and when he saw Rowan slowly descending the stairs, looking like a gorgeous, forties film star, he stopped his pacing and let the roses fall limp and forgotten to his side. She moved gracefully and elegantly, her small hand lightly skimming over the banister, and Max's attention became fixed on the length of slender calf that was exposed through a side slit in her dress with every other step she took. Her eyes held his uncertainly when her foot touched the bottom step, and as Max's mouth dried up and his throat constricted, all he could think was, *Wow*.

Rowan wasn't sure how to take his silence while his dark, unreadable eyes swept over her from head to toe. The longer she waited for his response, the more apprehensive she became. He was disappointed, she thought. She wouldn't measure up to the other guests tonight. She couldn't stop the slight droop of her shoulders as she nervously bit her lip.

Her action finally snapped Max's attention back to the present. Gazing at the slight, creamy swell of her breasts above the dress, noting how the soft fabric clung lovingly to her curves, sneaking another peek at the hint of leg revealed by the side slit, Max said the first thing that popped into his head.

"You wore *that* to your senior prom?" he gasped in disbelief. Her teenage date must have had hormones steaming out his ears!

Rowan became defensive at Max's remark and tone of voice. "Look, Max, just because this isn't the latest creation from the desk of Albert Nipon that sells for five grand in finer salons, it doesn't mean you have the right to criticize me. I happen to like this dress, and I think it's perfectly appropriate for tonight." Of course, she wasn't sure of that at all, she realized. But it seemed vitally important right now that Max not detect her uncertainty about the evening, or about their relationship as a whole, for that matter. She suddenly felt as if she were stomping around on very thin ice, and no matter how careful she tried to be, she felt as if she'd already made a substantial crack on the surface.

For a moment Max was puzzled by Rowan's outburst, then realized how his words must have sounded. "No, Rowan, I didn't mean it like that," he tried to explain. "I meant... Look, just forget it," he added, not wanting to get caught up in misunderstandings and hasty apologies. "You look ravishing," he added with a smile he hoped was disarming.

Rowan relaxed a little. "Thank you," she said quietly.

"You're welcome," he rejoined, pulling up the somewhat battered roses for her inspection. "These are for you," he announced softly, feeling his smile growing warmer by the minute.

His eager expression and the curiously jumbled-up bouquet of very beautiful roses dissipated whatever anger was left in Rowan. "Oh, Max," she said on a nervous chuckle, taking the flowers from his hand, "they're gorgeous. No one's ever given me roses before. Thank you." She inhaled deeply of their sweet fragrance, closing her eyes as she did so. When she opened them again, Max's expression had changed, as if he were weighing some very important consideration.

"What is it?" she asked quietly.

But Max shook his head and remained silent, his smile becoming even broader and warmer. "Nothing," he told her finally. "Just that we better get going."

She quickly retrieved a large porcelain vase from its perch atop the china cabinet in the dining room and arranged the roses in water. The conversation during their drive to The Brown Hotel was quiet and subdued. Did he, too, sense the electricity and excitement in the air? Rowan was still preoccupied by her unshakable misgivings about the evening, and try as she might to talk herself out of them, her doubts remained firmly entrenched in her mind.

The Crystal Ballroom at The Brown Hotel was every bit as sparkling and elegant as its name implied. Rowan had been here once before, years ago, when she was sixteen, for her boyfriend's junior prom. Even back then she had fallen in love with the old hotel, had been dazzled by the frothy cascades of crystal that made the ballroom chandeliers glisten like thousands of diamonds. Tonight the windows were festooned with scarlet curtains, and the numerous tables, draped with red linen and white lace, were enhanced by centerpieces of red roses and carnations and white baby's breath and lilies. Waiting at the ballroom's entrance while Max checked her wrap for her, Rowan inhaled deeply and could almost smell the sweet fragrance of the flowers, could nearly taste the fresh effervescence of the abundantly flowing champagne, could feel the sizzle of excitement in the air.

But when several minutes passed and Max did not come back to collect her, Rowan's apprehensions began to return, and she felt herself starting to panic. As she looked out over the crowd of people sitting at tables or moving gracefully on the dance floor, the world seemed to tilt a little askew from its axis, and reality began to shift. Suddenly the sparkle and splendor of the chandeliers paled beside the glitter of jewelry and designer gowns. The sweet fragrance of the centerpieces was overpowered by the pungent aroma of old money reeking from every corner of the room. The sizzle of excitement became a tension Rowan felt must be a result of the presence of a commoner amid so much nobility. The splendor and sparkle began to look excessive and gaudy, and as she gazed down at her own simple gown and pearls, she heard Max's voice echoing his apparent displeasure of her attire, and felt a lead weight sink coldly to the pit of her stomach.

What am I *doing* here like this? she demanded of herself. This was crazy. She felt so far removed from these people that at that moment, God help her, she felt an ugly, involuntary reaction threatening to overwhelm her. All she wanted to do was pick up a tray of champagne and thread her way through the throngs of people, offering them a drink with her best server's smile. This is America, you idiot, she had to remind herself, home of equality. There is no caste system, no feudal fiefdom to keep you in your place. You belong here as much as anyone. Your manners are impeccable.

But the little pep talk helped not at all. She wasn't comfortable in this society. Prom night at the Brown had been fun, because she'd been among a group of teenagers pretending they were high-class. But Rowan wasn't a teenager anymore. And high-class wasn't what she wanted to be, in real life or pretend. She wished she'd gone bowling instead. At least she'd be having fun.

"Rowan? Is that you?"

She turned to the familiar voice and was horrified to see Stacy Logan, one of her co-workers from September's presenting her with a tray of champagne. After the thoughts she'd just been entertaining, it made Rowan feel as though she'd stepped into a twilight zone, as if she'd made Stacy appear before her, just thinking about her job at September's.

"Stacy," Rowan said breathlessly, surprise evident in her voice. "No, I'm not working tonight," she added, indicating the tray the other woman still held up to her, thinking Stacy meant her to take the whole thing and begin serving.

The cute, blond waitress rolled her eyes and smiled at Rowan. "Well, obviously you're not working tonight, you big goof. You look incredible! I meant for you to take one glass, not the whole tray!"

"Oh." Rowan felt color creeping into her cheeks. "I'm here with a date," she told Stacy as she carefully picked up one of the crystal champagne flutes. "He was invited," she added, in case the other woman didn't believe her.

"Hey, go for it," Stacy said with a brilliant smile. "It's good to see one of our own on the other side for a change. Have fun," she added over her shoulder as she turned to make her rounds.

Great, Rowan thought. Now on top of everything else that was making her uncomfortable and ill at ease, she was going to be served cocktails and canapés by all her closest friends. The urge to pick up a tray herself and start weaving in and out of the "real" guests suddenly surfaced again before she could stop it, and Rowan cringed and gulped a mouthful of champagne.

Max finally rejoined her with an apology for having abandoned her, explaining that unfortunately, these affairs for him were usually little more than glorified business meetings. Rowan tried to smile, but knew her lips froze somewhere short of one. Luckily Max didn't notice, though, as a man with an extravagant mustache clapped him on the shoulder and offered his congratulations on the deal.

For much of the evening, Rowan found herself swinging precariously from mood to mood. On the rare moments when she had Max to herself, while they were dancing or touring the hotel, she felt happier than she'd ever felt in her life. But just as those moments were reaching their peaks, someone would snatch him away from her, demanding "just a moment" of his time. With an apologetic smile and the phrase, "I'll be right back," Max would disappear into the world of big business, and Rowan would be left to forage alone among the guests.

At one point, a bald man with a big cigar told Max he needed a word with him, taking an extra minute to introduce Rowan to his wife. The thin, grayish, bored-looking woman in a silver dress, had, Rowan discovered, an enormous chip on her shoulder.

"My name is Mrs. Emerson," she informed Rowan through her nose after the man who'd introduced her as "My wife, Grace" had left with Max in tow.

"I'm Ms. Chance," Rowan countered, feeling her back go up involuntarily at the older woman's air of superiority.

"Chance," Mrs. Emerson repeated, clearly feigning thoughtfulness. "*Ms.* Chance. Well, I'm afraid I don't recall ever having made your acquaintance. Oh, Maude," she called to another woman of similar age and appearance before Rowan could reply.

Maude and the group of straight-spined women she was with all turned to Grace Emerson. "Yes, Grace?" Maude muttered, apparently equally bored with the evening's events.

"Do you recall ever meeting a *person* named Chance?" Grace asked her.

Rowan opened her mouth in anger at the woman's blatant rudeness. She'd said the word *person* as if she'd meant *rodent*.

Maude's eyes raked over Rowan as if she were a drape being considered for the guest-room decor. She came to stand beside Grace Emerson and said in clipped tones, "We had a gardener named Chance once. We had to let him go, though. He was a drunk and a thief. Made off with some of my best pieces. He wouldn't be a relative of yours, would he?" she asked Rowan pointedly. "Some of those things *were* heirlooms."

Rowan's mouth snapped shut in outrage. She clamped her teeth together and tried to remain civil when she said, "Excuse me, but I find your behavior abominable." With that she turned, nearly running over Stacy again.

"Whoa, Rowan," the other woman said with a chuckle, grasping her tray with both hands to steady it. "Where's the fire?"

Rowan snatched a glass of champagne and emptied half of it before asking, "You wouldn't happen to have any hemlock on you, would you, Stacy?"

"You contemplating suicide or homicide?" the other woman rejoined lightly.

"It's for Mrs. Grace Emerson," Rowan told her. "The thin, grayish piece of meat in the Gee-vahn-shee over there." Actually Rowan had no idea if the gown was Givenchy or L. L. Bean, for that matter. But Grace seemed the type to go for French couture.

"Problems with one of the guests?" Stacy asked.

"Problems with *all* of the guests," Rowan responded glumly. "Here I always thought serving rich people was such a drag. Now I know partying with them is even worse."

"If you're talking about the dragon-lady society behind you," Stacy said, indicating the group Rowan had just left, "they had you targeted earlier."

"What do you mean?"

"I mean I was serving them a little while ago, and they were talking about the woman with Maximillian Donovan, wondering about your designer and your jeweler. It was

driving them crazy, trying to figure out if you were way below them on the social ladder or way above. Frankly, I think
they're jealous because you've outshone them.''

''Oh, that's silly,'' Rowan said, trying to make light of her
friend's speculations.

''Come on, Rowan,'' Stacy told her, ''you know how it
is when you work these functions. Eavesdropping is the rule
of thumb. You've managed to make quite a stir among the
beautiful people tonight.''

''But—''

''There you are.'' Max's voice caught her attention from
behind. ''Did you have a nice chat with Grace?''

Rowan whipped around and glared at her companion.
''You mean *Mrs. Emerson*? I found her and her cronies
unspeakably rude. What a bunch of—''

''Now, now, dear,'' Max cautioned with a grin, wagging
his finger at her playfully. ''Don't lower yourself to the behavior of the upper classes.''

''Max, can we go home?'' she asked him quietly, losing
all the anger that had been building since Grace Emerson's
appearance.

His expression told her he couldn't imagine why she'd
want to leave. ''Home? But the evening's barely started.
Why would you want to go home?''

Rowan wanted to tell him it was because she was uncomfortable among the glitz and showiness that seemed to accompany wealth. Because she couldn't abide such an excess
of excess and such an abundance of superficiality. She
wanted to tell him it was because his friends weren't very
nice. Instead she remained silent, knowing that after doing
whatever she'd wanted all week, this night was his, reminding herself that she'd wanted to prove she could get along
just fine among his society.

"I'm just kind of bored, I guess," she finally told him evasively. "I don't really have much in common with anyone here."

"That's because you've been stuck with old bits of dust like Grace Emerson. Come on, we'll mingle with the younger set for a while."

The younger set turned out to be five or ten years older than Rowan, but included people who were as friendly and agreeable as Grace and Maude had been antagonistic. Rowan found especially appealing two women named Claire Coopersmith and Lynn Brannon, who were married to two of Houghton's executives, but wonder of wonders, who had careers of their own, as well. Claire was a vice president of one of the city's leading banks, though to see the tall brunette tonight, dressed in a clingy, red sequined dress, Rowan never would have guessed it. Lynn, on the other hand, seemed every bit the owner of an immensely successful consulting firm. Blond and conservative-looking, she wore a long-sleeved, dark blue velvet gown. When Rowan mentioned her own business that she was soon to open, the other women applauded her, but offered some words of caution.

"Be prepared to get lost in your husband's shadow, though," Lynn warned her.

"I'm not married," Rowan told them, thankful this time that Max had again been pulled away.

"Well, then marry a guy who's a street sweeper or burger fryer," Claire counseled with a smile.

"Why?" Rowan asked.

"Because *nobody* takes you seriously when you're married to one of the wealthiest, most successful men in town, regardless of how wealthy and successful you were before you were married."

"This is true," Lynn agreed. "And everyone treats you like you're crazy to be working, when you could be home sleeping late every day...."

"Watching soaps," Claire added.

"Eating chocolate," another woman in the group chimed in.

"Having babies," yet another piped up.

"Because your *husband* makes enough money to support a small sovereign nation," Lynn completed with a dubious laugh.

"But that's ridiculous!" Rowan protested.

"That's life," Claire assured her. Then, with a sudden change of topic she added, "If you're not married, who did you come with tonight?"

Rowan hedged, not wanting the women to realize how completely and utterly overshadowed by the man in her life she would be. "Uh, no one local. He's a friend of mine from out of town. You probably don't know him. It's his first time here."

"Rowan, sweetheart," Max said softly but audibly as he came up from behind her and draped an affectionate arm around her waist. "I'm sorry I disappeared again. I promise I'm completely yours for the rest of the evening." To seal the promise, he leaned over and kissed her gently on the cheek.

As happy as she was to see him, his timing couldn't have been worse, Rowan thought, closing her eyes in chagrin. When she opened them again, all the other women in the group were grinning at her with the bright, knowing grins of a bunch of Cheshire cats.

"Ladies," Max greeted them with his formal, impeccable, gorgeous smile. "Mind if I reclaim my heart's desire here?"

"Of course not, Mr. Donovan."

"By all means, Mr. Donovan."

"Please do, Mr. Donovan."

"We've enjoyed her company, Mr. Donovan."

"Uh, you go ahead, Max," Rowan said sheepishly. "I'll join you at the table in just a minute, okay?"

"Don't be long, Rowan," he entreated. "I've missed you tonight."

With a gentle squeeze on her shoulder and a smoldering look in his eyes, he was gone, and Rowan turned back around to face the laughing expressions of her new *compadres*. Before she could say a word, Claire and Lynn burst into a fit of good-natured giggles.

"You're here with Maximillian Donovan?" Claire squeaked. "Oh, honey, you *do* have your work cut out for you. If you marry him, you might just as well kiss your credibility as a businesswoman goodbye."

"Yeah," Lynn chirped in agreement. "The only reason people will come to you is to get to him. Oh, Rowan, I'm sorry," she added, appearing to register the other woman's crestfallen expression. "I shouldn't have said that."

"Look, it doesn't matter," Rowan said defensively, lifting her chin a little in defiance. "Because there's nothing serious between me and Max."

"Oh, no?" Claire lifted her dark brows. "That isn't the impression, uh, *Max* seems to give."

"Listen, Rowan," Lynn offered, "why don't you just marry ol' Max, stay at home, watch soaps, eat chocolate and have babies?" Her half smile told Rowan she was only half joking.

"I don't like soaps *or* chocolate," Rowan asserted. "And I've already had a baby. So work seems the obvious next step, as I have no intention of marrying *anyone, ever*. Certainly not Maximillian Donovan."

Before the other women had a chance to doubt her, and in an effort to hide the look of uncertainty she knew must be obvious in her eyes, Rowan turned around quickly and ran smack-dab into that tuxedoed chest the size of Cleveland, whose owner had of late become such an important part of her life.

"Max," she whispered into his starched pleats on a breathless sigh, inhaling great gulps of the spicy, expensive cologne he wore. When she finally gathered enough courage, she tilted her head back to meet his expression. Shocked by the unmistakable look of hurt and anger in his eyes, she stammered, "I thought you were going to wait for me at the table."

"I thought you weren't going to be long," he responded in clipped tones. "Just what was all that about, anyway?"

She feigned confusion. "What was all what about?"

"I heard you use the words, 'marrying' and 'Maximillian' and 'never' in one breath."

"But not in one sentence," she pointed out.

"The meaning was still there."

Rowan's shoulders sagged, and her eyes fell to the ground. "I'm sorry, Max," she began hesitantly, knowing her comments, along with those of Lynn and Claire, had put him in a dangerously uncomfortable and awkward position. "I know what you just heard put you on the spot, and I apologize. They were only teasing me. No one meant anything by it." She laughed a little nervously before she added, "It was just a joke, that's all. Not a very funny one, granted, but then, that's rich people for you."

She looked up at him again then and tried to smile reassuringly. But Max continued to scowl at her. Well, at least she knew now how enthusiastic he was about the topic of matrimony. Trying to hide her hopeless feelings with a careless shrug, she pushed past him and returned to their seats at the table, in time to hear the announcement that the mayor and some others wanted to say a few words to the guests. Max joined her a moment later, but remained silent and apparently thoughtful throughout the numerous speeches.

As the evening drew to a close, Lynn and Claire approached Rowan once more to say good-night, this time with another woman, a soft-spoken blonde in a clingy, revealing dress, who had the most beautiful green eyes Rowan had ever seen. She was introduced only as Shelley, and Rowan got the immediate and distinct impression that the newcomer wasn't well liked by the other women.

"I just wanted to tell you that Randy and I are having a Derby party tomorrow afternoon, and we'd like you and Maximillian to come," Lynn told Rowan as she threw a dark blue velvet wrap across her shoulder.

"I'm sorry, but I have another engagement," Rowan declined, knowing she had to work at September's. "But Max doesn't go back to New York until tomorrow night. He might take you up on it," she added somewhat ruefully, knowing, too, that he seldom turned down an opportunity to party with the rich and famous.

"*You're* the one who's here with Maximillian Donovan?" Shelley asked incredulously, her voice as sleek and smooth as silk.

"Yes, I came with Max," Rowan told the blonde.

But Shelley had clearly already brushed her off as something unimportant and turned to Lynn. "Of *course* you should invite Mr. Donovan," she cooed. "Since Mark can't make it, I'll be odd woman out. Mr. Donovan can be *my* escort."

"Cool it, Shelley," Claire muttered with a sneer.

A new thought must have struck Shelley then, and she turned back to Rowan with a sly grin. "Tell me something, Ellen," she started.

"Rowan," Rowan corrected her, feigning tolerance.

"Yes, whatever. Does it bother you, your boyfriend's reputation as a notorious womanizer? I mean, every time I see him on TV or in magazines, he's with someone new. Doesn't that ever bother you or make you wonder?"

What is this, cat's night out or something? Rowan thought. "Shelley," she began, her feigned patience wearing thin, "Max isn't my boyfriend, all right? We met last week, and I've been showing him around town. You want a crack at him? Be my guest. But a word of advice—he's not into bimbos."

Rowan saw Claire bite her lip in an effort to keep from smiling, but Lynn didn't bother.

"Looks like you're out of luck, Shell," she said simply, slapping the other woman on the back in a less than comradely way. "Stay in touch, Rowan," she added with a wink.

"I will," Rowan assured her, turning to find Max approaching with her wrap.

Shelley's words had topped off the evening perfectly, Rowan mused as she and Max found their way to the car. They'd upset what dubious comfort she had finally managed to feel when seated beside him at their table, and reminded her that things were not as perfect as they might seem. As Rowan settled herself into the Jaguar's plush interior, her mood grew morose. It wasn't just the rude reception she'd received from Shelley and Grace Emerson that had shot holes in her hope that maybe things could work out between Max and herself. This entire evening had emphasized how wide the chasm between them was. No matter how much she cared for Max, Rowan told herself, it was time she faced an ugly truth: the two of them simply didn't belong together.

As her stomach clenched into a tight fist, she sighed inwardly and gazed blindly out the window at the passing buildings of downtown. Maybe the high life was exactly what some people wanted to lead, and maybe dressing up in finery to drink French champagne and dance the night away to a live orchestra was just peachy for some. But quite frankly, Rowan was not one of those people. She was more comfortable wearing casual clothes and staying home in front of the fire with a bottle of inexpensive, domestic wine, listening to music on the stereo while snuggling with someone who loved her exactly for the person she was—Rowan Chance, an average, middle-class woman with simple tastes.

She glanced over at the man beside her in the sleek, black car, the man with the perfect tuxedo and expensive haircut, the man who had thoroughly enjoyed himself among the people she'd found so foreign. Max had belonged utterly and without question at that party tonight. She'd followed him with her eyes throughout the evening, had watched as guest after guest wandered up to greet him, every one of them clearly dazzled by his Maximillian Donovan smile. He'd been totally at ease, had never missed a beat, completely confident in his surroundings. Max was born to a life of luxury, and born to be the center of attention, she realized. He was one of the lucky few who were destined from birth for a life of greatness. And he deserved it, too, of that she had no doubt. She only wished that somehow she could share that life with him.

She was suddenly struck once more by the odd and hopeless nature of her situation. How many times had she sworn to herself she would never, ever get involved in a relationship without a future, and how many times had she promised herself she'd live a nice, steady, *stable* life? Yet she had allowed herself to fall in love with Maximillian Donovan, had become caught up in all the splendor and greatness that made up his life. Splendor and greatness that were essential parts of the man, but that were things she had wished to avoid in her own life at all costs. When had matters gotten so completely out of hand?

Thinking about the party they had just left, Rowan found herself visualizing the future. What if...? she began to think, indulging in an excessive fantasy, letting her mind wander at the prospect of a future with Max. She would have to give up everything she had in Louisville, because Max's center of business was New York and always had been. She'd have to sell her house and let someone else enjoy all the hard work she'd put into it, would have to surrender the business she hadn't even opened yet, would have to say goodbye to all her friends. Of course, she could still visit here, and they could come see her, but ... It wouldn't be the same.

She wasn't sure she'd like living in New York, Rowan realized. Having grown up in a quiet, suburban neighborhood, surrounded by huge trees, chatty birds and silent nights, she wasn't certain how she'd be able to adjust to city life. She and Miranda would have to give up their evening strolls around the neighborhood, and they wouldn't be able to make snow angels in the front yard anymore. The backyard gardens would probably wither and die without the two of them out there, tending to them all the time.

Of course, she'd have Max, and he was certainly well worth some sacrifices. Except that he'd probably be gone much of the time; he'd told her he traveled extensively for his job. Even when he was in New York, he seemed the type to put in long hours at the office. She'd probably end up as bored with and indifferent toward life as Grace Emerson.

Rowan shuddered at that thought. No, she'd go ahead and open her business as planned, maybe even call it The Warehouse. Except this Warehouse would be different, because she wouldn't have struggled so hard to see it come about. Thanks to Max's money and position, she'd have a state-of-the-art business, stocked with expensive antiques and fixtures that she could order from a wholesaler or catalog. She wouldn't have to search for those occasional treasures, the ones that somehow always made her feel more triumphant because she'd stumbled upon them amid worthless bits of trash. And certainly her business would flourish, if not because hers was a store that stood alone and apart from others—no doubt New York had dozens of businesses comparable to The Warehouse—then because she was Mrs. Maximillian Donovan and something of a celebrity.

And of course, Miranda would always have anything her little heart desired. She would attend the best schools, wear the most elite labels, vacation in the most exotic locales and live in the poshest surroundings. "Spoiled rotten" would be the words that followed the little girl everywhere she went, and Miranda would never get a chance to appreciate the basic values Rowan wanted so badly to instill in her daughter. Instead, Miranda would be a rich, city kid, who would cringe at the concept of gardening or walking or playing in the snow. And instead of growing up with a deep appreciation for simple things, she would probably learn early on to scorn them.

Ah, yes, Rowan could see the future quite clearly, and it was nothing but bleak. No matter how she and Max might feel about each other now, their ways of life were far too different to ever mesh. And when that fact became obvious, Max would want nothing more to do with her. With a sigh of defeat, Rowan forced herself to realize that their relationship could never work out. It was just as well Max had to return to New York tomorrow. She didn't want to prolong the heartache she knew was imminent. She wished things could be different, but she had to be realistic. She had been on an even track, approaching a good point in her life when Max had come along, and with any luck at all, she'd be able to maintain her stride when he was gone. So why did it suddenly feel as if the hurdles she'd been convinced were behind her now loomed so menacingly ahead?

Chapter Eleven

By the time they entered the house, Rowan's thoughts had caused her to become angry and morose. Angry at herself for having gotten into such a hopeless situation after promising for years it would never happen again, morose precisely because it would never work out between Max and herself. She was aware of him watching her with silent and frank speculation, but she said nothing as she kicked off her black patent flats in the kitchen and padded soundlessly in her stocking feet to the den to rouse Debbie.

After the sitter was gone, Max moved from where he'd been hovering at the entrance to the den to approach Rowan, who, he noted, was trying to busy herself by fluffing up sofa pillows and picking up scattered sections of the newspaper. There was so much he wanted and needed to discuss with her, a question he wanted to ask, a promise he wanted to offer, but he wasn't sure how to go about it. What he wanted to say to Rowan was something he'd never said to anyone else before, and he was a little uncertain of how she might react. His normal calm confidence eluded him now. This was entirely different from settling a deal or putting up a building. He was scared and full of apprehension, and those were feelings he'd never experienced in his adult life. He was at a loss as to how to deal with them.

"Rowan, we have to talk," he finally said quietly.

His words brought Rowan's attention up with a snap, so gravely were they offered. So he felt it, too, she thought, as an empty pain permeated every major organ in her body. He'd settled his deal and celebrated it, and in the silence that had filled the car on the drive home, his thoughts had obviously mirrored hers. He saw as well as she how fruitless it would be to continue their relationship and, like herself, sought to end it cleanly and completely. She should be happy they agreed on the subject, she told herself. So why did she feel as if she were slowly coming apart at the seams?

"What about?" she asked him on a shallow breath.

"About...things," Max told her vaguely, still uncertain how to bring up the topic he so wanted to discuss. "About...us," he clarified.

Rowan sighed and moved toward her desk, hoping to shield herself from what she knew was coming. "I...I don't see that there's anything to talk about," she said lightly, unable to meet his eyes, wishing they could just get it over with. "You have to go back to New York, and you want to say goodbye. So...goodbye, Max. I enjoyed the last two weeks a lot. You're a nice man, we've had some wonderful conversations, and I want to thank you for helping me face up to some things I might not have faced up to otherwise. I...I had a nice time."

Max couldn't believe what he was hearing. *A nice time?* he echoed to himself. I'm a nice man? We've had some wonderful conversations? If she thought she could make him believe that what they'd shared together had been nothing more than wonderful conversation, that he was no more to her than a nice man, then she was out of her mind!

"So that's it?" he muttered petulantly. "You'd actually just say goodbye and watch me leave? Why don't you just say, 'Get lost, Max,' or 'Beat it,' or something?" He wove his fingers furiously through his hair and began to pace anxiously back and forth. "How can you speak so lightly of what's happened during the past two weeks? How can you make it sound like nothing more than a brief friendship?"

Rowan watched and listened to him with a growing sense of panic, not understanding the vehemence of his words or the nervousness of his actions. "Because that's all it has been, Max," she asserted, feeling not nearly as confident as she wanted to be. "We *have* been friends. It's been fun. But now it's over."

"It is *not* over," he assured her.

She dared not let herself hope that his words meant what she wished they did. "Are you saying you're going to stay here?" she asked him cautiously.

Max was clearly taken aback by her question, and it showed in the surprise that filled his eyes. "Well, no," he stammered uncertainly. "I have to go back to New York tomorrow night."

Rowan's shoulders sagged involuntarily with hopelessness, her eyes falling defeatedly to the floor. "Then it's over," she told him.

Max was fast becoming frantic. This wasn't going at all according to plan. He had hoped they might come home and enjoy a nightcap after the party, then after a little bit of mellow chitchat, he could have steered their conversation toward a discussion of the future and asked her the question he'd been rehearsing in his mind all day. There wasn't supposed to be this antagonism between them. Rowan was supposed to be receptive to him now, not mired in denial. As he thought about what he wanted to say, he tugged sav-

agely at the bow tie around his neck that suddenly felt like
a confining leash, then shrugged out of his jacket and tossed
it over the arm of the couch.

Rowan saw his actions as a preparation to do battle and
steeled herself for what was about to come. The ball was in
his court, though, and she waited without speaking to see
what he was going to do with it, all the while mentally dig-
ging in to take and make her stand against him.

Max continued to gaze at her silently as he undid the
buttons at his throat and wrists, then rolled the sleeves of his
pleated shirt to his elbows. Finally, unable to discern exactly how to go about saying what he had to say, he placed
his hands on his hips in challenge and told her decisively, "I
thought you might come back to New York with me, Rowan. As my wife."

The fist curled about Rowan's insides clenched even
tighter, and her lungs were quickly emptied of air as it
rushed past her lips on a ragged breath. For long moments
she heard nothing but the blood pounding wildly between
her ears, felt nothing but her heart threatening to jump out
of her throat. She saw all of her nightmarish visions of the
future flash into her mind once again, and knew without
doubt that she had to put a stop to this now. Taking a deep
breath, she whispered, "Then you thought wrong, Max."

Wrong? he repeated to himself. *Wrong?* No, what was
wrong here was her answer. How could she not want to
marry him, after everything they had enjoyed for the past
two weeks? Before his desperate thoughts could overcome
him, he asked calmly, "Why is it wrong?"

Rowan felt like crying. Why did he have to make things
more difficult than they already were? He had to see as well
as she did that any future they might have would be short-
lived and pointless. Why did he want to prolong their suf-
fering? Trying to steady her runaway heart and erratic

breathing, she said lamely, "I don't want to live in New York City."

Max's confusion was obvious. "That's it?" he asked. "That's the reason you won't marry me? Because you don't want to live in the city?" He threw up his hands in surrender and offered, "Fine. We'll find a place upstate or in Connecticut or something. Hell, I don't mind commuting."

"I want to live here," Rowan told him softly, realizing that there was more to her reluctance than that. "I like it here. This is my home. It's Miranda's home."

"I know it's a lot to ask of you both," he pleaded. "But my business is and always has been in New York. And I won't settle for a long-distance relationship."

"Neither will I," she agreed.

Max looked at her through narrowed eyes. "What are you trying to say, Rowan?"

She met his gaze levelly as she responded, "I can't marry you, Max."

He said nothing at first, just looked at her without blinking, then took several slow steps toward her. When only scant inches separated them, he lifted his bent index finger to tip back her chin, and met her eyes steadily with his own. "Can't?" he asked her pointedly. "Or *won't*? There's a difference, you know."

Rowan frantically searched his eyes, drawing her brows together in confusion at his choice of words. "How can you ask that?" she demanded softly. "You know as well as I do that it would never work out between us."

"No, I don't know that."

Rowan shook her head slowly back and forth, and her voice was low when she spoke. "There's no future for us, Max. We've come from two different worlds, we move in two different worlds, and we both want to live in two different worlds. It will never work out," she repeated emphatically.

"I thought we settled this a long time ago, Rowan," Max said. "Whatever *small* differences we may have are not significant enough to warrant keeping us apart."

"The differences between us aren't that small," Rowan assured him. "And they *will* keep us apart."

The hand under Rowan's chin settled on her bare shoulder as Max roped his other arm around her waist. "Not if we don't let them," he pointed out.

Rowan doubled her hands into loose fists and placed them against his chest in an effort to keep some barrier between them. "How can we help but let them?" she asked desperately.

Max pulled her closer. "Don't you mean how can *you* help but let them? I'm not the one who has a problem with our differences, Rowan. I never was."

"That's because you don't have as much to lose if the future doesn't work out the way you plan," she acknowledged. "What happens if I marry you, sell this house, give up my business, pack up my daughter and move to New York, only to have you decide you liked things better the way they were before you met me?"

"That will never happen," Max said quietly and with complete conviction.

Rowan wanted to believe that the look in his eyes backed up his words, but she couldn't allow herself to do so. "You don't know that for sure," she said hollowly.

"Yes, I do," he assured her without a doubt. Then he added with a note of defeat in his voice, "But evidently you aren't as certain of that as I am."

Rowan remained silent, but the fear that darkened her eyes told Max everything he needed to know. Reluctantly he removed his hand from her shoulder and unwound his arm from her waist. She took several steps backward, as if physically emphasizing the distance she obviously felt was still between them. Max watched her movements silently, feeling her hopelessness and unwillingness seep coldly into his bones, wishing he knew what to say that would convince her to change her mind.

"So that's it, then?" he asked quietly. "You aren't even willing to make an effort? You're just going to throw away everything that's happened between us? Has it meant nothing to you?"

It meant everything to her, she wanted to tell him, and that was the problem. Her life had begun to include Max in every facet, and she'd begun to feel that it would be meaningless without him. And she couldn't allow that to happen. Because when he did see the futility of their situation, which she was quite certain he would, then her life without him would cease to have meaning. She had struggled too long, had overcome too many obstacles and faced down too many hard truths to just hand herself over to Maximillian Donovan. She'd wandered lost for years after her parents' deaths and Joey's desertion, and was only now beginning to find herself again. She didn't want her struggles and search to be in vain by getting lost all over again in Max's shadow.

"Everything has been wonderful, Max," she told him honestly. "Better than it's been in a long, long time. But I've been forgetting one crucial thing for the past two weeks, an important rule that I've always tried to follow."

"Oh?" he asked sardonically, unable to keep the edge from his voice. "And what's that?"

"You're out of my league, Max," she said softly. "And I don't box outside my weight."

Max's jaw twitched at her statement, but otherwise he remained motionless. "You've chosen an interesting analogy," he finally said, his voice low and menacing. "But it's a completely inappropriate one. You haven't been fighting anyone, Rowan. Except maybe yourself."

Rowan shook her head slowly. "Just let it go, Max," she urged him. "We weren't meant to be together."

"You know that isn't true," he insisted. "Nothing has ever been more right, more perfect, than the two of us together. I've never met a woman like you, and you've said I'm like no one you've ever known. Doesn't that tell you something? Like maybe whoever's responsible for our having met in the first place wanted to make it perfectly clear to us that we'd found what we've been searching for for so long?"

His words were full of urgent pleading, and Rowan almost let herself believe what he said was true. But the pictures she'd painted for herself earlier in the evening rose up to haunt her once more. What they had together now was tenuous, at best. It would not last. She would never be happy in his world, and he would never fit into hers. He would overshadow her until every last scrap of the independence and self-sufficiency she'd striven to achieve was gone. Before long she'd be bored and bitter like Grace Emerson and her entourage, or the predictions of Claire and Lynn would come true, and her identity would be determined exclusively by his. People would see her as Maximillian Donovan's wife and nothing more, and soon that would be all she'd feel like. And as Max became more and more engrossed in his work, Rowan's place in his life would grow smaller and smaller, until she was little more than a household accessory. When she thought of the future, she realized again that they had none, and it reinforced her conviction that she was doing the right thing by ending it all now.

"It'll never work out, Max," she said simply. "We're just too different from one another, have entirely different perceptions about life in general and the future in particular."

Max groaned in exasperation, grasping great handfuls of his hair in frustration. "Rowan, listen to yourself," he pleaded. "Listen to how *lame* your reasons are. Our differences aren't that significant. You're just using them to hide the fact that you're terrified of letting yourself love me. Because no matter how often you try to deny it, you *do* love me. I know it as well as I know *I* love *you*. And I will *not* leave here until you admit that the reason you won't marry me is because you're afraid I'll abandon you. Like your parents did, like Miranda's father did. Once you face that, we can start to deal with this whole situation a little more rationally."

"My parents and Joey have nothing to do with this," Rowan insisted.

Max laughed mirthlessly, his eyes full of fight. "You're wrong, Rowan," he told her furiously. "Until you face up to your fear of rejection and abandonment, you'll never be able to commit to anyone. You're just lucky that this time you had economic differences to blame. If I'd been poor or middle-class, you'd have had a hell of a time coming up with some excuse why you couldn't commit yourself to me." When she said nothing to deny or confirm his allegations, he continued adamantly, "I won't stand here and beg you to marry me. But if you don't face up to your fears now, you could lose the one person who'll love you for the rest of your life and beyond the way you need and deserve to be loved. I'm that man, Rowan. *Don't* blow this. Please."

For long moments they stared at each other in silence, neither giving an inch. Rowan thought about his cautiously uttered warning, tried to believe what he said was true. But no one could predict the future, she realized. Her parents had told her they'd always be there for her, and Joey had said time after time that she was the only woman for him. Yet they had all left her alone. And no matter what Max had to offer, no matter what he promised, Rowan knew from experience that there simply were no guarantees. Things changed. People changed. Feelings changed. And the thought of giving herself over to Max only to wind up consumed by him and his life-style, then rejected by him when he lost interest, gave Rowan all the strength she needed to turn down his proposal. Definitely and finally. It simply would not work.

She took a long, deep breath and said softly, "I'm sure you have a lot of packing to do before your flight leaves tomorrow. Have a safe trip, Max. I...I'll miss you. Goodbye." Rowan turned her back as she offered her hasty farewell, trying to prevent the tears she felt gathering. She would not cry, she ordered herself. Not now. Not in front of Max.

He remained where he was for some moments in stony silence. Then, realizing nothing he could say tonight would change her mind, he snatched up his jacket from the sofa and made to leave. At the doorway to the den, he turned once more, gazing sullenly at a rigid-spined Rowan, wanting more than anything to cross the room and take her into his arms. "This isn't finished, Rowan," he assured her on a ragged whisper. "Not by a long shot."

And with that he did leave, slamming the kitchen door behind him as he went. Not until she heard the quickly fading sound of the Jaguar's engine in the street did Rowan allow herself to relax, and the first things she let go were her tears. She dropped into a chair and propped her elbows on her desk, burying her face in her hands. As her tears tumbled one after another into her damp palms, Rowan felt caught in a trap of her own making. As hopeless and impossible as she was certain a future with Max would be, the thought of living without him now tore an even greater hole in her heart, and made her wonder how she was ever going to enjoy life again.

Chapter Twelve

July was without question the most hideous month of the year, Rowan decided as she swiped at a trickle of sweat that ran down her neck and over her shoulder to pool between her breasts. And it had barely begun, she remembered, rubbing more perspiration off her forehead. The temperature must be ninety degrees outside right now, which meant that here in the attic, it more than likely exceeded one hundred. She was crazy to start renovating her third floor in the middle of the summer, she realized, especially when business at The Warehouse was better than she could have anticipated and growing faster every day. But twelve-hour days at the shop hadn't been enough to keep her busy, and on Sundays like this one, when the shop was closed, she felt almost useless. Worse than that, though, she still found herself thinking far too often about Max, so in an effort to divert her thoughts, she'd added projects to her already overpowering work load.

She had spent the morning dragging plywood and bits of lumber she'd been hoarding in the attic down to the third floor, gasping for breath in the close, dusty heat of the small room, feeling as though she'd lost ten gallons of moisture through her pores. The ragged, red bandanna she'd tied pirate-style over her hair did little to contain the wet, lanky strands plastered to her forehead, and Rowan knew that the black streaks of dirt on her bare legs and arms only hinted at the ones that must be smudging her face. She wiped her hands on her sleeveless, red midriff top and tugged at her short, faded cutoffs. This whole project was nothing but an exercise in futility, she knew, as thoughts of Max still assailed her heat-muddled brain.

It had been nine weeks since she'd said goodbye to him. Nine weeks since he'd left her house to go back to New York. Of course, she'd heard from him since then, she reminded herself. He'd called her at all hours of the day and night, both at the shop and at the house. At work it hadn't been a problem. She told Tara, who was working for her until that big theatrical break came along, to assure him that she was busy and couldn't come to the phone. But at home his calls posed a considerable problem. At first she'd simply told him they had nothing to say to each other and had asked him to please stop calling and leave her alone. When that had proved fruitless, she'd purchased an answering machine so she could screen her calls, but that had just made the situation worse. Max had made it a point to leave incredibly erotic messages, usually two or three a day, and when she'd come home from work at night feeling tired and lonely, the sound of his low, sexy voice telling her things he wanted to do to her made Rowan's already sleepless nights become even more impossible.

Yet she was still strong in her conviction that she had done the right thing by ending her relationship with him. She was still quite certain that there had been no chance for a future between them. Soon Max would see that, too, she told herself. Soon he'd understand the impossibility of their previous situation, and he'd stop his silly insistence on maintaining contact with her. And then she would be alone. Which she assured herself was exactly where she wanted to be.

She dropped an armload of plywood onto the floor with a ragged groan, feeling a tendon in her arm strain against the angle at which she'd been holding the boards. As she made a fist and pumped her elbow to ease the pressure, she cocked her head at the sound of a frantic knocking at her back door. She stubbed her toe painfully as she raced toward the stairs, then had to hop down them on one foot as she massaged the injured appendage. By the time she reached the bottom step, her toe was throbbing, and along with her arm, which still stung with a shooting pain, it made Rowan feel a little testy.

"I'm coming!" she shouted crossly at her unknown visitor as she limped through the dining room, but whoever it was apparently did not hear and the ceaseless, annoying rapping continued.

She thrust open the swinging door that connected her dining room and kitchen with a crash, then stopped suddenly and stared, speechless. Since Rowan's house was not air-conditioned, she'd left her back door open to allow in what little breeze there was. The screen door was still latched, though; otherwise she was sure her guest would have taken it upon himself to come barging right in, as the man obviously did not understand the meaning of words such as "no" and "go away." If he did, he wouldn't have come back to her now.

"Hello, Rowan," Max said, feeling a tremendous rush of déjà vu as he did so. Had it really been only eleven weeks ago that he'd come knocking at her door for the first time? He felt as though he'd lived a lifetime since that day. She looks wonderful, he thought, curling his lips into a smile, feeling a warmth spread through every fiber of his being. He let his gaze rake slowly and freely over her body, starting at her slender ankles, finally settling on the blue eyes that held his so intently. "Did you miss me?" he added softly.

Rowan didn't know what to say. What was he doing back in town? she wondered as she took in his khaki trousers and white cotton shirt. She noticed, too, that he was surrounded by various pieces of matching, designer luggage. "What are you doing here?" she asked him with a frown.

Here we go again, Max thought. Only this time things were going to wind up a little differently than before. This time, the ending was going to be a happy one. "Can I come in?" he asked her. He wrapped his fingers around the door handle and rattled the screen door against the frame impatiently. "It's locked," he pointed out unnecessarily.

Rowan approached him slowly, her brain scrambling furiously for reasons to turn him away. She raised her hand cautiously to the hook that latched the door, but before she lifted it, she asked him again, "What are you doing here?"

Max's eyes held hers through the screen as he told her, "I need a place to stay for a little while."

When he offered no further explanation, Rowan demanded softly, "Why?"

Max looked down at the ground quickly, then back at Rowan once again. "Can I please come in?" he repeated quietly.

Warily Rowan unlatched the door, and Max hastily pulled it toward him before she could change her mind. Quickly he picked up his bags and began tossing them one by one into the kitchen, until they rested in an unceremonious heap by the door. When he was finished, he straightened and smiled.

"Thanks," he acknowledged.

"Max, you can't stay here," Rowan told him, utterly confused by everything that had transpired in the past several minutes.

"But there's some huge, weird convention in town this weekend," he told her. "Trucks, RVs, trailers, tractors, school buses, you name it. The only place where I could find a room was this dump downtown that showed nonstop dirty movies and had a very, uh, unusual concept of what room service involves. I knew you wouldn't want me to stay in such a morally questionable atmosphere, so—"

"Max," Rowan tried to interrupt, but failed.

"So, I thought maybe I could use your spare room."

"Max, why are you back in town in the first place?" she asked him, thinking it was an excellent question. She knew all about the new development for which he'd been responsible going up down on the river, because almost every day there had been an article concerning it in the paper. She'd been telling herself that the continuous news coverage was the reason she'd had so much trouble forgetting about Max. But from the things she'd read, she'd been under the impression that the development was moving along quite nicely without his presence. Why would he be appearing on-site and out of the blue now?

His eyes sparkled as he took in her disheveled appearance, and he lifted a hand to wipe away a smudge on her cheek. "You look beautiful," he told her on a quiet breath. "More beautiful than I remember."

Rowan brushed negligently at his hand with hers. "I do not," she denied, knowing she'd never looked worse in her life. "I look like hell."

Max smiled cryptically at her. "If this is hell," he said, "I don't ever want to be saved."

"You're crazy," she whispered breathlessly, feeling her heart run wild at the look in his eyes.

Max broadened his smile as he shook his head slowly in disagreement. To himself he said, not anymore. I was crazy before, to have left you behind. But I won't be stupid enough to make that mistake again. To Rowan, however, he said nothing.

Rowan sighed at his silence and tried one more time. "Why are you here?"

He gazed indifferently at his fingernails as he spoke. "You, uh... You remember The Houghton Complex that's going up down on the river?"

When Max looked up, Rowan nodded but said nothing.

"Well, Old Man Houghton decided the plans I designed for it were way too ambitious for his tastes," Max explained. "And he felt that the complex would just be too damned big to solely house his corporate headquarters."

Rowan shrugged slightly. "I still don't understand why that would bring you back to town," she admitted honestly.

Max studied his hands absently once again as he spoke. "Well, *I* really liked the plans just the way they were. I think my ideas for this complex are the best I've ever had. So I made Houghton an offer and he accepted, so instead of The Houghton Complex, it's going to be The Donovan-Houghton Complex."

"Meaning?" Rowan asked, still afraid to allow herself to hope.

Max finally looked up at her again, his eyes fixed intently on hers as he spoke. "Meaning I'm moving my corporate headquarters from New York to Louisville."

"You're what?" she gasped incredulously.

Max strode casually past her, farther into the kitchen, then turned around to face her. "Yeah, New York has just become so crowded and noisy, I'm beginning to feel lost in the shuffle," he explained. "And Adrienne's been badgering me to change locations, so she can be near this guy named Michael Canadian she met when she was here before. Apparently she's crazy in love with him or something.''

Rowan's spirits sank a little at his admission. "Those are the only reasons you came back?" she asked him; this time her gaze dropped to the floor.

"Well, that and the fact that my life in New York was becoming unlivable," he confessed.

Her head snapped up again, her mind surging with frantic thoughts at the implication of his words. "Spell it out for me, Max," she entreated.

For long moments he didn't speak, not sure whether he should reveal his intentions yet. It hadn't been many weeks since they'd parted ways, and he saw no indication that she'd ever faced up to her fear of rejection and her consequent unwillingness to get involved. What if nothing had changed? What if she still balked at the idea of making that final commitment, of marrying him? Could he stand it if she said no twice? Would he have it in him to keep on asking her until he became lovelorn and pathetic? After quick, careful thought, he made a decision.

"I'm moving to Louisville," he told Rowan simply. "I'm tired of New York, and I made some good connections during my visit before. It seemed a logical conclusion to move here."

"Oh," Rowan said softly, feeling a coldness chill parts of her that had begun to grow warm. "I see."

"I'll be living in a penthouse suite at the Donovan-Houghton when it's finished, but until then, I was hoping you'd loan me your spare room," he added cautiously. "I really hate the thought of staying in a hotel that long."

"Max, you can't—" she exclaimed, she started to deny him, but he cut her off before she had the chance.

"Look, I know how you feel about things," he said quickly, "about us, our differences and everything. I know you think it will never work out. And I'm not going to pressure you, Rowan, or even mention what we once had, if you don't want me to.''

What we once had, she repeated hollowly to herself. So he *had* gotten over it, she thought with growing despair. And pretty fast, too, apparently. She should feel happy and relieved that she'd stood by her convictions and ended things when she had. Otherwise she'd have been out on her duff faster than she'd come into his life. She should pat herself proudly on the back. So why did she feel so much like kicking herself instead?

"Can I stay, Rowan?'' Max asked again. "I, uh, I could help you out with whatever it is that's given you that handywoman aura you wear so well.''

She lifted her chin defensively at his jab. "I'm working on my third floor,'' she stated proudly.

His eyebrows went up in surprise at her assertion. "Already? I thought you said that was a long way off.''

"I needed something to do in my spare time,'' she told him evasively, not daring to admit she had needed the hard work to keep her mind off him.

"From what I've heard, you've got plenty to keep you busy at your shop,'' he revealed. "Too much, in fact. I hope you're not overextending yourself again, Rowan. Twelve-hour days, six days a week, can wreak hell on a person. Trust me, I know.''

"How do you know what my schedule's been . . . ?'' Her words trailed off as realization struck her squarely in the brain. "Tara,'' she guessed.

Max smiled unashamedly. "A veritable fount of information,'' he confirmed. "Although I had to weed through a lot of other stuff to get to it,'' he added.

"What else did she tell you?'' Rowan wanted to know.

Max shrugged innocently. "Just that The Warehouse is an enormous success and the money's flowing in, so you quit your job at September's to work ten times harder at the shop. And that Miranda's birthday is coming up next month, so I brought her a little present from New York— I hope you don't mind. And she also said that her cousin Enid tried to fix you up with some guy named Cyril, but you said no."

"If you knew Enid, you'd understand why I said no," Rowan muttered.

"Hey, whatever your reason was, I'm sure it was an excellent one."

"It was," she assured him.

"Tara *didn't* tell me, however, that you had started renovating your third floor," Max added, and Rowan thought she detected a note of disapproval in his voice. "So let me help you out where I can. Until the corporate move is complete, I'm going to have some spare time. I'm between projects."

Rowan felt her resolve slipping and made herself admit that it wasn't because he could help her out with the third-floor renovation that she wanted Max to stay. It was because she was happy to see him again, because he was coming to town to live. But apparently his intentions for coming back weren't precisely the ones she'd hoped to hear. She was beginning to see that maybe she had made a colossal mistake in letting him go, without even giving what they had a chance. Max's words of that night echoed in her mind, as they had so many times during the past nine weeks. Perhaps she would never be able to commit herself to anyone, until she gave up her fear of being abandoned again. Perhaps Max *was* the one man who could and would love her the way she needed to be loved. And perhaps she had blown it when she'd turned down his offer before. Her throat closed around her heart as she realized the revelations that came now, came too late.

"All right, Max." She ceded, telling herself she was only creating a masochistic hell for herself by doing so. "If you help with the third floor, you can stay until your apartment's finished."

"Thanks," he replied graciously, moving toward his bags. "You won't regret this, I promise."

Oh, Max, she thought to herself. You can't even imagine the regrets I have already.

For the next three weeks, Max and Rowan cohabitated in the strictest sense of the word. He stayed in the spare room, she in her bedroom. Many were the days they didn't even see each other at all, but there was always something, some telltale sign to reassure one of the other's presence. For Max, it was the lingering fragrance of Rowan's perfume that seemed to reach to every corner of every room. For Rowan, it was a simple knowledge that she and Miranda were no longer alone in the big house. A quiet sense of comfortable togetherness developed. Slowly the loneliness and emptiness that had plagued both of them for years fled, replaced by feelings of security and peace.

When Rowan came home from work on Saturday evening, entering the house silently to find Max in her kitchen, barefoot and shirtless, wearing only khaki shorts thanks to the summer heat, Rowan couldn't help but observe him. He stood over the stove, lifting the lids of steaming pots to inhale the tantalizing aromas escaping from beneath. Miranda sat on a high stool by the sink, chatting away to him about her birthday next week. For a moment Rowan only stared at the sight, feeling as though she were suddenly living a new life. And in a sense, she supposed she was. She was a businesswoman now, with her own shop to run. She kept regular, though extended, hours, and came home at night to relax in her home with her family. Only this wasn't her family, she had to remind herself. At least, Max wasn't, much as she might want him to be.

"Hi," she finally said softly, breaking the solemn spell that had hung so briefly in the air.

"Mommy's home!" Miranda squealed, scrambling down from the stool to hurl herself at her mother.

Max looked up from the stove with a warm smile and said, "How was your day? You look beat."

Rowan bent to hug her daughter, but her eyes never left Max's. She felt like breaking into hysterical giggles, so innocuous and domestic were their words and actions. Why couldn't she come home from work to this every day? "It was busy," she told him. "I'm glad tomorrow's Sunday."

He nodded his agreement. "Miranda and I had fun today, didn't we?" he asked the little girl, who was still crowding against her mother.

"Yeah!" Miranda responded enthusiastically. "We finished the third floor!"

"Already?" Rowan couldn't disguise her disbelief. "Boy, you guys worked fast."

"Well, we haven't done the painting yet, have we, Miranda?" he asked the little girl. "We still have that to do."

Miranda nodded her head vigorously. "We waited, 'cause Max said you should help him choose the color, Mommy. Since it's gonna be—"

"Miranda," Max interrupted her quickly with a look of mock sternness on his face.

Miranda smiled and slapped both tiny hands over her mouth. "I forgot," she mumbled from behind them. "It's a s'prise."

Rowan's eyes widened at that. "A s'prise?" she asked curiously, imitating her daughter's language. "What kind of s'prise?"

Miranda looked first at Max, then back at her mother, and her smile grew brighter. "A big s'prise," she confirmed.

Rowan's gaze wandered to Max, but he, too, smiled and said nothing to give it away.

Turning back to the stove, he asked, "Do you want to change your clothes before dinner? This will be ready in about five minutes."

Accepting the fact that her curiosity would not be assuaged until after dinner, Rowan gave Miranda a final squeeze and rose. "Okay, I'll change my clothes and be right back. But as soon as the dishes are done . . ." She hoped her intention was clear.

"No peeking!" Max called out after her.

Rowan had looked forward to their dinners together in the past weeks, and tonight was no exception. The hours of Max's job weren't as demanding as she had thought they would be, and he frequently took advantage of being the boss by cutting out of work an hour or so early, so he could come home and relax. He frequently had dinner cooking when Rowan arrived home, explaining it away as nothing more than enjoying the opportunity to cook again, after forgetting how much fun it used to be. Max had also told her that he religiously avoided working on the weekend when he wasn't traveling. Whatever crisis arose on Saturday or Sunday could almost always wait until Monday, he'd pointed out, and weekends to him were sacred days. He worked hard during the week to earn them, and he would cherish them like the precious, temporary things they were. His philosophy had surprised Rowan at first, but when she thought about everything she'd seen of him so far, she supposed it wasn't such a fantastic concept at all that Max would be the kind of man to relish his free time.

Tonight was apparently no different. Max was all laughter and smiles as he filled everyone's plate, and as Rowan watched him exchange a wink and a secret smile with Miranda, she couldn't help but become infected by his good humor, too.

"I can't believe you finished the third floor in such a short time," she said again as they sipped coffee and watched Miranda consume a huge helping of chocolate chip ice cream.

Max gazed at her warmly over the rim of the stoneware mug that was nearly eclipsed by his big hand. "I ducked out of work early a few times," he admitted negligently. "And having Miranda's assistance helped a lot," he added, playfully nudging the little girl's shoulder, and being rewarded with a childish chuckle.

Rowan laughed, too. "Yeah, I'll bet."

"So you want to see it or not?" he asked eagerly, his eyes shining with excitement.

"Of course," she told him. "Let's go."

Miranda mysteriously disappeared after some quietly whispered words from Max, and then the two of them ascended the stairs to the top floor of the big Victorian. All the while Max explained what he'd done, and all the while Rowan nodded at his suggestions.

"Now remember, it still needs paint," he reminded her. "I've only put on a white base coat, so we can go with any color you want. And I hope you don't mind, but I had a guy in one day to take measurements for a stained-glass inset that I think will look great in the round window that faces the street. It'll get the morning sun. The floors were in better shape than you thought, so they only needed minimal work, but the fireplace is definitely going to need professional cleaning. I did what I could with it, though." He concluded his speech at the closed door at the top of the stairs, waiting for some sign from Rowan.

She offered him a disarming smile and challenged, "Well? Let's see if you're as good as they say you are."

He returned her smile with a smug one of his own. "Better," he assured her, then threw open the door with a flourish.

Rowan preceded him through the doorway into the huge room, lighted by a floor lamp that Max had pilfered from her den. The soft, sweet aroma of lemon oil filled her nostrils as she gazed in wonder at her surroundings. The walls at either end of the room were paneled in dark, rich mahogany that now gleamed with a loving finish, where before they had been scarred in places and covered with filth. The ceiling-high windows facing the backyard were clean and warm with the pale amber light of evening, and opposite them, where the ceiling sloped down somewhat, a circular one looked onto the street. Max was right. Some stained glass would be wonderful there. The fireplace sported a different mantel than the badly damaged one that had leaned against it before, the new one also fashioned of mahogany, beautifully and intricately carved with leaves and grapes and bacchanalian satyrs. Rowan's eyes filled with tears when she saw it, and she crossed the room quickly, then ran her fingers lovingly over the frolicking figures.

"Recognize it?" Max asked her softly when he saw her actions, knowing, of course, that she did indeed.

"It's from the living room in the house where I grew up," she whispered quietly. "My father made it." She turned quickly to face Max, wanting to express her gratitude, aware that her eyes were full of tears. "Oh, Max," she said brokenly, "where did you . . . ? How did you . . . ?"

"When I explained things to the current owners of your old house and offered to buy it, they accepted my offer. They were reluctant to part with it, but I told them about this great place down on Main Street called The Warehouse, where they could—"

"Oh, Max." Rowan hurried across the room toward him and threw herself into his arms. "Thank you," she mumbled against his chest.

"You're welcome," he rasped out on a ragged breath, wrapping his arms tightly around her, burying his face in her hair. He'd waited so long to hold her like this, had spent so many sleepless nights wondering if he would ever be able to do so again.

Rowan let herself be held for a moment, drinking in the warmth and strength that emanated from him, feeling the loneliness chased from her soul, loving the sensation that came with having Max this close again. When she lifted her face toward his, he wasted no time in pressing his mouth against hers, crushing her body to his as he did so. Immediately she kissed him back, threading her fingers through his dark gold hair, coming up on tiptoe to give herself better access to his mouth. Only the need for breath finally separated them, and as their chests rose and fell in irregular rhythm, only one thought echoed in Rowan's muddled brain. How had she been stupid enough to let this man go before, and how was she going to handle it when he left again? There had to be a way that she could convince him to stay.

"How am I supposed to rent this room out as an apartment, when you've gone and made it the most beautiful one in the house?" she asked him dreamily, cupping her hands possessively at the back of his neck.

Max dropped his arms to settle them on her waist and shifted his gaze toward the floor at her question. "Ah, Rowan?" he ventured a little uncertainly. "I, ah, I sort of have a few confessions to make, before we get bogged down in some kind of meaningful discussion." His eyes came back to fix on hers. "You *do* want to have a meaningful discussion, don't you?"

She nodded slowly, letting a smile spread across her lips, but remained silent.

"Good," he said on a quick, relieved sigh. "But before we do, I should own up to a few things."

"Such as?" she asked mildly, knowing there was nothing to which he could confess, short of being a repeat felon, that would even begin to question her new conviction that they were perfect for each other.

"Well, I know how important it is to you that you be the one to provide for yourself and Miranda, but... Actually, your third floor isn't the only thing I, ah, *fixed* this week."

"Oh?"

"You'll probably be getting some phone calls next week about things you're going to consider very curious."

"Will I?"

Max's arms tightened around her waist, lest she try to escape from him when she heard his admissions. "Yes, you will," he told her. "Let's see, there's Currier Roofers about putting on your new roof, Leyton-Smith Investors about your new stock portfolio, The Hawthorne Academy about Miranda's enrollment in their kindergarten class next year...." His voice trailed off at Rowan's reaction. Or rather her lack of one. She just gazed at him with that dazed, delighted expression that she'd been wearing for the past several minutes and said nothing.

"Max, what have you done?" she finally asked him after a minute, her voice indicating nothing about what she might be feeling.

Max decided to tread cautiously until he could fathom what she was thinking. "You remember that conversation we had a few months ago, where you mentioned some things you needed?" he asked experimentally.

Rowan shook her head slowly. "No, but I remember one where we brought up a hypothetical situation, in which I told you what I'd *like* to do if *I* had the money. And these are things I can take care of when *I* have the money, which should be pretty soon, at the rate things are going.''

Her words were plainspoken, without the accusation or defensiveness Max had been prepared to hear. Her calm reaction and even-mindedness set him on edge. He wasn't sure now how *he* should act. Before he had a chance to decide, Rowan was talking again.

''Oh, well, at least these are things I can reverse with a phone call. I guess I should be relieved you didn't buy me a car, too.''

Max's eyes fell quickly to the floor at her statement, and he dug his bare toe into a crack between the floorboards.

Rowan pulled one hand from behind his neck and covered her eyes with it, then took a deep breath. ''You didn't,'' she said softly.

Max, too, took a deep breath, then let his eyes wander up to the ceiling. But he remained ominously silent.

''You did,'' Rowan groaned.

''Look, it's not a very big car, Rowan,'' Max coaxed.

''What kind?'' she asked quietly.

''Well, I know you said something about a Toyota or Chevrolet that night....''

''What kind, Max?''

''But you really can't beat German engineering, so...''

''A Volkswagen?'' she asked hopefully.

''A, ah, a Mercedes,'' Max confessed. ''It's out in the garage. I had them haul your old one away.''

''Oh, Max.''

''Rowan—''

''And this thing with The Hawthorne Academy is just too much,'' she interrupted. ''That school is far too expensive and snotty, and Miranda will fare perfectly well in the public school system.''

''Not if she wants to go to Harvard,'' Max pointed out.

"Harvard?" Rowan asked, feeling the world growing more surreal by the minute. "Trust me, Max, when I tell you there's very little chance of Miranda going to Harvard. And we certainly don't have to worry about it right now. She's only three years old."

"She'll be four next week," he reminded her. "No need to wait until the last minute. I could call in some favors."

"You what?"

"I'm one of their more famous grads," he told her matter-of-factly. "Why? What's wrong? Isn't Harvard acceptable? Surely you don't want your daughter going to *Yale*?"

"Max!" Rowan finally cried out, squeezing her eyes shut and doubling her fists loosely against his chest. This conversation had gotten way out of hand.

"What?" he responded softly.

"You can't do this," she told him quietly after a moment, opening her eyes to see his reflect genuine disappointment.

"Why not?" he wanted to know.

Rowan sighed and tried to explain as rationally and calmly as she could, hoping her uncertainty at his intentions didn't show through. "Because you have no right," she said simply.

"I have every right," he countered. "I love you and Miranda. I want to take care of you. Both of you."

Rowan felt the fist that held her stomach reach up to clench her heart, too. "Miranda and I can take care of ourselves," she told him on a shallow breath, knowing he probably realized as well as she did what a liar she was. "I appreciate what you're trying to do, Max, but . . . but our welfare isn't your responsibility." She let her eyes fall, when she feared her hope that he would contradict her might show in them.

"But that's just it, Rowan, don't you see?" He tipped back her chin with the crook of his finger and looked intently into her eyes. "I want to *make* it my responsibility."

Rowan was afraid to believe he meant what she wanted him to mean. "You do?" she asked quietly.

"I want to marry you, Rowan," he told her. "I always have. Why do you think I moved to Louisville, anyway? Why do you think I wanted to stay here at the house with you? There's no excuse you can make now, no risk you have to take, besides trusting me. And I want to prove to you, once and for all, that I will love you forever. How can that be such a surprise to you?"

She shrugged uncertainly. "I'm not very preceptive?" she asked lamely in lieu of an explanation.

"Maybe it just takes you a little longer than most," he offered magnanimously.

"Maybe," she said with a smile.

"So?" he encouraged. "What's your answer?"

Rowan laughed softly with satisfaction at the question that clouded his eyes. "Yes," she said finally.

"Yes, what?" he asked, knowing he'd posed more than one question that needed her approval.

"Yes to all of it," she responded happily.

Max couldn't believe she was giving in so easily. "You're going to let me do all those things for you and Miranda without putting up a fight?" he asked, relieved.

Rowan looked at him as if she couldn't understand why he was so puzzled. "If we get married, what's mine is yours and what's yours is mine, right?" she reasoned.

"That's usually the way it works," he agreed, still not sure where she was taking the conversation.

"So it won't be *your* money paying for all those things, it will be *ours*," she explained.

"You'll pardon me if I find your sudden change of position a bit odd, won't you?"

Rowan airily waved a hand at him. "Max, you're just trying to make things more difficult than they are. You'd never catch *me* doing something like that."

"No, not you," he agreed. "Never."

"But, Max," she said carefully, "about that Mercedes..."

"Okay, okay, you get yourself a Toyota or Chevrolet. *I'll* drive the Mercedes."

She smiled her gratitude. "Thanks." After a moment she added, "And, Max?"

He looked at her with mock impatience and said, "What now?"

"There's a private school besides The Hawthorne Academy that's much less expensive and really very good, with a significant emphasis on the creative arts. I think Miranda would enjoy it much more. As for Harvard, well, I think it would be best for her to decide when the time comes, okay?"

He smiled again and nodded. "Okay."

Rowan felt herself relax at his acquiescence.

"So what color would you like to paint our new bedroom?" he asked, pulling her close once more to drop a number of light, leisurely kisses along her cheek and jaw. "Because, of course, you realize what your daughter was about to give away earlier was the fact that this isn't meant to be an apartment, but our bedroom."

Rowan sighed with contentment and draped her arms lovingly around his neck once more. "Oh, I don't know," she said absently, concentrating on the delicious thrills that were rippling throughout her body like circles on the water. "Something significant."

"Significant?" he asked as he tasted her earlobe, then the curve where her neck joined her shoulder.

"You know," she said softly. "Something symbolic of the way we feel for one another. That represents this . . . this tremendous emotion we have for each other."

"Love?" Max asked, pulling away only far enough to gaze into her eyes.

"Yes, that's it. Love," she confirmed with a smile.

"So we're going to have a red bedroom?" he asked, considering the color on the two walls that weren't paneled.

Rowan followed his gaze with her eyes. "I was thinking more of a deep crimson. Because my love for you is as hot and vital, as necessary for life as the blood that runs through my veins."

"Wow," Max murmured. "You must love me a lot."

"Probably as much as you love me," she told him.

"That much?" he asked. "I'm impressed."

"And I'm in love," she rejoined.

"That makes two of us."

She looked at him for a long time, wanting to say so much to him, but feeling he probably already knew it all. Finally she placed her palm against his warm cheek and said softly, "Thanks, Max, for giving me a second chance."

He smiled and covered her hand warmly with his. "Thanks, Rowan, for giving me my only one. Let's neither one of us blow it."

She pressed her lips softly against his before assuring him, "There's absolutely no chance of that."

Epilogue

The morning sun shone warmly through the stained-glass rosette of the window above the big, black, cast-iron bed. Rowan nestled more comfortably against the pile of crimson- and ebony-printed throw pillows behind her back, pulling up the matching quilt over her gray sweatpants and Bullwinkle T-shirt. Beside her, her husband loafed comfortably on top of the quilt, wearing only black silk pajama bottoms. There were still a lot of differences in their characters, she thought with a smile, but they were nothing with which they couldn't live peacefully.

Max looked up at her then, curious about the reason for the slight smile playing about Rowan's lips. Before he could voice his inquiry, however, the small child in the red bunny sleeper, who lay on her stomach at the foot of the big bed, called out to him.

"Daddy, will you read 'Calvin and Hobbes' to me?" Miranda asked as she rustled the brightly colored page of Sunday comics at him.

Max looked at his wife and whispered, "I love it when she calls me that." Without waiting for a reply, he pulled Miranda into his lap and did exactly as she asked.

Rowan gazed up at the ceiling for a long moment, listening as Max read to her—no, *their* daughter—smiling at the way he changed his voice to accommodate his interpretation of different cartoon characters. How had she ever managed to get this lucky? She closed her eyes for a moment, sending a silent inquiry heavenward. Mom? Dad? she asked wordlessly. You guys see all this? If you had anything to do with it, I just want to say thanks.

"Rowan?" she heard Max's voice laced with concern. "Is anything wrong?"

She opened her eyes and gazed at her husband with frank adoration before shaking her head back and forth. "I don't think anything will ever be wrong again," she told him honestly.

"Damned right, sweetheart," he concurred adamantly.

"Oh, Mommy! Daddy said a bad word!" Miranda covered her mouth with her hand, her eyes wide with laughter.

Max had the decency to look sheepish. "Oops. I keep forgetting." Rowan chuckled and picked up the Arts section of the paper, scanning the review of the play they'd gone to see the previous evening. When she spied her name among the reviewer's list of local celebrities present at the premiere, she couldn't help but laugh in delighted surprise.

"Listen to this," she instructed Max before she proceeded to read from the review. "'Also attending the opening last night was local businesswoman, Rowan Chance-Donovan, accompanied by husband, Max. Ms. Chance-Donovan is the owner and manager of the hip, new shop on Main Street known as The Warehouse, and this reviewer would be lost without her incredible selection of fixtures and faucets to enhance his new home.' Wow, what a nice plug, don't you think? I'll have to send him a thank-you note.''

"Looks like you've made it to the big time," Max congratulated her. "How do you like it?"

She ogled him openly then, settling her eyes on the dark gold scattering of hair across his brawny chest. "It has its perks," she said. "I especially like the groupies."

"Groupie?" Max gasped. "Me?" He gave her a sly look and said slickly in his best Humphrey Bogart voice, "Come on sweetheart, you know I loved you when you were just a little nobody waitress without any prospects."

Rowan laughed out loud, getting into the spirit of the game. "Admit it, Max. You only married me for my money."

He looked affronted. "How can you say such cruel things to the only man you ever loved? I *am* the only man you ever loved, aren't I?"

She smiled enigmatically. "Maybe."

"Maybe?" he gasped in affected horror. *"Maybe?"*

"Oh, all right," she said, giving in. "If you must know, you *are* in fact the only man I've ever loved. But don't let it go to your head."

Max leaned back against his pillow, looking very smug. "I'd never do that," he assured her.

Rowan grinned at her husband, thinking what a bright future they had. That thought in turn reminded her of something else. "Have Adrienne and Michael set a date yet?" she asked suddenly.

"April 30," Max told her. "It will be the one-year anniversary of the day they met." After a thoughtful moment he added, "You know, I never knew Adrienne to have a romantic streak until she met Michael. Funny how love can change a person's way of thinking."

Rowan nodded in agreement. "Yes, isn't it?"

"Adrienne's going to have September's cater the reception," Max mentioned in passing.

"She isn't," Rowan said doubtfully.

Max threw her a funny look. "She is," he insisted. "Why? Is that going to be a problem?"

"It's just..." Rowan began. "Remember that night I collapsed at work, and you said Adrienne talked Louis out of firing me?"

"Yes, I remember."

"Well, after that, I don't think I ever worked a shift where Louis didn't mention Adrienne." Rowan chuckled a little sadly. "Oh, Max, I think Louis fell in love with her after that."

Max lifted the sports section to scan an article about the University of Louisville's new recruits for the upcoming basketball season. "He did," he confirmed.

Rowan's eyes widened in surprise. "He did? How do you know? Have you been holding out on me?"

"Uh-huh."

"Max!"

"All right, all right." He surrendered. "Adrienne didn't want me to say anything to you, because she didn't want Louis to be embarrassed."

"What happened?"

"After that night he started sending Adrienne flowers and candy, offering her a ten- to fifteen-percent discount on anything she might want catered."

"That sounds like Louis," Rowan remarked dryly.

"Anyway, they worked through it all, and now the two of them are very close friends."

"The epitome of the 'strange and wonderful relationship'?"

"Something like that," Max agreed. "Did you know his real name is Lester Shoemaker?"

"I suspected something of the sort," Rowan admitted. Then an ad for a local wallpaper store caught her attention. "Look, Max, Morgan's is having a sale."

"So?" he asked absently.

"So I thought I might turn my old bedroom into a parlor-type sitting room."

Max let the newspaper fall into his lap and glared at his wife.

"What?" she asked him.

"I, uh, I sort of had plans for that room," he hedged.

Rowan frowned in confusion. "Did you want to make it your office? I thought we were going to share the den downstairs."

"Actually I had something else in mind," he confessed.

She raised her hands palm up and shrugged, indicating she did not know what he was talking about.

Max rolled his eyes and sighed in exasperation. "Ms. Chance-Donovan," he said through gritted teeth, "I thought it would make a very nice nursery."

"Nursery?" Rowan gaped at him. "But Miranda already has one, and she's about to outgrow it, as it is."

Closing his eyes in an attempt to remain calm and patient, Max went on slowly, "It wouldn't be for Miranda."

"Then what . . . ?" Her eyes darkened as understanding dawned on her like a summer morning. "You want to have a baby?" she asked him softly, breathlessly.

"Well, frankly, I was kind of hoping you'd do the actual *having*. Not that I wouldn't if I could, of course."

"Of course," she agreed, her eyes shining at the prospect of yet another reason to be happy.

Max loved the look in Rowan's eyes and a thought suddenly struck him. Turning to the little girl, who was using her crayons to color in the black-and-white photographs of world leaders in the front section of the paper, he said,

"Miranda, why don't you take those pictures of the president and British prime minister downstairs?"

"Why?" Miranda asked him pointedly.

"Because," Max told her with a smile.

She looked back up at him and grinned from beneath her long black bangs. "Because why?" she insisted.

"Because I'm your daddy and I said so, that's why," he told her with an affectionate smile.

"You just want to be alone with Mommy, don't you?"

"Uh-huh," Max replied.

"Okay," Miranda gathered her things and padded out of the room then, closing the door behind her.

"We've got a great kid," Max said when he turned back to Rowan.

"Yes," she agreed with a smile, feeling her temperature rise when she saw the fires igniting in his eyes.

"Wanna make another one?"

"Yes." She nodded eagerly.

"Just so we'll have something to do with that extra room, of course."

"Of course."

He gathered her close then and gently kissed her mouth and cheeks. "You know," he murmured quietly as he nibbled her earlobe, "if we do this right, we won't even have to change the blue wallpaper that's in there now."

And with a throaty chuckle, Rowan agreed that she was certainly willing to give it a try.

* * * * *

Silhouette Special Edition

proudly presents
the long-awaited "prequel" volume of

★ LOVE AND GLORY ★

by
LINDSAY McKENNA

Dawn of Valor

In the summer of '89, Silhouette Special Edition premiered three novels celebrating America's men and women in uniform: LOVE AND GLORY, by bestselling author Lindsay McKenna. Featured were the proud Trayherns, a military family as bold and patriotic as the American flag—three siblings valiantly battling the threat of dishonor, determined to triumph . . . in love and glory.

Now, discover the roots of the Trayhern brand of courage, as parents Chase and Rachel relive their earliest heartstopping experiences of survival and indomitable love, in

Dawn of Valor, Silhouette Special Edition #649.

This February, experience the thrill of LOVE AND GLORY—from the very beginning!

DV-1

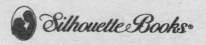

Silhouette Books

**Star-crossed lovers?
Or a match made in heaven?**

Why are some heroes strong and silent . . . and others charming and cheerful? The answer is WRITTEN IN THE STARS! Coming each month in 1991, Silhouette Romance presents you with a special love story written by one of your favorite authors—highlighting the hero's astrological sign! From January's sensible Capricorn to December's disarming Sagittarius, you'll meet a dozen dazzling heroes.

Sexy, serious Justin Starbuck wasn't about to be tempted by his aunt's lovely hired companion, but Philadelphia Jones thought his love life needed her helping hand! What happens when this cool, conservative Capricorn meets his match in a sweet, spirited blonde like Philadelphia?

Take 4 bestselling love stories FREE

Plus get a FREE surprise gift!

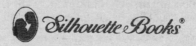